Snuff

Also by Kirby Farrell

The American Satan
Cony-Catching

Snuff

Kirby Farrell

Walker and Company
New York

First published in the United States of America in 1991
by Walker Publishing Company, Inc.
Published simultaneously in Canada by Thomas Allen & Son
Canada, Limited, Markham, Ontario

Library of Congress Cataloging-in-Publication Data

Farrell, Kirby, 1942–
Snuff / Kirby Farrell.
p.   cm.
ISBN 0-8027-5782-0
I. Title.
PS3556.A77S68   1991
813'.54—dc20   90-22044
                     CIP

Printed in the United States of America
2 4 6 8 10 9 7 5 3 1

Snuff

1

"I HAD TO DRAG his carcass over the fence," Rachel wisecracked. "He didn't want to come."

Me, she meant. Dear old dad. From the breezeway of the ranch house we could look back across the rail fence to the red saltbox I still thought of as our house, even after four years of divorce. A hammock sagged like taffy in the hot August sun. A black cat with white paws was melting into the grass. Day after day of peaceful, murderous heat; newscasters were scolding us about the greenhouse effect, itemizing our polluted sins with thrilling hints of doomsday.

Through the screen door Rachel greeted her friend Amy: "I told him what the guy said about your sister sucking things and being killed."

Rachel knew how to get a father's attention. On the Vermont farm where I spent the first years of my life, kid's lingo could be as violently matter of fact as the Christmas hog slaughter, but Rachel could still shock me. A face appeared behind the screen.

"Look, Amy," I said, "whatever Rachel's told you, I'm a business investigator — credit card fraud, that sort of thing. And I work mostly in New York. I wouldn't know how to find anybody's sister around Boston even if I had the time."

Amy looked pained: "That's all right, Mr. Ames."

"Everybody calls my father Duncan," Rachel prompted.

"Sshh," Amy hushed, "my mother'll hear us." Amy came out from behind the screen door and hustled us into the backyard. "She's got that panic thing where you're scared to go out —"

"Agoraphobia," Rachel put in.

Amy nodded. They were both high school seniors, yet with her solemn mouth, solid calves, and indispensable bra, Amy seemed older than the lightfooted Rachel. She had a touch of fuzz on her upper lip, a dot of acne cream on her nose, and worry in her eyes. In exploding letters her yellow tee shirt screamed STEAM THIEVES — a rock group evidently. On her thumb she wore the red rubber thimble she used as a supermarket cashier.

In the backyard we stood around the rusty gas grill. The Virgin Mary kept an eye on us from her spot by the weathered rail fence. From out here Amy's house looked a bit ratty — peeling green paint, a cracked storm window. For years Joan Biondi had been living on stingy alimony.

"Duncan, listen." Rachel took off her sunglasses and wiped them on her shirttail. She has her mother's eyes, the same way of zeroing in on your soul when she's moved. "Somebody's going to kill Amy's sister. That's what the guy was telling her. That's why—"

"Amy, really—" I began, trying to head off the appeal.

"Wednesday night," Rachel cut in, "right after work, Amy picks up the phone and a voice says, *'Tell Dawn, she doesn't get this thing straightened out, the next thing she sucks is gonna be a bullet.'*"

"I thought you said Amy's sister's name was Donna."

"She calls herself Dawn. In high school she started it, like a stage name, because she wanted to be a movie star."

"What year did she graduate? How old is Dawn?"

"Well, she didn't actually graduate." Rachel's voice raced. "Senior year she got into this play at BU and it flipped her out. I mean, this Natick high school kid asked to star in a college production. She cut a lot of classes and flunked things and never came back to graduate. Even the yearbook has just her name, no clubs, no friends, no nothing. She even missed the picture sittings."

"So she went into what? Movies?"

"She'd come home and say she was in some play, like summer stock up in Ogunquit. But you couldn't actually be sure."

"So nobody really knows what she's been doing for—?"

"Six, seven years."

"Which would make her about twenty-four?"

"But she wasn't just a liar. Like, one time she actually had a program for a summer playhouse in—Saratoga, wasn't it?—and her name was right there as First Servant. And another time her picture turned up in a men's magazine." My eyebrows must have twitched because Rachel hurried to add: "I saw it. The magazine's called *Spread*, and Dawn's on a sawhorse pretending to ride. It's this dumb piece called 'Meanwhile back at the Raunch.' Dawn's got a buckskin vest on so all you can see is her bare bottom. It's got to be airbrushed. Nobody's can could be that rosy."

Rachel would know about flesh tones and retouching: she had a darkroom in the cellar and she was headed for the Boston Museum School next year. And since the day she rescued all the pillows off the sofa wearing her overcoat and Meg's bra for earmuffs—*Saving baby seals from trappers! Get back!*—she's been intrigued by the stage. In the high school *Diary of Anne Frank* she was Anne's mother.

"When strangers phone to discuss the cemetery," I said, "the cops should hear about it."

"I'd tell the police," Amy offered, "but they'd start questioning my mother, and god, if she has another breakdown I'll die. Like, when I was in junior high, she was a basket case."

"When did you last hear from your sister?"

"A few weeks ago. Like, every month or two she'd call us."

"And that was the last time?"

Amy nodded: "I've been calling and calling and nobody answers. Even this morning I tried. She usually goes to sleep real late."

"What's her address?"

"Dawn's always moving. She's been living with a rich guy."

"You catch his name?"

"He let her drive his silver Porsche. But then the last time I saw her, she'd moved out on him—"

"Broke?"

"You kidding? She had a little red sports car and she gave me this rap about how she was about to turn the world upside down but it was too risky to talk about it yet. So I asked her, I said 'Who's involved?' And she says, 'Everyone. The whole country.' Can you believe that? What a family. A mother too scared to get out of bed, and a sister who thinks she's, like, Superman."

"Is she really unstable?"

"Ha. No way. Just trying to impress me. And I didn't want to hear it. You know? But then"—Amy threw up her hands—"this envelope comes with three hundred-dollar bills wrapped inside. Very bossy. Pay for my college boards and buy some clothes for my mother and me."

"And the postcards," Rachel coached.

"And then, really weird, I got a postcard from the Pyramids, and one a couple weeks later from I think it was Peru." Amy twisted the rubber fingertip grimly. "And now I'm scared about this phone guy saying they'll kill her. You know he meant killing. Shooting her in the face, it sounded like."

"I get the picture." In a world of horror flicks and headline rapes the girls' effort to be casual spooked me.

Amy shrugged: "Dawn's sloppy about guys. She likes them all."

"Sweet romance? or fun and profit?"

"What?"

The way Amy winced made my heart wince. The world was full of thoughts she couldn't bear to think. Before she could answer me a voice from the porch complained: "Amy? Why's the door open? You're letting the heat in."

"I'll be right there, Ma."

3

Behind the screen the woman's face was a ghostly blur. She talked in a calm, strangled voice. Joan Biondi. I remembered her from neighborhood barbecues years ago when the girls were small: a petite brunette with a handy smile and hair-trigger giggles that made you feel unbelievably witty. But she kept her family and her house fanatically clean and shunned strong opinions as if they were germs. Once at a neighborhood cookout she burst into tears when her husband, Joe, the cheapskate contractor, picked up a hamburger patty that had fallen in the grass and plopped it on the hot grill. I can still hear Joan screaming at him in a panicky whisper: *"Joe! There's dog dirt in that grass! Somebody could die!"*

Now Joan Biondi flitted back into the shadows of her house without asking who we were. Rachel grabbed both my wrists and pushed into me — the same bulldozer determination she had as a kid — and backed me across the grass for a little one-on-one.

"Duncan," she muttered, "this is too much for Amy. She's scared, it's all she thinks about. Can't you at least get something started? Give her some hope?" Rachel grabbed my elbows: "Hey, watch it."

I sidestepped to avoid kicking the statue of the Virgin by the fence. Frost had cracked her pink cheeks and bobbed her plaster nose. She stood at a tipsy angle staring at the hot dry grass.

"Just this one favor," Rachel was repeating. "Then we'll go to New York and move the airplane."

For over a year I'd been building an ultralight plane in a friend's loft around the corner from my office in New York. He'd lost his lease and I'd promised to clear out my junk by this weekend. I was in Natick today to pick up Rachel and the nylon tail surface she'd been tailoring for the plane. There's never enough time. Rachel saw me hesitating:

"I'll help you move and so will Amy. Come on, look me in the eye. Just say yes. Say, 'Yes, Rachel, I'll try to save this smartass before some creep shoots her in the face.' Okay?"

4

$\triangledown$

2

I AGREED TO MAKE a couple phone calls.

As any horoscope could have predicted, Saturday is no day to fish info out of Boston City Hall or Boston Edison's billing department. The Natick cops did fish the Registry of Motor Vehicles for me and gave Dawn Biondi a red 1986 Alfa Romeo with a vanity plate: ACTRYST. "A pun," Rachel enthused. "She can't be a total airhead."

Kevin Hollings, the young cop on the desk, remembered me from a year ago, when a dissatisfied customer of mine had fired two bullets through the front door of our Natick house. When Kevin realized Dawn was Donna Biondi, he also remembered a buddy of his brother's who'd just sold her the Alfa Romeo: "His name's Red LeBeau. Owns an auto body shop off 135 in Framingham. He went with her in high school."

Amy began telling Kevin Hollings how Dawn had grabbed all the family snapshots of her. "When she acted in her first play at BU she used one of the photos on posters. She plastered the campus – total publicity freak. We stapled fliers to phone poles on Comm. Ave. I was right there helping her, just a little kid – Dawn was supposed to be baby-sitting me. It was about the time my mother had her first bad breakdown."

"Any of those posters left?"

Amy shrugged. "You kidding? You put up hundreds of posters with your face on them, and next day" – she snapped her fingers – "all gone. Like all these election ads they spend millions on."

The day before the Democrats had nominated Senator Daniel Merriam to run for the White House. A cop had taped one of the President's campaign posters over a crack in the plaster wall like a red, white, and blue Band-Aid.

On the Gloss Auto Body sign a stylized tow truck hook had snagged the *G* and was tearing it away from the *loss*. The sign advertised welding, used cars. Half a dozen maimed cars waited on the lot for Red LeBeau's plastic surgery. The office window still had spray-on Christmas snow at the edges and a sticker proclaiming

GUNS DON'T KILL PEOPLE
PEOPLE DO

which missed the point.

Inside the shop a kid with a crew cut was spray-painting a van. The wet caramel lacquer looked delicious. The kid didn't look up: "Red's out back."

"Don't you need a spray mask for that job?"

He threw me a dirty look: "Too goddamn hot."

In the weeds behind the cinder-block shop were fenders and other unburied body parts. Red LeBeau was sitting in a junked bucket seat naked to the waist, putting to death a row of beer bottles with an ugly-looking CO_2 pistol. The gun would give a gaseous pop and thirty feet away a beer bottle would jump to pieces. He was preparing new targets from a live six-pack of Rolling Rock. Freckly guy in his early thirties, with sun-pinked skin and deltoids that stood up sharply when he turned his head to wonder: "You the one wants the estimate?"

"Kevin Hollings tells me you might know where Donna Biondi is these days. I'm trying to reach her."

He thought for a minute, then a smile stretched his mouth. His voice turned dreamy: "Ahh, you want to pork her. She'll yank you for big bucks these days, I gotta warn you."

"She's in business now?"

"Now? Ha. She started out when she was fifteen, servicing guys down at the Legion in Natick. Twenty bucks a bang. She's wiggled her ass in every kind of backseat ever made." He squeezed the pistol with both hands and another beer bottle shattered. "I used to be all over her to clean up her act — I liked her. But what the hell. Even a spotless clean toilet, you wouldn't want to eat out of it. You know? Jesus, she was a kick. She'd be out in the parking lot all dolled up like Jeeves was coming for her in the limo. She'd stop anything — wheelchair case, anybody with a buck. And what a knockout. She had this soft, soft mouth, and knockers, these Dairy Queen knockers you wouldn't believe. Fifteen years old. And always kidding around with you like you two just won the Megabucks. Putting on foreign accents and like that. Finally the cops started hassling her, so she wised up and kept a little address book. Went pro."

"And you saw her recently?"

"I've seen her stick things up there you wouldn't believe. Ballpoint pen. Sundae spoon. Plastic saint off a dashboard. She'd try anything. Even niggers she'd go down on. One time, a Marine. His car got loose and ran into the Charles River while they were inside this motel over in Dedham. Asswipe sent her home in a cab when she wouldn't ride with me. He would have kicked my face in if there hadn't been four of us in my Camaro."

"You put his car in the river."

"Did I say that?"

"You beat him up?"

"Nah." Red turned again, one workboot up on the edge of the seat, his bicep flattened out on his knee. Tattoo on the bicep. "So you know little Kevin the Cop." He grinned: "You a cop too?"

"Friend of the family."

He cocked a surprised eye at me: "She dead already?"

"Should she be?"

"If you went where Donna's been, you'd last about as long as a Popsicle up a bear's ass. Though she's got bucks now. I just sold her a nice sporty Alfa Romeo Spider, almost new. Pussy red. Wire wheels. Custom leather seats. Scarcely any rust. Paid me cash American bucks too. Drove off looking like a movie star. Car like that's got classic looks, just right for her."

"She used an address on Hemenway Street in Boston to register the car. Think I'd find her there?"

"Good luck, pal. She slapped the bread on me and shot out of here. I let her use one of my repair plates, to get her over to the registry. She still hasn't returned the plate."

"Maybe she's on the run."

"You know how much they bag you for a repair plate now?"

"What's she doing these days? She say?"

"You kidding? Same old crap about acting. Says she's made sexy videos. But five'll get you ten she's putting out for a buck. Big dreamer. Your basic Natick wop coming on like Princess Di there. Well, up hers."

Red LeBeau flexed his bicep. The tattoo squirmed over the muscle: a heart filled with rust-colored freckles. He sighted down the pistol barrel. It gasped. Against the back wall of the neighbors' cinder-block garage a beer bottle twinkled to nothing. He offered me the pistol.

"You any good? Wanna do some recycling? I hate this goddamn bottle bill law."

"Know anybody who'd threaten to kill Dawn?"

"Donna?" Red weighed her life gravely: "Like I say, she's a million-dollar piece of ass. Sure, she can get on your nerves, but nothing a piece of tape over the mouth wouldn't fix."

"You sleep with her this time?"

"It came up. She wanted to go to Switzerland to get laid."

"Switzerland."

"Yeah, you believe that? Saint Something, where they ski and drink fancy shit. I'm supposed to close up shop and take her there. To get my

7

rocks off. She'd just come back from London and climbing the Pyramids or whatever you do to them. What an asswipe. Like I got bucks up the hog, you know? I offered her a discount on the car for a little nookie."

"But?"

"What does she care about discounts? She peeled off a wad of hundreds. She's carrying it around in her handbag like Brinks, for christsake. I made her drive over to the bank with me, I says: 'Hey you crazy or what? There's some heavy types out there.' "

"So she can afford to be choosy now."

He sighted along the gun barrel at an invisible bird gaining altitude: "You see me losing any sleep over it?"

"**Y**OU LOOK RIPPED," Rachel said when I got back to the car.

"Very ugly guy," I grumbled.

"Looks like a hunk from here."

"Well up close he's not a girl's best friend."

"So you're not going to introduce us."

I pointed the car toward Boston: "Let's check out Dawn's address in Boston, and afterward I'll introduce you to some Ethopian food in the South End."

Amy made a squeamish face: "I'm allergic to spicy foods."

"The fried locusts taste like Rice Krispies."

"Ignore him," Rachel muttered, "he's always joking."

Hemenway Street is just off Mass. Ave., an eighth note or two from Symphony Hall, a choice address if you love Beethoven or you work the big hotels. It was a two-story brick building that had settled unevenly in the Back Bay soil, giving the granite lintel over the door an unsettling tilt. Nothing in Dawn's mail slot. I was leaning on her bell when a curly-haired extrovert in a purple shirt pushed into the entryway with us and demanded: "Who you looking for?"

"Dawn Biondi," I said. "You a neighbor?"

"Sort of."

"I'm her sister," Amy blurted.

"Hey really. She leave any of her things with you?"

"Are you a friend of hers?"

He parried the question: "You live around here?"

"Oh no," Amy began, "I live out in—"

"I'm Duncan Ames," I said glad-handing him, helping Amy step aside. "And you?"

He was flustered, nodding his head and shoulders slightly, in time to rock music only dogs could hear. Up close he wasn't so handsome. Football or a fist had adjusted his nose. A watery paleness made his eyes eerie. The purple shirt had thin gilt stripes and showed lots of tanned Latino chest to match the flavor of Spanish on the tongue. It occurred to me that he didn't live here. Didn't work here. Didn't really know Dawn. Didn't endorse the nonviolent principles of Mahatma Gandhi. He gave me a competitive handshake like Indian wrestling. I said:

"And your name is —?"

"Yeah, well. I gotta go."

"Wait a—"

"Have a nice one."

He flung his hand behind him in a sort of wave, skipped out onto the sidewalk, and kept going. Rachel said, "You see that little chunk out of his ear? Like something bit him?"

Amy curled her lip in disgust: "You suppose he was watching the building?"

Not a bad guess. I rang the super's bell and Mr. Henry let us in. Little guy in his sixties with a shiny no-wax head. In his white shirt he wore a pocketful of ball point pens in a plastic liner stamped GREAVY REALTY. I showed him my business card and a ten-dollar bill while explaining that Dawn was a severe diabetic: her sister Amy was worried about her, could we have a look, make sure she wasn't on the kitchen floor in a coma?

Mr. Henry conscientiously wrote the date and time on the back of my card and unconsciously folded the ten into his shirtpocket. His keyring must have weighed five pounds.

With the shades drawn Dawn's place was gloomy inside. What caught my eye first were stacks of books on the floor by the living-room windows: *Cognitive Theory*, *Introduction to Psychometrics*, *Affective Disorders*, Freud's *Civilization and Its Discontents*. Each title page sported a neat ballpoint signature: Lynne Dresser. Lynne was gunning for a degree in psychology.

Wrong apartment. I was about to retreat when Rachel motioned me into the bedroom. The security grille on the back window had been bent aside by King Kong. The King had also jimmied the sash lock. If the damage was fresh, it had been a polite entry: no wreckage, no smashed valuables. No kids on a rampage. But then, there wasn't much to ransack. A few dressy dresses, a flock of shoes. Under the bed a pack of peanuts, frilly briefs, a glittering foil condom wrapper, and *Victoria's Secret* — a mail-order catalog for fancy lingerie. On the wall hung a photo poster of breasts and smooth peaked hips that made a succulent shadowy landscape: undulant Sahara sand. Artsy stuff, sympathetic to the human body.

The furniture took me back to my grandmother's house in Vermont: fiberboard wardrobe, black mahogany dresser, one iron lamp, one bloated armchair, one very depressed sofabed. The coffee table held a batch of presidential campaign literature. Out in the kitchen Amy turned up ketchup and a brutally sour quart of milk in the fridge. On the sink drainboard stood a steam iron—quite warm when I pulled the plug. Who knows how many hours or weeks it had been ironing the air. The wastebasket revealed that human life can be sustained by blueberry yogurt, granola bars, Beth Durkee's Homestyle Cupcakes, and peanut butter patties.

Snippets in the bathroom wastebasket told us that Dawn had blond and eskimo black hair, with some reddish brown curls. Or girlfriends sharing the rent. "Or wigs she trimmed," Rachel suggested. More condom foil. The medicine cabinet held a tube of topical anesthetic, some skin preservative, premenstrual pills, a manicure set, and a hose-wrapped rubber douche bag.

On the living-room wall was another artsy photo poster, this one of reclining curves so eerily backlighted that the flesh colors died to black and white, creating the female horizon of some gorgeous, impossible planet. I wondered if the posters revealed sensitivity in Dawn, or if they were the whorehouse equivalent of the yuppie's classy BMW. "Nice nudes," Rachel shrugged. "Sexy but hard."

"Yeah." Amy agreed grimly. "And no TV. She's gone for a while."

Rachel wiped sweat out of her eyes. "Anybody getting hungry? It's sweltering in here."

Thumbing through the Boston phone book I found a scattering of numbers circled, so I slipped it into a plastic supermarket bag from the kitchen. I looked back at the room full of stuff. Suffocatingly ordinary stuff. The stuff of a woman who was going to turn the world upside down.

Good luck.

$\triangledown$

4

ETHIOPIAN GRUB USUALLY MEANS stews served with sourdough bread, *injera*. Chicken, lamb, or fish and the odd veggie. Garlic, ginger, and cardamom among other spices. The Upper Nile squeezes into a narrow storefront on Tremont Street. My old friend Larry Millman, the travel writer, had put me onto the place. Hourglass-shaped wicker tables, excruciatingly authentic African chairs, and taped Ethiopian music that marries black Africa and the Middle East. You begin with a hot cloth to wash your hands, and dine by swabbing up dabs of savory stuff in pieces of injera. If you liked hands-on dining as a kid, you're in heaven.

Amy ordered with a gusto that surprised me. I had the impression that for years she'd been defining herself against her reckless older sister. Today for some reason the Good Daughter had decided to live it up a little. Rachel was feeling a little rambunctious too: "So how come we stole this phone book?"

"Don't pick on the old man," Amy said, patting my shoulder.

We began logging into my notebook phone numbers Dawn had circled. Restaurants, taxis, hotels, a couple Newbury Street boutiques. Then Amy said: "Hold it, there's a page ripped out."

"Wait," Rachel said. She skipped out to the car and came back with my flashlight. She skimmed light over the phone book page at a severe angle: "Look. Someone wrote on the missing page and the ballpoint made an impression on this one under it." She blinked hard on her new contact lenses: "Looks like *Lynne*. And a phone number."

I wrote it down: "There's a pay phone by the ladies' room. Call information. Find out the exchange."

Amy was so excited she drained my glass of Asmara beer. "I just knew if you helped things would start to happen."

The waitress brought another beer and a honey pastry something like baklava. Nectar of the gods, messenger of tooth decay. Rachel and Amy wafted out the door licking their fingers.

As I was pocketing my credit card something slammed into the plate glass window. Amy. Her skull crashed against the glass and she collapsed. I leaped through the door.

"It's him!" Rachel pointed at a shadow sprinting along the dusky sidewalk. "I'll take care of Amy."

12

Even in the failing light you couldn't miss the purple shirt.

I was gaining on him when he cut into the mews behind the row houses on Dwight Street. By the time I made the corner he was halfway into a parked car. Big Buick, murky platinum in the dusk. As I yanked the door open, the fanbelt screeched and the car lurched into the van behind it with a tinny crunch. He shifted. Armpit hooked over the door, I kicked wildly at him as we lurched forward. Then we were careening toward somebody's back door, and I realized he was too busy aiming a pistol to steer. In the stupidity of the moment I had a sense of death as mistake even as my shin was bashing the guy's forearm and he twisted over into the passenger's seat with a squeal of rage more terrifying than the glimpse of the pistol coming around to meet me. His left arm wrenched the steering wheel and the car broke back into the alley. Without thinking I shoved backward, let go of the door, and dropped on my ear.

My skin burned against the pavement and my funny bone went berserk, but I was able to roll and then stagger toward the row of garden plots opposite the row houses.

As I was getting a fix on his license plate the Buick braked. Purple shirt swung out the door in a shooter's crouch. More amazed than panicky, like a deer jacked in a spotlight, I watched. In the instant it took his joined hands to bring up the pistol, my legs threw me sideways over a skimpy hedge. Sprawling forward, I plunged through green-smelling waist-high plants and knocked headfirst into an arbor trellis of old iron pipe. His footsteps trotted toward me.

On my left was a fence too high, too exposed, to vault. No time. Even if I could sprint across the alley without making a blatant target, back doors would be locked. Nobody would let me in. Trapped, feeling sick, I hopped a wire fence, then a ramshackle board fence that fell apart behind me, and feinted left and right among tomato plants and pole beans till I scrambled under a rickety garden lean-to, among garden tools and buckets, holding my breath.

His footsteps scuffed around the gardens for a minute, then he stepped up to the lean-to to listen. His shoes creaked a yard from my nose. His teeth struck soft, angry *fucks* off his lower lip. His thumb clicked the pistol's safety catch on and off. For some reason I remembered a client of ours, a New Jersey sports clothes wholesaler who entertained a Bergen County grand jury one Tuesday and on Saturday, in the desolate industrial park where he had his warehouse, was cut off in his Caddy by a couple of strangers who chased him on foot till he ran out of breath and then put a sawed-off shotgun in his right eye.

Vera—my partner—and I read the account in the *Times* over hot scones and coffee one Sunday morning at her place, and I said: "Remind me never to leave home without some hardware." Instead of arguing, Vee said in her dry Brit way: "I'm a pacifist, love, but in a pinch I'd want you to be able to express yourself."

If I could express myself now, the guy standing on my head would have a .38 slug climbing his pant leg.

Out on Tremont Street a siren whined. My man took the hint, sprinted to his car, and floored it. The relief lasted until I breathed in again. Stink.

Cat.

I was hiding in a cat comfort station. I wiggled out trying to be philosophical. Next time I met the purple shirt I'd be sure to have mother's little helper on me. As I stood up so did an Asian woman, a grandmother, quite hunched, in the next plot. She had a fat tomato in each hand. Shades of Vietnam. I waved and limped back to Tremont Street repeating the Buick's license plate to myself. Above the scrimpy garden plots the lights of downtown Boston flowered in the night sky.

Cops crowded around Amy. The small, very black waitress had her hands clamped together and her voice seemed crushed in her throat: "Her eyes are oopen, boot she don't see us, do she?"

"Here's the ambulance."

When I saw Amy's face I felt sick. Her eyes stared through me with terrifying passivity. I knelt beside Rachel, who seized my aching arm so hard I yelped. "Don't touch her," one of the cops ordered.

"We didn't move her," Rachel insisted. "She'll be all right if we don't move her."

"Just what happened?"

"We came out the door and this guy—the one at the apartment this afternoon—he comes up and grabs the bag with the phone book from Amy. Only Amy managed to snatch it back. So he slammed her into the window with all his might. Look."

The plate glass was cracked. Rachel grabbed my arm.

"You catch him?"

Her faith in me made me ache in a couple new places. "No," I said, "he stuck a gun up my nose."

But Rachel wasn't paying attention. Her eyes shimmered with tears. I looked down at Amy, at the tee shirt logo STEAM THIEVES. The helplessness crushed me. I knelt:

"Hey kid, you hear me?"

The girl's mouth slowly slumped open to one side, as if gravity were pulling her down through the sidewalk. Her eyes looked right through my face into the meaningless black sky.

An hour later I caught up to Rachel across Huntington Ave. at Brigham & Women's Hospital. In the meantime the cops diagnosed the episode as one more pointless mugging. Assault. Theft of property under $50. The purple shirt, I found out, was tooling about in a stolen car. Figured he'd been watching Dawn's apartment and followed us over to the South End thinking we might have the key to her whereabouts in the plastic bag.

When I described the situation, one of the cops shrugged and said: "Likely her pimp."

"I can't be sure she's hooking."

"She's doing something controversial."

"Where would you go looking for this guy?"

He patted his hip: "You packing?"

"The hardware's in my office in Manhattan."

"You want my advice, forget it. What good is finding him if we can't get a conviction? On the other hand, the sister may take a turn for the worse. She dies in the hospital and it's in the papers, then we got a whole different ball game."

Brigham & Women's is part of the Harvard Medical complex, just off the Fenway. It was ten o'clock when Rachel phoned her mother. When I took the receiver, Meg mixed sympathy with an ex-spouse's I might have known. At the mention of the hospital she gave a pained sigh: "Oh great." The year before a tipsy priest and his drunken Oldsmobile had run Meg off the road and into Brigham & Women's for weeks. She sounded so rueful I changed the subject:

"How'd your date go tonight?"

"Bill was feeling really run down. We postponed it."

Meg's steady guy was an electrician with weak batteries that only his drinking buddies could recharge. I sympathized cautiously, so my sympathy wouldn't put her on the defensive.

Next I dialed my partner Vera in New York, who worried because I was worried and wondered if she needed to reschedule our week's work. When I told her I'd take an extra day to see what I could do in Boston, she wondered some more, very softly: "Does this mean you've slept with Meg again?"

"Uh-uh, that was strictly an odd moment. A relapse."

"Don't protest so much, love. You're both adults. Or at least one of you is. And I don't mean to be possessive."

15

"Possess me, Vee."

"Give my love to Rachel. And for godsakes, be careful."

I smacked some kisses into the phone, and Vee quipped: "You sound like my auntie's budgie."

After which I had to face phoning Amy's mother, Joan.

"*Who* is it?" she demanded. I tried again:

"Duncan Ames. Rachel's father."

"Duncan! It's been years. I've been meaning, I — Amy's late. She was supposed to finish the laundry. I have my hands full around here. I haven't been well."

"I'm afraid Amy's in the hospital. In Boston."

Joan dived to the bottom of her mind. I tried to fill the silence:

"She cracked her head on a plate glass window."

"What kind of — ?"

"They're doing a CAT scan now."

"My poor baby!" she groaned.

"Why don't I pick you up?"

As I expected, Joan Biondi suffered a rush of anguish. She had a million powerful reasons why she shouldn't leave her house, and she named all but the real one. Instead of getting hysterical, she insisted I shouldn't have dragged Amy into a dangerous place like Boston: "Amy should've told me she was going. That would be the considerate thing. Should have asked me. And if I'd said no, she'd be safe at home now, wouldn't she? Is she all right? God, I hope she's all right. Bring her home as soon as the test's done."

Hopeless to explain.

I promised to report back in an hour. In the waiting room Rachel ate peanut butter crackers from a vending machine and remembered the weeks we'd spent here the year before waiting for Meg to heal. On TV one of the mega-conglomerate junk bond kingdoms of the 1980s was collapsing with a foul smell. An air quality alert was making breathing inadvisable. The ongoing taxpayers' revolt was locking up public libraries in the state's poorer neighborhoods. The presidential candidates were working the crowds, pumping hands with the theatrical urgency of X-rated sex.

Amy remained unconscious.

The nurse I cornered said, "She could begin to respond five minutes from now. Or five months. Too soon to tell. So far she's stable, that's a good sign."

In fabulous detail the neurological workup began to identify skull fractures, intracranial bleeding, and the like, leading to the irresistible prognosis: wait and see. When we looked into Intensive Care, Amy was hooked up to monitors and catheters, tubes in her arm and her mouth too: a living store-window mannikin, facsimile of life.

Down in the lobby I phoned Joan Biondi again. By now Joan was in tears, choking on her fear. Feeling clotted in my throat like peanut butter or dirt.

I did what I could.

On a hunch I called Lynne Dresser, the woman whose books were in Dawn's apartment, but the phone rang on and on.

We drove out Route 9 in gloomy silence until Rachel sniffed a few times and stammered: "By the way—this sounds silly—but, well, I mean, have you maybe stepped in something?"

I laughed: "I forgot, I've been rolling around in a catbox."

When I explained, Rachel burst out laughing, a hiccuping uprush of hilarity that kept on and on, soft and wild in her throat, until she was wiping tears on her coatsleeve.

$\triangledown$

5

SUNDAY MORNING I WOKE up on the sofa in our house in Natick—really Meg's house now. Meg was on the side porch picking through the *Globe* with a pungent cup of French roast coffee balanced on Rachel's easel. Her "Good morning" came with a questioning squint—maybe it was the sunlight. Hard to say sometimes whether Meg welcomes or tolerates these weekend visits. On some Sunday mornings she goes to church and then I take the three of us out for brunch. Over waffles we catch up on each other's news and silently practice saying goodbye to Rachel's childhood and the family we used to be.

This morning I pirated some of Meg's French roast and fed my aches and pains a couple aspirin. Then Rachel drove me and a trembling Joan Biondi into Brigham & Women's.

Amy's mother had tweaked her eyebrows thin and firmly marked her mouth with lipstick. You could see every muscle in her face. She was graying and to my eye underfed. "I went to Mass," she said scraping at her dress. "What's good for a soup stain? Look at you, Duncan. You haven't changed at all. You're not even fat. Remember the summer we had the blue wading pool in the yard when the girls were little? How's Meg? She get out much? It's hard for me to get out these days. I have a nervous problem, it gives me bad adrenaline to go outside my house. I just can't do it. It's not that I don't care about Amy. Do you—can you understand that?"

"Rachel's told me."

"I haven't been out of Natick for years. Literally. It sounds weird, but it's the truth. It's like house arrest. I'm okay as long as I don't leave my little nest. I get panic attacks."

"It's a disease. It's not just you."

"I love my girl, Duncan. Oh my god—"

I glanced at her in the rearview mirror. She rode with her eyes closed, hands clutching the edge of the seat.

"Amy's not a butterfly like Donna," she insisted. "You can count on Amy, you really can. God, they used to fight like cat and dog. Donna was the type who'd just snatch things from other kids. Not mean, just grabby. Full of herself. Totally full of herself, from day one. Very creative. And now where is she when I need her?" Joan winced: "I'm gonna need a ladies' room pretty quick; my insides are all messed up today."

When I pulled into the hospital lot, Joan started to get the shakes, so I hustled her inside before she could think too much and Rachel parked the Volvo.

Up on the fifth floor you couldn't tell one day from another. Amy was unchanged. Her body lay precisely in the middle of the bed where the nurses had placed her, as if the tubes were feeding her embalming fluid. In a squeaky voice Joan Biondi leaned close to her daughter: "Can you hear me, baby? You listening?"

I gave Rachel a hug: "I'll be right back, you two. Don't worry."

From the hospital I dialed Lynne Dresser's phone number, which turned up a cautious, intelligent voice: "How did you get this number? It's unlisted."

"You've stayed at Dawn Biondi's apartment in Boston?"

Silence.

"I found your name in Dawn's telephone book."

"Who let you in?"

"Someone's threatening to kill her. You're a friend of hers?"

Silence.

I took a chance and told her the whole story, from the ugly phone call and Amy's appeal for help, to the casual viciousness that put Amy in the hospital. The voice on the phone gave a groan: "God, the poor kid."

"Do you know where Dawn is?"

"She goes by the name Dawn Ashland now. And no, I don't know for sure where she is at the moment."

"But you hear from her."

Silence.

"Look, neither you nor I want to read about mangled remains in tomorrow morning's *Globe*. But I can't do much alone. I don't even have a photo of her to work with. You at least know what she's been up to."

"I'm a graduate student at BU. During the semester I stayed with Dawn on Hemenway Street to avoid the long commute out to—where I live." She hesitated, then suddenly broke out of her indecision: "Look, what time is it? Eleven? Can you meet me at two-thirty in the lobby of the Copley Plaza? Just you."

"Can I tell Mrs. Biondi that Dawn's still alive?"

"Two-thirty. At the front desk. What's your birthday?"

"I'm forty-three and I have more than two gray hairs."

"No. What's your sign?"

"Leo, I guess. Why?"

"So I'll recognize you."

"Look, shall I reassure Dawn's mother? She's on the edge of a nervous collapse." Which was true, though Mrs. B had no idea Dawn was in trouble. The line buzzed a moment then the voice came back:

"Yeah, Dawn's alive."

6

INSIDE THE COPLEY PLAZA the wood-paneled lobby dozed in smug Bostonian luxury. The shops yawned with fancy gold doodads suitable for burying pharoahs. I figured Lynne Dresser chose the place because you couldn't imagine violent surprises in here.

She came through the Dartmouth Street entrance patting her curly brown perm and thanking the doorman as if he were doing her a personal favor. Country mouse in the big city. Cute mouse. With her red pumps, trim skirt, and frilly white blouse, she might have been a remarkably pretty schoolteacher. She headed right for me. The expressiveness of her mouth told you she was thinking all the time. Interesting that she'd pick the swanky Plaza for a rendezvous then show up toting a favorite beat-up leather handbag. Her manner was just as unpretentious: "You want to hear about Dawn."

"How'd you pick me out so fast?"

"You're the only Leo in the lobby."

"I thought psychologists didn't believe in superstitions like astrology."

"If it works, don't knock it." As she shook my hand her eyes locked me in, sizing me up. "Besides," she grinned, "as you know, all psychologists are a little dingy."

She tapped her forehead, clowning, but her eyes were auditing me. I said: "Want a drink?"

"Sure," she shrugged. She fell in beside me like an old girlfriend, walking with a subtle bounce that made you feel you'd both whiffed laughing gas. "See, my family never had a cent. I went to Fitchburg State, a nothing school, and what I did" — she shrugged — "hey, I did nothing. Only one day my ed psych professor took me aside. She said, 'Lynne, stop hiding out.' Just like that. Next thing I know I'm trying things."

"And now?"

"Besides grubbing away at a degree? Well, I've been interviewing kids in Dorchester for a study on juvenile crime. Part of an NIMH grant."

"Enlightening?"

"About what you'd expect. Most of them are so poor it's like a foreign country. The only jobs are one step from slavery. Chump change. You can see why — what is it — one out of every four young black guys in America's in prison or the courts. I mean, shit."

"That's a scary number."

"It's sick. Like South Africa or someplace. The guy running for president, Senator Merriam, his wife, Caddy, keeps blurting out all this taboo stuff. Like, why don't they get serious about violence against women? Look at the wives and girlfriends beat up and mowed down every day on the news. How come you can go outdoors at night in Canada or Europe and not get raped or stabbed, whereas here it's all threats?"

"Especially if you're Dawn. Any idea where she is?"

"She's called me once or twice."

"From where?"

"She doesn't like me asking."

End of discussion.

In the dim hotel lounge Lynne scanned the darker corners for trolls. "Brrr, funeral parlor in here." She hugged her elbows. "Or a theater before the lights go up—that's how I met Dawn, you know. At tryouts for *Pygmalion*. I was doing a paper on role playing in child development, and I wanted to interview some actors. So Dawn and I got talking about acting. She wasn't even a BU student, but she'd starred in campus productions. In fact she was real tight with Frank Fascelle, the director. It was a trip to see them together—the rest of the cast was crazy jealous."

"And you?"

She shrugged: "Every move Dawn made, there were eyes on her. She was so uninhibited she was a little nutty. She made you sense how much of your life is habit. Dead moves. Even when you try to break out a little, have some fun, in the end it's so routine. Like a wedding is the biggest day of your life. But in the end there's the fancy white dress and a photo album. Well, Dawn wouldn't play along with that. She drove the BU feminists crazy. Because she'd actually do things they'd only talk about. The wildest thing I'd ever done in college was have a butterfly tattooed on my—well, kind of a dumb working-class thing, you know? And there was Dawn telling these yuppie feminists she wanted to make good porn movies. Can you believe that? Sex is too important to let men fuck it up, she used to say. They need to learn how to feel sex way way down. I mean, how naive can you get?"

"She slept around?"

Lynne shrugged: "You know how theater people can be."

"Was she sleeping around for money?"

"Ah. So you know about that."

"About what?"

"How she supported herself then." To the waiter Lynne said: "I'll have a gulp of Jack Daniels in my coffee, okay? Enough so you can taste it." She lit a long pink cigarette: "These are British. Dawn left them behind so I have to keep them from getting stale. I'm a real addictive personality. I'd give anything to quit."

"A cry for help," I said snatching the burning cigarette. "Habit. Dead moves. Let me call you back to life. Shall I ditch this?" She was speechless so I crushed the weed into the ashtray.

"My hero," she mocked. "Ever been addicted?"

"In the army. Tobacco and other plants. My daughter tried smoking last year."

"You bullied her out of it?"

"Her mother and I. Tough cop, soft cop."

"You're married."

"Once upon a time."

"What happened?"

"I got tired of carrying a boss to the bank so I dropped him and wormed into law school and debt. So Meg went to work for the boss and ended up marrying him. Which lasted six months."

"No alimony there."

"She married him to punish me and reward herself. And six months after the wedding she saw that and ran for the door. She called me in a panic and we talked nonstop for two days."

Lynne shrugged: "But you guys never got back together."

"For some reason, no. Maybe by then I could see how Meg kept confusing me with her old man."

"What, she wanted you to solve all her problems for her?"

"Uh-uh. She was just learning to get him off her back, and I was encouraging her. But then it felt so good to be pushing back after all those years that she pushed too hard. If you ask me."

"You still see her?"

"Sure. We take turns pulling the wagon."

"So now you're a, what did you say? Some kind of investigator? That's a big jump."

"I had a nitwit lawyer job and I met a woman with a lot of savvy. And we decided to be curious together."

"You have credentials you show people?"

I produced my billfold. As she studied its contents she lit another cigarette: "Back then I think Dawn was addicted to men. Maybe having missed a father growing up. He was a pretty cold customer, from what I hear. And she had too much feeling for anyone to snuff."

"Not everybody with feeling and no father works a mattress."

"In high school she found out that men pay when they're happy. So she began sneaking out of the house to make them happy. The way she tells it, she just barely escaped being handed over to DYS as a wild child."

"She have a particular boyfriend?"

"In high school. He turned out to be a car freak."

"Red LeBeau."

"Could be. Then when she started acting she was close to Frank Fascelle. Like his, what is it, protégée."

"I take it he's not the kind of boyfriend who takes money from his girl after a busy night."

"Oh." She was flustered. "You mean a pimp."

"Someone who might threaten to shoot her in the face."

Her eyes flinched: "The creep who called, he really said that? That's sick."

The spiked coffee arrived. "Dawn know any sickies?" I asked.

Lynne patted my billfold as if it were a hamster and nudged it back across the table to me. "Over the years," she said, "Dawn must've gone with hundreds of guys. Accountants, baseball players, media types. One night she brought home this government fish and game bigshot who had a cardboard box full of weasels in his car, and him and her shook the bed like an earthquake, then the three of us sat up all night drinking and feeding the weasels crackers. See, Dawn's an actress. Like, sex for her could be a role. Dirty or heavenly. Whatever turns you on—Anthony and Cleopatra."

"Professor Fascelle drive a silver Porsche?"

"That's someone else."

"Named?"

She tossed her hands in the air: "You're the one getting paid to find out this stuff."

"Amy and her mother haven't got a nickel."

"Suppose Dawn offered you something to help."

"I'm way off my turf. With no time. I'd recommend cops."

"Why not you?"

"I'm not a public servant."

"Nobody is." She gave a little puff of disgust. "It's all money and pushing other people around these days. Besides, you know how many women get threatened by drunk boyfriends every day? The cops are going to yawn."

"Dawn have some reason to avoid the cops?"

"I didn't say that." Emotion tightened Lynne's mouth. Her sudden

24

silence challenged me: "So that's all you can say? *Keep your fingers crossed?*" She stabbed out the cigarette and picked up her weathered handbag. When I opened my mouth she cut me off: "I know what you're thinking. *She got herself into this.*"

"What I—"

"Well, screw that." The disgust in her voice was startling. Suddenly she was on her feet and aimed for the door. When I started after her she turned and said coolly: "Don't follow me out of here or I'll scream for every security cop in the house."

"Let's not throw a—"

The bartender's eyeballs swiveled. Lynne leaned into my face with a furious whisper: "If she turns up—what did he say, shot in the head?—we'll know who to thank."

"All I kn—"

She patted her naked elbow: "You don't know this from—"

Her bottom gave a stylish twitch as her hand smacked it. She flicked out the door into the lobby. I slapped a ten on the table and hustled toward the other entrance, out onto St. James, hoping she'd leave the way she came in. There were doormen on the sidewalk, a few pedestrians across Copley Square in front of the Boston Public Library. Up on the John Hancock tower the sun was burning in the mirrored windows—when the place was new the wind would suck out the occasional wafer of glass and spit it down onto the street.

I saw Lynne Dresser and the platinum Buick in the same instant. She was moving so fast that she brushed past the car without seeing it. Looking for me over her shoulder, she skipped out into the traffic, headed past Trinity Church toward Boylston Street. The Buick inched away from the curb. Two heads, front seat. Too much glare to make out the driver, but I pictured a purple shirt. In the moment I hesitated he raced the engine and suddenly dropped it into gear. With a shriek the Buick shot into the street swerving toward her. In the same moment I was running.

I sprinted from the curb and ran with my hands out, dodging fenders like a maniac convinced that magic rays from his fingertips can stop cars. I ran with a vivid mental picture of my holster in the file drawer under Vera's computer printer. Cement barriers funneled Lynne around new construction outside Trinity Church. The car squeaked up beside her and braked hard. The passenger knifed out the door and hurdled the barrier next to her. You couldn't mistake him. Halfback body in a khaki safari shirt this time. The driver threw open the back door of the Buick for the snatch.

"Lynne!" I yelled.

In one movement she turned, saw him, cut left, and raced toward the church doors, away from the street. He'd have to drag her screaming to the car.

The safari shirt slowed. As his head came around I hurdled the barrier and jumped into him, missed the nose, boxed his ear, fell over his staggering body. Kicked. Kicked again and rolled on the pavement. I was afraid I'd see a gun barrel when I looked up, so I scuttered at a crouch past the church entrance, sweeping Lynne ahead of me. I heard tires but I didn't look back.

We did three months' aerobics in two minutes, into the company of a couple cops on Newbury Street who were shackling a scofflaw Cadillac with a Denver boot. To Lynne I panted: "You — want to — explain this — to them?" She shook her head, eyes searching up and down the street. In wild relief we squeezed each other's hands. My ankle throbbed. I said: "Where's your car?"

"Out in — Auburndale. Took — the trolley. So nobody would — follow me."

"Back there," I wheezed. "That was the car, the driver, that put Amy in the hospital. Last night."

"You don't have some kind of gun or anything?"

"In New York. My office. We're used to business fraud, cheesy bank tellers. Not these guys. I mean, it's broad daylight." Together, stupidly, we looked up at the irrelevant sun. "These guys are commandos. Like sicarios in Columbia. The ones who whack you from a motorcycle. Like the Vietcong used to do."

"Yeah, great. What about the gun? Could you use it?"

"How did I get involved in this?"

"Well, it was you they followed to the Copley, not me."

"But they wanted the pleasure of your company."

She smiled to calm her own fears. Thought played silently on her lips. I took my eyes off her thoughtful mouth long enough to notice her bare feet:

"Lost your shoes."

"Kicked them off. Couldn't run in them."

"Shall we go back for them?"

"You crazy? Get killed for Filene's basement shoes?"

"I'll give you a ride out to Auburndale."

"What if they're watching your car? Let's do the trolley."

"Your feet must be sore."

"Are you kidding? I'm still alive. I'm walking on air."

$\triangledown$

7

O**N THE TROLLEY TO** Auburndale we kept a nervous eye on the other riders. As the train swayed through shady backyards, neighborhoods that hadn't changed a lot in fifty years, Lynne sat across from me. Though her eyes were nearly closed, as if napping, she was studying my face.

Riverside is the end of the line west of Boston: a parking lot with a loop of track to turn trains around. Somewhere out here years ago was Norumbega Park, with a penny arcade, caged bears, a few amusement rides like the Caterpillar and the Lindy Loop, and the Totempole ballroom, where you could make out in sofas comfy and private as a kangaroo's pouch while a revolving mirrored ball tossed out a thousand fake moonbeams. I was in love with a Pine Manor Junior College girl who talked a lot about her oil exec father and proved to be as wholesome and slippery to squeeze as expensive soap.

Probably condos now.

In the parking lot, Lynne steered us toward a red sports car, an Alfa Romeo Spider with the vanity plate ACTRYST. "Dawn borrowed my big old Ford," she shrugged, "and left me this toy car. Can you scrunch in?"

Squeezed down beside her I found her eyes on me again. "Why the stare?" I said. "What's on your mind?"

"Hold me. I'm shaking apart inside."

I obliged. After a moment she gave my right pants pocket a shy pat and started to say something. "Come on," I said, "out with it."

"Sorry." She lowered her eyes. "I'm thinking how you risked your neck today. I'm excited." She gave my shoulder a soft pat. "I'm thinking I'd like to slip your pants down and show you how I feel."

"What?"

"It's okay, there's nobody around."

"Here?"

"I won't make a mess."

"In this toy car?"

"I can curl right up in your lap. God I was scared back there. Hold me." When I clamped my hands on her shoulders she stroked the back of one hand with her cheek the way a cat marks you with its whiskers. After a minute she reached for my zipper. "It's just pleasure," she mused. "Affection. No big deal."

27

"Lynne, I hardly know you."

"So? You took a risk for me, for no reason. I mean, most men talk a big battle, but that's it. Next thing you know they're punching their wife. But you actually saved my skin. Here, help me with this zipper."

"I just did what I had to do."

"Don't ruin it with the phony modesty. I saw your face, you were scared to death. But you did it. For me." Her eyes danced.

"I've had cashiers offer sex when we catch them stealing." I squeezed her to me, alarmed at her vulnerability. Full of unexpected feeling. I couldn't help smiling: "But christ, I think you really mean it. You really want to."

"Look, Duncan, don't be a shit. I don't do what I don't mean. You think I come on to every man I meet?"

"You're not as shy as you look."

"What a bullshit thing to say."

"All I meant was—"

"Let's drop it."

"Ever get paid for showing your gratitude?"

"What's that supposed to mean?"

"Dawn ever start you doing tricks?"

"*Turning* tricks. Dogs *do* tricks."

"No comment."

Her hand flashed. A moment too late I caught it. My nose stung, my eyes watered. I blinked as much in surprise as pain.

Lynne knotted up her mouth in consternation: "Sorry. You shouldn't have said that. Sometimes my temper gets away from me." She flung her fingers open as if shaking off dirt. I said:

"In my experience—maybe it's a hang-up—this isn't such a generous world. When someone offers you something that goes straight to the heart, it's usually a sales gimmick. There's fine print."

"Yeah well. If you're always on guard, when do you actually live?"

I told her a bit about Vera. I said: "If she knew, Vera would admire your strong feelings and hurt like hell. For starters."

"So you really are married in a way."

"Look, let's not get technical."

Her hand snugged into my crotch and held me softly. After a moment she said with quiet satisfaction: "Well. So you do care. That's interesting."

It was an eerie moment—half ecstasy, half army physical—and I had to swallow a grin. I kissed her forehead, which in these cramped circumstances was all I could reach anyway. I gave her a teasing nudge: "You were about to say something about Dawn."

"Dawn?" She slumped in her seat with a sigh: "I was dead broke when I met her. How was I ever going to finish school? I still had that false feeling. Big dreams but born to be a waitress. So sex for money—it didn't seem so deranged. Finally I even let Dawn fix me up. Once. It wasn't much different from a couple of blind dates on a weekend. Except on Sunday morning you bought your coffee and danish and had over a hundred bucks left. One guy was a lawyer and the other runs an employment agency. For Dawn it was fun. But me, I had this nagging voice in the back of my mind.—It's all how you're brought up, I guess. Anyway, a couple of days later, out of nowhere, I panicked."

Her eyes followed a string of green MTA cars as they snaked up to the terminal building. She fingered her earrings: silver daisies with glittery stones in the middle. "I read about AIDS symptoms and that night I had the sweats and a hundred-and-three-degree fever and I was hysterical." She grimaced: "Little yeast infection probably. Anyway, next day, we were both spooked. Dawn went for the HIV test, and we sweated it, and she swore if she got a negative, she'd quit. Which she did."

"Was that when she went out to the coast to make films?"

"Mmm. Videos actually. Erotic videos. She did walk-ons, then leads, and she was really good at it. I mean, all around her were these muscle zombies and gorgeous flakes with boobs out to here." She showed me where. "But see, Dawn had imagination. She wasn't into, like, meat and power trips—there was this scene where she had to—well, and she was tired of having to screw every sleazeball in the industry to get noticed. So after four, five months she let a guy talk her into coming back East with him."

"Mr. Silver Porsche."

"Yeah, but it wasn't like that," she protested, "not just money."

"But she was broke, right?"

"Boy, you really know how to get under a person's skin."

"Lynne, I have to try to be realistic. That's all I've got going for me."

She twisted the ignition key and the little Alfa sputtered to life: "Where do I drop you?"

"Wait. Where's Dawn now?"

"Who knows?"

"Help me find—"

"You want a ride or not?"

"Hold on. Let me phone Rachel at the hospital. Then we can go someplace very private. I'm getting excited thinking about all the questions you can answer."

"Duncan, you are so straight. You and your rubber-soled shoes and your Timex watch. Who the hell are you?"

"A very ordinary son of a bitch."

"Like hell," she said suspiciously.

Her hand was on mine, squeezing hard.

She drove us over to the pay phones at the terminal building, and I dialed Brigham & Women's.

"Gawwd," Rachel groaned, "where've you been? Amy's mother's going to pieces."

"Can you hold her together an hour or two longer? I'm right in the middle of some hot questions."

"Well, I don't know. She's in there sitting by Amy's bed with her eyes closed, sucking on her knuckle. She's pestering the nurses for tranquilizers. You better get here quick."

Behind me I heard tires shriek on asphalt. I took a few steps to see what was going on. In the receiver Rachel's voice squawked: "Hello? Hello? You there?"

"Yeah, but some hot questions just ripped out of here at a hundred miles an hour."

▽

8

AT AMY'S BEDSIDE JOAN sat with her ankles hooked around the chrome legs of her chair as if a storm were about to blow her out the window. She was still sucking on her knuckle, blotches under her arms, sweating it out. Her eyes avoided mine. "Is it true what Rachel says, you're searching for Donna?"

Rachel winced: "I had to explain how we —"

"She's in trouble," Joan croaked. "She doesn't have any fear; she always goes too far."

"Donna's fine. Just keeping her head down for a while. I just talked to her roommate."

"So she is in trouble."

"Maybe avoiding trouble."

"She really is a good kid, never mind what I've said, may God strike me dead, I love my —"

The words fell apart; she was sweating tears.

I hugged her, and Rachel was still squeezing her together half an hour later while we drove her home. Getting out of my old Volvo in front of her house, Joan said: "Don't worry about me. Once we find Donna, once I'm in my own kitchen, I'll be fine."

She ran into the house.

At home Meg offered us chicken sandwiches. It gave me a twinge to realize she was wearing a pair of Rachel's jeans. Rachel was a woman these days and they could borrow each other's clothes and not even squabble over it. They sported the same lush dark red hair and the same shoe size. They no longer fought off the resemblance. They even enjoyed each other. As Meg put it the night we slept together — one of two times since the divorce; neither of us approved of it — she said, "We're too old to fight. We can afford to be kind."

She meant Rachel and herself, and maybe me too.

On the other hand, when she offered me the chicken sandwich she added, "I thought you had an airplane to move in New York."

"Right after supper."

Meg smushed her mouth up under her nose — her equivalent of blushing. "It takes a certain extra energy, having to be aware of you around the house when you're not —" Her shoulders gave an embarrassed little hitch. "Mustard on your chicken, not mayo, right?"

31

"Hotter the better."

"I don't keep the horseradish type in the house anymore."

I was still chewing when I reached for the phone to dial Vera in New York. "Finish your sandwich," Meg scolded. "I didn't mean to push you. It's just that Bill's coming over tonight."

"He still going out to Oregon to work for his brother?"

"They're building fifty houses. They need electricians." Meg's thick red ponytail twitched as she shook her head: "But he won't be back. This is last rites. Bill's still a kid. I can see why his wife left him. Some men can't help it."

"That's a shame. I mean—"

"By the way, I think I may have a new job." She put up her hand to block questions: "When it's official I'll fill you in. Make your phone call."

When I took my thumb off the receiver I heard not a dial tone, but Rachel's voice on the upstairs extension. She introduced herself as a friend of Dawn's and hesitated: "You might—would you remember her?" I heard teeth bite an apple and chew, then a good-natured masculine grunt:

"How's she doing? I always stay for movie credits thinking I'm going to see her name one of these days. How is she?"

"Well, that's just it," Rachel said. "She's missing, and her family's, you know, they're getting concerned. And I was wondering if you could sort of suggest some people who know her? You know, people we could ask about her?"

The other voice turned grave: "This the usual disappearing act? Or is this what we've always worried about?"

They made a date to wonder.

After she hung up Rachel swooped downstairs and scooped a mouthful of chicken: "Can I have the car tonight for an hour or two?"

"I'm not sure you should be nosing around for Dawn by yourself."

"I thought we agreed it's not polite to listen in on other people's calls." You could feel her check the anger in her voice: "And besides, that was Frank Fascelle, the theater professor at BU. And since he was her friend, somebody should talk to him."

"Dawn's traveled in some sleazy—"

"Hey, he's not some hood. He's at a rehearsal tonight. Some summer theater program." Rachel flicked a finger in the mayonnaise and then popped it in her mouth. Meg couldn't resist:

"There is such a thing as etiquette, you know. And you're not chasing around after Donna Biondi, so get that right out of—"

"Besides," the mouthful of chicken argued at me, "you're going back to New York tonight."

I put down the phone. "Look, Dawn's got a mind of her own. And the Boston cops know she's in a fix."

"What can they do? Look what's happened to Amy. Nobody official gives a—banana."

I could hear heels digging in, so I said: "Okay, suppose I help you wag Frank Fascelle's tongue tonight. Then we call it quits."

Rachel gave a noncommittal shrug: "Well, he might say more to another guy than he would to me. We can see."

She was putting on her favorite earrings, little silver cameras with synthetic pearls for lenses, when Meg said: "If you're filling in for Amy, you have to be at work early tomorrow, you know."

"Okay, okay." Rachel snatched up a paperback titled *In Search of the Real America*. "I'll read this in the car," she breezed, "so I'll get lots of sleep."

These days mother and daughter could struggle like bulldogs and not get a hair out of place.

On the bare gloomy stage in the BU theater, a couple collegiate wrestlers were locked in a clinch while the ref studied the holds.

On second thought, no. One mouth was licking and nibbling its way down from earlobe to rib cage. Female rib cage. An erotic clinch. The director leaned over, egging them on. The lovers rolled over now, hips jostling for joy, hands caressing. From time to time their Nikes softly thumped the boards.

A dozen cast members in the front rows sat silhouetted by the dim footlights. A couple toddlers were running up and down the aisle, intrigued by the rake of the theater floor.

Up on the bare stage Frank Fascelle hovered over the lovers, waving his arms, coaching. Big guy, Frank, in his mid-thirties, with a white V-neck jersey that set off his bushy black hair and dramatic black eyebrows. He wore jeans and leather sandals, and talked with eloquent hands.

"Tammy," he was coaxing, "this soldier takes advantage of you. Sex he wants. Behind the bushes in the park, for crying out loud. And afterward you appeal to him for love, some sign of human feeling. But he's had his thrill, what does he care? So you hurt. We've got to feel you hurt. Try it again."

With noisy lips the couple clinched again—very erotic unless you thought of a CPR demonstration. Finally the soldier shuddered and got up. The girl buttoned her blouse, rose on one elbow, and reached out a hand, which the soldier was too busy lighting a cigarette to take. Tammy's voice fluttered: "Tell me, do you—like me?"

The toddlers pranced up the aisle hooting.

"Come *on*, Tammy," Fascelle coached. His hands swept the air. "It's an evil moment. This isn't the suburbs. You're a servant. You feel worthless. You're *begging* him for love. This donkey in his hot-shit army uniform and gold buttons. You *beg* him and he's giving you VD. Which is what *La Ronde* means, eh? Get *into* it."

"Tell me," the girl fluttered again, "do you—like me?"

Fascelle stamped his foot, his hands flinging passion: "Come *on*, kid! You're nothing! You *hate* yourself! You want to spend your life swabbing rich people's toilets? This guy's your only chance to escape. You tremble if he looks at you." The coach was crooning now. "It's gotta be '*Love me. Oh christ, love me.*'"

Tammy objected: "I just don't want to overdo—"

Frank Fascelle was pleading: "Hey, corrupt we need. Sex we need. Power. Not this nice girl who worries does he like her Esprit jeans!"

"Well if that's how you feel"—Tammy pushed to her feet—"then just forget it!" She dropped off the stage and marched up the aisle, Frank Fascelle calling to her:

"Tammy, knock it off with the ego. We got work to do." When she didn't relent he cut his losses: "Okay, who wants to fill in for the servant?"

No takers. I leaned into Rachel's ear, teasing: "Here's your big chance, kid."

The girl in front of me hooked one of the romping toddlers by the straps of her jumper. The other kid, the boy, climbed up on the armrest of her seat. He teetered there, amazed, and when she reached for him, toppled into my lap and let out a howl.

"Gotcha," I said, and handed him across the seat.

"This is Mario," the girl said, "one of Frank's twins. He's a busy little monkey."

I noticed Rachel had sauntered up to the stage and was thumbing through the script. I said: "How's Frank as a director?"

The woman twisted about to get a better look at me: a picturebook face with a glum-looking mouth. "Frank? He's great. He was with Joseph Papp for a while. He's done a PBS Tennessee Williams and some Off Broadway. You have any idea how cutthroat the competition is for a job like this?"

"You know an actress named Dawn Ashland?"

"Sure, only I haven't seen her in ages. Maybe her singing career took off"—hint of sarcasm?—"or maybe they're cutting a record."

34

"Who?"

"Her band, Steam Thieves. They gig over in Kenmore Square sometimes. Like tonight."

"She's a musician?"

"She's got an okay voice. But the way she uses it, like Frank says, you can feel her breathing in your ear — here he comes."

He hunkered down close, with an easy intimacy: "How they behaving, Sherry? Want me to get you a ride home?"

"I'll stick it out awhile longer."

When I introduced myself, Frank Fascelle clapped a handshake on me while rubbing little Mario's head. He was sweating, giving off energy like a steam radiator too hot to touch. Vigorous bush of hair, plenty of chin. Confident mouth. He reminded me of an athlete in an aftershave ad I'd seen. Around his neck he wore a chain with a small gold medallion of the Holy Virgin.

He set Rachel and the Soldier to work rehearsing together. To talk about Dawn he walked me backstage: "She was supposed to do *La Ronde* with us, but she hasn't shown up."

"Someone's threatening to kill her," I said. "Her family hopes I can find her first."

"Who would hurt her?" He stopped to face me and blurted his own answer: "One of her guys, huh?" And that was the trickle that broke the dam. "Dawn doesn't listen. She'll try anything. I used to be amazed she never got clobbered out there."

"Keep your fingers crossed."

He lit a cigarette, tapping the ash into a tiny brass ashtray he carried, compromising with the No Smoking signs up on the walls.

"So she slept around for fun and profit?"

"It's amazing, isn't it? I mean, sex is so available these days — like junk food. You've seen the teenage pregnancy rates. It's amazing any woman could get money out of a guy for sex now. And yet Dawn" — he gave a little sigh — "she had the moves. The magic. She could play along with anyone."

"Party girl?"

The phrase pained him: "Not stupid like that. It was more she could read wishes, fears — your particular dumb idea of love." His hands scooped the air for words. "She has imagination."

"Where'd she find her customers?"

"You couldn't predict. A professor over in chemistry. Some hotshot in the fire department. Some bozo, his car turns her on. Some jerk with a knife collection. Used to scare the hell out of me, some of the guys

35

she'd take — I let her crash in my office or backstage here sometimes, just so I'd know she was safe. The campus cops killed that option."

"You gave her parts?"

"Damn right."

"Even though she wasn't enrolled at BU?"

"She could act. Here's one middle-class kid who had a life away from the boob tube. While other kids waved silly signs at football games, Dawn was out learning about life. She came here on a visit with a friend. Read Desdemona for us, I think. And holy shit, she forgets herself. All these little touches with the hands and the catch in the throat, and — alive. Just to watch her mouth. Her *lips*, for christsake. What a relief from these suburban cows trying so hard to act. Going through the motions. I could have kissed her."

"Word is, you did."

"Who told you that?" He was flattered.

"Friend of hers."

"Ah, don't tell me. The one with the wire notebook — the psychologist. Lynne. She followed Dawn everywhere. If you told me she was in love with her, I'd buy it."

"You were in love with Dawn yourself?"

"Sure. You'd be too." In trying to be blunt, he couldn't help boasting a little.

"Would I have given her up by now?"

"Ahhh." He was kind enough not to laugh in my face. "You picture yourself in control. Well, you could be — if you had handcuffs and enough rope. I mean, this kid hated routine. For a week she'd be so close it was like she'd unzipped you and climbed inside. Then poof. Gone. Note written with a bar of soap on your mirror. Or nothing. Just a breeze where she'd been standing a minute before."

Out front I could hear a woman begging for love. The urgent, queasy seduction in the all-too familiar voice gave me the creeps. Frank pricked up his ears. I said, "You weren't married then?"

"When Dawn left, in a way it helped nudge me toward marriage. These little guys are mine."

"Cute kids," I said. "Sherry's your wife?"

"We're in separate apartments at the moment. If you want a peaceful home and hearth, don't go into theater. It's insane."

"So Dawn hit the road what, five or six years ago?"

"I'd see her from time to time. I helped her find parts in summer stock. In Ogunquit, in Saratoga, in — "

"In porn movies?"

He ignored the cue: "She always had ambitions. Summer stock bored her. Too cute. Too safe. *Auntie Mame. The Philadelphia Story.* Cotton candy, she called them."

"But she did make porn flicks?"

The twins came romping backstage. They swung on the curtain ropes whooping like orangutans. Dad crushed his cigarette into his little brass ashtray and snapped the lid: "I hear rumors. But I've never seen her bare ass onscreen. Although I can tell you. If you had your clothes off together—used to happen all the time—she'd want to try out lines with you. Improvise scenes."

"Such as?"

"Oh, a reunion from prison. Maybe some terrible jealousy. Or her baby's just died, she begs you to give her another baby." His eyes twinkled at the idea of all that playacting, but his hands were talking passion. "All the time different moods, new feelings. Always pushing you toward, what—?" He stopped and gaped at his dancing hands. I couldn't stand the suspense:

"Make-believe?"

His face turned so grave I was afraid he was winding himself up to say something like *ecstasy.* Instead he broke into a grin: "Not just make-believe. She'd push you outside yourself. Make you wish. Both of you. Like two kids sometimes. Like you were the only survivors of this long lost family—that was another one of her favorite scenarios."

I tried to imagine it. Frank Fascelle let out a poetic sigh:

"Terrifying woman. Unless all your feelings have been snuffed out or you've got middle-class prejudices to hide behind."

Little Mario raced toward us and plunged headfirst in between his father's knees. Frank scooped him up onto his shoulder so he could examine the red fire extinguisher on the black brick wall. In a glass box next to it hung a vicious-looking fireman's ax. I said:

"As far as you know, then, Dawn's still hooking."

Frank Fascelle winced: "I hear she joined up with some kind of glorified escort service for a while. Computer appointments, photo brochures. Send four girls to my sales convention—that type. Expense account nooky. Did you know Japanese executives make about forty percent what Americans get?"

"They have geishas."

"Dawn has a weakness for money."

"You must have been angry when she left."

"Of course, of course. I told her she was an idiot, listen to me. But she already knew what I knew. Maybe she's only half-crazy. Maybe she'll make a million doing erotic films. The way TV and Hollywood's going, that's all that'll be left pretty soon. Everybody's addicted to happy endings these days. Good-bye theater."

Mario was hypnotized by the fire ax. He gave the glass case a scientific tap. Frank slid him to the floor, then took out another cigarette.

"See, Dawn's hung up. It kills her that sex is money in this society. And not just in ads. She'll tell you romance novels teach little girls to use sex as a tool to marry money. And porn—she thinks porn treats bodies as sex machines so you can forget that some day the body you're trapped in is going to shrivel up and die on you. And good sex—in case you're curious, good sex is—"

"Well?"

He threw up his hands. "Why make fun of her? She's been through enough, she's got a right to her obsessions. Believe me, she's read a lot of intense stuff. And she wants to talk about it all night long—if you can stay awake."

They were calling for him out front. I said: "Let's hope she turns up before someone switches her off for good."

I fished out one of my business cards. He gave his head a little shake as if waking up from a nap. He gave a gravelly whisper: "If she comes here, how can I protect her?"

"Call me." I handed him the business card.

"But this is a New York address."

"I can only afford to keep an eye on this problem from a distance. I have to work for a living."

"Look. If she's really in harm's way, we need to find her. I'll come up with whatever money you need. Somehow."

I admire people who can make a clean decision to do what's right even if it costs. Maybe directing Hamlets onstage frees you from to-be-or-not-to-be agonies. Maybe a guy like Frank could feel his way through a divorce without a lot of tapdancing and hallucinations and cheesy regrets. "Let's give it a few days," I said. "I've found someone who'll pass on the warning, and maybe Dawn will check in by phone."

"Okay if I ring you for an update? It'd kill me if anything happened to her."

"Sure. Good luck with the play."

We shook hands.

For the next twenty minutes I watched an Austrian soldier negotiating a nerve-racking quickie in the bushes with a maidservant I'd known years before, in another life, as a rescuer of seal pups.

When she hopped off the stage afterward, Rachel faked a yawn to hide her excitement: "Guess what? He says I can have the part."

"I heard."

"Don't look so thrilled."

"I thought we were here to look for Dawn."

"We are. We just did." Indignation started to smoke behind Rachel's eyes: "Hey look. I got a shot and I went for it."

"It's not a good idea."

"It'll be a great experience. And Dawn may turn up here."

"I thought you were filling in for Amy at the supermarket."

"Part-time," she huffed. "God, I can't believe it. You sound just like—" Suddenly she was steaming. "I have the rest of my life to rot in a supermarket. All I—"

"I'd feel better if—"

"What about how *I* feel?" She glanced over her shoulder, softening her voice: "Let's argue outside."

But of course the walk to the Volvo turned out to be chummy and conspiratorial, with Rachel crooning in my ear: "So. You get anywhere with Frank?"

As I say, chummy.

Stubborn as a goat.

9

STEAM THIEVES WAS SHAKING up the Richter scale at The Rat's Hat a block off Kenmore Square. A stage lurched out of one corner into the cellar, and the smoke was thick as steel wool. The band turned out to be three brutal amplifiers and a set of drums powering four stagily disreputable guys with vests and stubble. Their lips moved during most of the songs, though the sound system blew the words to kingdom come. The scraps I caught went:

> *Let the rich bitch*
> *Suck my fist*

and ended with an explosion of keyboard synthesizer noise. College kids in their New Age smocks and flattop hairdos were eating it up. Nothing like a little wash-and-wear brutality to relax you.

During the break we went backstage to the dressing room. The lead guitarist had both hands inside his tie-dyed shirt like a straitjacket — wiping his armpits with a red kerchief and a white sock, it turned out. I didn't rush him the glad hand.

"I'm Barry," he said. "You here about the album?"

"Got one ready?"

"Frigging record companies, man. We cut this monster album couple years ago. Dermott and me wrote the songs, Ryan did the cover photo — you should see it, it's this Uncle Sam, you know, in the hat and the suit, only between his legs what he's got, he's got a syringe, like in the hospital, like junkies. Trick photography, see — and it's shooting out stuff: nickles, dimes, lightning bolts, musical notes."

"Not your average party band," I said.

"It's a mock, see? We're mocking the whole commercial music scene and all the power shit that's going on out there. That's why they killed the album. Frigging Japs buy out the conglomerate. All contracts down the tubes."

Rachel nodded: "They never released the album?"

Barry flung his hand in the air like Jimmy Swaggart poking Satan's eye out. "It's in the can, all mixed. The assholes are *sitting* on it. Some subjects are off limits, see? Like how the rich get richer and the poor get drugged out. You do Top Forty about getting laid tonight and you get airplay. You do shit about who's cracking the whip behind the scenes and you never get out of the can. They tell you to make it symbolic. Or the audience'll be offended, some such shit."

"Who's they?"

"Fucking six corporations, man, they control the whole industry. You go to the small labels, shit. Guess who owns them."

His fist pounded the wallboard partition with such a racket that the bassist leaned into the cubicle: "Hey Barry, cool it. Don't give that dork upstairs any excuse to hold back the bread for this gig."

"Screw you," Barry drawled. "This guy's—what are you, an agent? You scouting for somebody?"

I didn't deny it. The bassist, Dermott, came in to sniff me over. He had bluish hair, lazy eyes, and a peachfuzz chin. Two tiny gold skulls in his ears and one tiny gold skull in his left nostril. Leather vest over his skinny torso. The weed in his hand smelled like a burning jockstrap. Behind him came a short pouting brunette with sour skin, hairline eyebrows, and a buckskin jacket. She was dipping paper cups into a bucket of orange juice and handing them out. "Christ, Barry," Dermott grunted. "This guy isn't the agent."

"I'm looking for Dawn Biondi. Dawn Ashland."

"Good old Dawn," Barry snorted. "She almost broke up the band."

"I hear she signed a separate contract and wouldn't take the rest of you along."

"What kind of bull is that!" Barry started to punch the wall again. Dermott grabbed his arm.

"You want the true story, man? Dawn couldn't sing."

Barry sneered down his long borzoi nose: "She sounded like a bazooka reaming out a pig."

"Any idea where she is now?"

"She didn't quit us. We blew her off. She went out to L.A. to do a movie, which of course was bullshit. All she could do was peddle her ass. Comes back screwing this rich sleazeball and telling us she's gonna make our album the soundtrack for a film that the sleaze and his mob friends are financing—"

"Bar—ry," Dermott growled. "Shut *up*. You don't want to offend anybody."

Barry stopped short: "Hey, well. No offense—"

To ease his mind I slapped my business card on him and said: "Let me tell you about an offensive phone call."

My spiel seemed to sober Barry a little: "You should talk to Ryan, he'll tell you. That broad's got evil friends."

Dermott shrugged: "Ryan's our regular drummer. Him and Dawn,

41

they were this tight." He folded his hands together like a kid praying or spiders getting it on. "And Ryan's got his head kicked in for her sake. Couple weeks ago. He's got doctor bills, Percodans. Codeine capsules this big—"

"Who clobbered him?"

Dermott passed the toke on to Barry: "Ask Ryan. Call him up, see if he'll talk to you. His name's Ryan Kassiotis. I'll dial the number for you. Got a dime?"

I did. Dermott positioned himself to block my view of the pay phone's keypad, and dialed.

So Rachel and I drove into Medford, to a duplex with just enough side yard for the tenants to park. Ryan made me show my business card and my driver's license through the mail slot in his front door.

Inside was a madhouse of empty bottles and savory clothes, fast-food litter and reading matter that ranged from *Mad* to *Scientific American* and *Rolling Stone*. A luan door turned table in the living room held up a video game, stereo gear, a Hasselblad view camera, and a telephoto lens the size of a fireplug. A kit-built astronomy telescope leaned in one corner, hemmed in by battered black drum cases. MIT decal on the bass drum case.

The clutter had a boy genius quality about it. And no end of surprises, including a cage composed of four storm windows webbed together with duct tape that sheltered a deep green tortoise with a mystic eye and a church-key beak.

Ryan was about as talkative as the tortoise. He was swigging from a jug of Almaden chablis: tall kid in his early twenties with brass-rimmed specs and a clunky plaster cast on his left arm. His whitish blond hair was clipped close to the sides of his head up to a puffy crown on top—sort of a hair beret. When I asked Rachel what they called the hairstyle she said under her breath: "Circumcised."

It's some kind of milestone when your kid is old enough to try out a dirty joke on you.

Up close Ryan's face was still pink and purple from the laying on of hands. No wonder he was cautious.

"Nice tortoise," I said.

"Yeah, in Central America the Miskitos eat them. They're almost extinct. Cost me a hundred bucks. I wanted to get one before they're all gone."

"Who was it tried to put your lights out?"

He waved the plaster cast at me: "They stomped me, man. I couldn't even get to one of my knifes."

On the wall, from a six-foot khaki strap, hung five scabbards with five brutal-looking knives in them. I said: "Give me some names in case I run into them."

"Forget it, man. Unless you want to get kicked in the face—the doctors thought I'd be blind at first afterward."

"What happened to you?"

"I talked to a guy in a parking lot."

"Which guy?"

"The wrong guy."

"Which wrong guy?"

"The one that kicked the shit out of me."

"You report it?"

"What for?"

Going nowhere in narrowing circles. Rachel tried a different angle: "I like your view camera. I have an old Hasselblad I bought at a tag sale for ten bucks. I had the shutter rebuilt."

"Ten bucks!" Ryan gushed. "Unbelievable." He turned and limped into the kitchen as if we weren't there. He'd hung olive drab canvas over the windows to make a darkroom. On the table stood an enlarger and developing trays. Rachel uncurled a print drying on the linoleum-topped counter: a Shirley Temple toddler holding a rose between her teeth and coming out of a cannon muzzle, in midair. "This a composite?" she asked.

"I put the two prints together," Ryan said, "so it looks like she's being shot out of the barrel." The subject loosened him up. He fingered Rachel's ears: "Where'd you get the camera earrings?"

"A gift," she shrugged.

"I want a pair."

"Have one." Rachel took off the left camera and dropped it in his open palm. He worked it into his earlobe. "Close the door," he said without a thank-you. And shut off the room light. We sank into dim red darkness. I said:

"You know Lynne Dresser?"

"Sure. She crashes with Dawn. Chases after black kids in Roxbury asking why they do stuff. You steal, you slash somebody, she interviews you to see what makes you tick. She gets *paid* to ask it, too. Barry thinks she just gets off on dark meat."

"Dawn sleep with everyone in the band? Or just you."

"What do you think, she's some kind of whore?"

"I'm trying to find out."

"Don't be so fucking judgmental." The enlarger lens snapped the

43

negative onto the board: white hair and black faces in a swarming background. Ryan fussed with the contrast filters, cursing the clumsy plaster cast. Rachel silently lent a hand, then took over the printing:

"I'm good at this," she said, "trust me." And before he could object: "I hear you did the surrealistic cover for your last album."

"Oh," he mumbled, "yeah. Uncle Sam and his needle. With the right darkroom technique you can put things back together."

"Back?"

"Yeah, back the way they'd be if people weren't so crazy to keep things separate and pure. Like Uncle Sam. Dawn and me laughed our asses off that night." He slipped a sheet of print paper onto the easel. His face was lumpish and incomplete in the glow of the red safelight. "We were so together, Dawn and me. Like you wouldn't believe. She'd wear my white socks, my shirts — she's still got this other earring." He pointed to the G clef in his right ear.

"How long an exposure?" Rachel asked. They negotiated. The enlarger flashed on, the timer ticked, then darkness again. Rachel slipped the print paper into the developer. The timer ticked again. Ryan coughed.

"But that got all screwed up. After Dawn left Steam Thieves, she went out to the coast to make some skin videos. And when she came back she had this guy Armand, she walked him around like a pet dog. She just about owned this house he had. And then she realized she couldn't get away from the guy, he was so jealous. So she asked me would I help, and we did a few things, and it seemed to work and then it didn't."

"What things?" Rachel asked.

"We had a good time though. In London. Then Egypt — we wanted to see the Pyramids, feel the psychic energy and like that. We stayed in this amazing hotel. Ten bucks for a Coke. Then she booked us to Tokyo because that's where the action's gonna be by the year 2000. But it's just swarms of people now. Did I tell you, the Japs killed our second album when they bought — I guess I did. Anyway, we flew back through Peru. She wanted to see that lost city in the mountains, maybe bring back some dope to sell. But that was a total washout. So I bought Montezuma, the tortoise there."

"But what did you do about the jealous guy?"

"See, Dawn's a high energy person. The way she thinks, she puts out high energies. The normal psychic resistors that control everybody, they don't stop her thoughts. So she —"

"Wait," I cut in, "exactly who is Armand?"

Ryan transferred the print to the stop bath. "Armand Fixler's a dealer. Not drugs. Papers. Historical shit. Treaties and presidents' letters. Movie star stuff. He's got George Washington, he's got Pope Pius, he's got Elvis. He happened to be in Hollywood buying up some estate. Some buddy of Reagan's."

"And he met Dawn there."

"What he did, he sucked up all her psychic energy. Because his whole thing is collecting. Scoop up famous shit and lock it in a safe. Sit on it. Sit on it and wait for the price to go insane. So a guy like that, he has nothing in himself. He has to tap power from a high-voltage profile like Dawn."

"So he wouldn't let her go. And when she came to you for help, he had some assistants stomp you."

In the dark you could feel him shrug: "Dawn didn't blame him. We were in this parking lot in Revere, nobody around, and they jumped us. Dawn dropped the mikes she was carrying and locked herself in the car, then took off looking for a cop —"

"She took off on you?"

"To find a cop," he repeated. Testy this time. "What was she gonna do, let them bash her too?"

In the fixer the new print turned out to be a close-up of the terrapin's can opener face grafted onto a guy in a dark IBM-style business suit. The eye sized you up from a million years ago: from the other end of the universe. Ryan slid him into the sink to rinse.

"When it happened I said to Dawn, I said, 'What do we do, hire bodyguards for the rest of our lives?' And Dawn says, 'If they were really into killing us we'd be dead now.' "

"I bet that cheered you up."

"Sometimes weirdness is ultimate reality, you know?"

"So you weren't really angry at her?"

"Why should I be?"

"Well, for starters, you got a facelift."

"In her old life she knew a lot of crazies. Guys who, like, feasted on her body. Geeks who'd give anything to touch her tit. And she probably told one of them no, not for no amount of gold now, and he went apeshit. So it was like her dead life coming after her. Like that movie —"

"*Night of the Living Dead*," Rachel whispered.

"Yeah, the undead. You like sci fi?"

"What I've read," Rachel said. She steered the conversation off into outer space. I took the hint and coughed:

"Ugh, these fumes. I'll be in the other room."

Ten minutes later they came out discussing cult rock groups with names that made me feel like a mutant from beyond.

"By the way," Rachel murmured. "Where's Dawn now?"

"I thought you came over here to tell me."

"I wish we knew." Rachel knows how to look touchingly wistful.

"How about Mr. Fixler?" I said. "Think he loves Dawn enough to kill her?"

"Hey look, I can't talk about him, it makes the whole side of my face ache."

"Where's he live?"

"Concord someplace."

"He in the phone book?"

Ryan shrugged. "I can draw you a map. Only do me a favor. If you find the guy, don't give him my name."

$\bigtriangledown$

1 0

W E SKIRTED SOMERVILLE ON the Alewife Brook Parkway, then
cut west on Route 2. "You know," Rachel said, "when Paul Revere did
his ride out here, it didn't happen the way the books tell it."
    "How did it happen?"
    She wasn't listening: "Boy, is Ryan high on Dawn or what?"
    "Bit caught up in himself, isn't he?"
    "Don't jump all over him," she huffed. "He's been going through a
bad identity thing. Even his name – Ryan Kassiotis – he feels it's like
his immigrant family pinning this WASPy name on him, trying to
belong. Which makes him feel freaky. Plus I bet he was a nerdy sort of
kid who took a long time to wake up. His old man was a machinist, and
he scrimped to send Ryan to study engineering at MIT."
    "But he didn't graduate."
    "Uh-uh. He went through this – well, he sort of spun out."
    "Spun out how?"
    "He lost it. Mentally." Rachel described a manic breakdown the kid
had suffered his sophomore year. He'd locked himself in his dorm
room and written a fifteen-hundred page sci-fi epic about Galactoids –
insidious creatures cannabalizing the citizens of . . .
    You get the picture.
    What cured him was quitting MIT and playing drums fifteen hours
a day with breaks to discover photography. He loved darkroom work
especially, since there you could compensate a lot for what was missing
or distorted in a negative, not to mention the world. Dawn had per-
suaded him that all that past confusion had actually prepared him for
a serious creative breakthrough – which was finally starting to happen.
    "Which is why," Rachel said softly, "he loves her."
    "He told you that?"
    "Couldn't you *feel* it in him?"
    "You trust him?"
    I felt her shrug in the dark beside me: "Well, he got beat up. That
must prove something."
    You could feel the pulse of Rachel's curiosity. She leaned forward
in her seat like a keen pointer on a first hunt. All at once I felt too old
for this. Sorry for Dawn but indifferent to whatever kinky sins or sincere
evil she'd stirred up. I wanted to be in Vera's bed with a bottle of

Guinness and her Mozart on the stereo, not following the white dotted lines down the highway like an idiot counter on an endless game board.

"Watch it," Rachel cautioned, "this is Concord. Better slow down. The new speeding fines in this state are murder."

These days the cradle of the revolution is sedate and classy, with a maintenance-free bronze Minuteman on a pedestal and lots of stately old houses. In the midst of suburban congestion there's still an illusion of farms—a landscape that says *gentry* and *squire*.

Armand Fixler's shack was a couple of miles west of the famous bridge, lighted up, behind iron gates, like the Love Boat. Exotic cars, including a Jaguar and a BMW Turbo-Bankroll, loitered in the circular driveway. I snugged the Volvo up behind a Saab, fellow Scandinavian.

PARTY AT ARMAND'S
COME AS YOU ARE WHEN CALLED

Leaving Rachel bobbing her head to a rap group, I made my way up to the front door, where a butler-type in a powder blue summer suit inspected me and my business card in the light. He had a droopy mustache and gravelly basso—I wanted to call him My Good Man. He took the card and Dawn's name further inside to Mr. Fixler. Nice house: One of those new designs that combines colonial simplicity with the extra closet space of Versailles. The formal living room was right out of the Sunday *Times* and sumptuously dead: the faint party sounds came from the back of the house.

Armand Fixler came out to shake my hand. He favored continental fashions for the male: fitted shirts, pleated pants, stately necktie. He was a mature thirty-seven or a tinted fifty: thin and wavy on top, with quick boyish eyes behind his bifocals. He pinched his lips as if trying to catch an invisible hair on his tongue. Not a bad looking guy really. As an exponent of the sincere handshake, he kept cranking my arm like Granny Ames's ice cream maker.

When I apologized for intruding, he protested: "Nicholas tells me you're looking for Dawn—she's all right, isn't she?"

I did my little song and dance about the phone threat.

His forehead furrowed and the corners of his mouth drew down in—what exactly was it, sadness? resignation? "I can tell you where she is," he offered, "or at least with whom. But you'd better be careful, this young man has a bad temper. And he collects some pretty fiendish-looking knives. Kassiotis, his name is."

"She's not with him now. In fact she's nowhere to be found. The kid tells me Dawn lived here for a while."

"Ah. You talked to him."

"I tried."

He smiled: "Exactly."

I pushed ahead: "You were pretty close to her?"

"When I met her, she was writing a screenplay. She needed a place to work and I have this big house. I'm sorry she got restless—let's face it, bored—though that's part of her charm. She was going great guns, but she got blocked." My Good Man came over to have a discreet word, and Mr. Fixler nodded: "Nicholas says someone's waiting out in your car?"

"My daughter."

"Invite her in."

Rachel was willing. As she was ogling the porcelain vases and canvases in the living room she whistled: "Whoa. The picture of the boy hauling fish, that's not a real whatsisname, is it—Franz Hals?"

Armand beamed: "You can tell?"

"Most artists got paid to paint rich people's faces."

"You're an art student?"

"I paint a little. You a collector?"

"A dealer. A broker really." Armand was making a bundle selling investment-grade Beauty to the me-first buccaneers of the Reagan years, the computer and finance hotshots who've built mansions on tax breaks, fiddling while Rome rots. "Sometimes," Armand said, "you work with the big auction houses to catch a real antiquity for a client. The Hals is here on its way to its new owner. Other times you just chase trivia. As Dawn says, it's never boring." There was an awkward silence, then: "She has genuine talents, you know. Not very educated or polished, of course. But the real thing. That's what's so exciting. She used my old Royal typewriter in the back study."

"Any financial arrangements?" I asked.

"I agreed to back a movie she was going to direct, if that's what you mean."

"Movies take a big investment these days."

"More exactly, videos. Dawn wanted to make erotic videos with a woman's vision of sexual feeling."

"Feminist porn?"

"I think she'd find that description a bit simple minded."

"Does she still owe you money?"

He shrugged: "As if I'd ever ask her for it. If she peeked in that door right now, I'd be"—he gave a pained, comic growl—"glad."

Rachel followed the line-up of paintings into the next room.

"So the relationship wasn't totally business?"

He couldn't resist bragging a little: "Under that brassy veneer Dawn's a sensitive girl. And no dummy. We used to lie on the, we used to listen to classical music and she'd get down on the rug. *Scheherazade* we listened to—you know the nineteenth-century fad for Oriental exoticism. Dawn was learning the sounds of the different musical instruments. Always educating her tastes. On the move. At least that's my take on her."

The wrinkle of his smile didn't go with his hushed discretion. He wanted to say *I introduced her to Titian's sublime palette and porked her bowlegged*. His eye scanned the room for Rachel. He took a breath: "Tonight I've been showing some interested parties a letter Lincoln wrote to his wife."

"You wouldn't happen to have any papers Dawn might have left behind?"

"I have a photo of her. But it's not what you expect."

"Anything would help."

"Don't be so sure. Here, I'll show you. You can give me your professional opinion of my security system while we're at it."

In the dining room Rachel was chatting with a very tall black woman not much older than she was. In her satiny blouse and salmon slacks, the woman stood in the glow of a chandelier with a thousand pinpricks of light.

I followed Armand through the kitchen and downstairs into an office with a polished steel door that would excite a banker. The outer walls were faced in firebrick. Inside, real rosewood paneling with a matching desk and a Chippendale guest chair. Against the walls were fireproof file cabinets. One rosewood panel masked a lavatory.

The desktop sported a telephone, intercom, fountain pen, magnifying glass, and a clutter of papers that included gallery catalogs and a cartoon about dogs eating cats—one more report from the mean streets. Nicholas, I noticed, kept an eye on us from the stairs.

"I'm fireproof down here," Armand enthused. "I've got a generator. My own air supply. The phone line's buried—I have a phobia about losing contact with the outside world."

"You could survive the end of the world down here."

"That's the idea." He beamed. "Well, here's Dawn."

From a file drawer Armand fetched a folder that opened on a five-by-seven black-and-white glossy: a pretty nude with the head of a red fox grafted on by some darkroom sleight of hand. Ryan's work, obviously. Beautiful and arousing and disconcerting. The pose might have been ballet, the woman leaning on one elbow, her leg trailing behind her. Or it could have been your girlfriend stretched out on the rug to read the paper on a hot Sunday morning with her breasts swooping free and an odd — well, a very strange — look in her eye.

"You see?" Armand said smugly. "It's all about desire."

"I'm used to a human face."

He hummed agreement. "A child's always fascinated by a mother's face. If you can believe the psychologists, that's the beginning of desire. But it's not all there is."

Dawn had given him the photo, and that was all Armand could — or would — tell me. I found myself swatting at the swarm of questions suddenly buzzing me.

Upstairs the tall black woman was nibbling at a fistful of Norwegian crackers. Her tightly wrapped hair and six-foot-plus elegance made her seem exotic. But when she spoke it was all husky New Yawk: "Minnie says you're out of pimento dip."

While Armand was out getting Minnie dipped again, Rachel whispered: "Giselle wants to know will we take her with us. I told her sure."

"She wants a ride?"

"Mmm. Armand doesn't want her to go."

"Just no hassles is all I want," Giselle murmured. When Armand came back Giselle was standing with us, not him. "They're giving me a ride to my sister's," she announced. "I think I told you, I got a sister in Boston."

She had a beautiful profile, Giselle, and heart-stopping eyes the color of figs: but she was a godawful liar. Armand had fast reflexes: "No problem, Nicholas will drive you."

"I'm going with these two," Giselle explained.

"Oh, that's an imposition," Armand protested.

"No problem," I assured him. We were all easing toward the front hall again. "If you hear anything about Dawn," I said, "leave a message at my office. Signs are that she's in trouble."

"That's terrible. Wait — "

Giselle dipped one knee to scoop up an Esprit bag from beside a dining-room chair. "I got everything. Call me sometime."

"Wait, wait — " Armand's hands wanted to grab me. "Let's agree to keep each other informed about Dawn."

In the doorway he reread my business card. Stalling. The night air felt clammy. I began to taste adrenaline. Halfway down the driveway I had a vivid sensation of eyes on me. Then Nicholas materialized out of the darkness. "He wants me to drive you," Nicholas murmured to Giselle.

"They're giving me a ride to my sister's," Giselle recited.

Nicholas took her arm. I tensed. "Nah," he pooh-poohed softly, "let me drive you."

Giselle lifted his hand away: "Those breath drops I told you about. They really work."

Nicholas took her arm again as we approached my old Volvo. "Okay kids," I said. "Time to boogie."

Nobody moved. As it happened I had my ignition key in my fist, between the knuckles, and when I gave Nicholas a friendly good-night tap on the bicep he hopped like a tiddlywink. Rachel threw the car door open.

Wheeling around in the driveway, the Volvo's lights picked out behind the steel fence the yellow alligator eyes of two watchdogs, and I began to feel better about my sixth sense.

$\triangledown$

1 1

Headed south on 126 past Walden Pond, where Thoreau loitered over the meaning of life and the woods are littered with computer companies, I thought somebody was following us, but the lights dropped away. "Giselle's headed for New York too," Rachel said. "Maybe you can give her a ride. Damn, I wish I didn't have to work in the morning."

"You need to learn your lines for the play too."

The thought consoled her.

In Natick Meg was already upstairs asleep. I looked in on her from the bedroom doorway, smelling the scented soaps in her dresser drawer. I felt bad that her evening with Bill had pooped out, though to be honest, it would've pained me to walk in on a well-deserved orgy.

At the kitchen table Rachel and I scratched the night into my notebook — pretty thin stuff. Giselle began to describe the inside of her stomach, so Rachel dished out her special mix of granola with dried fruit, nuts, seeds, newts, and puppydog tails. With napkins Giselle showed us how she tore tickets in half when she worked in a Brooklyn movie theater. Rachel refilled her bowl:

"How come you needed help getting out of Armand's?"

"He gets lonesome."

I nudged: "And then what happens?"

"He don't want anyone to go home."

"Giselle, we just saved you from a big pain in the ass."

She gave me a cocky smile. Her hands kept tearing smaller and smaller shreds: "I can handle Armand."

Under the table Rachel's toe gave my shin a kick of advice. She began talking about Dawn. Dawn as childhood friend, actress, hooker: Dawn as corpse in the trunk of a stolen car. Rachel drew in a painful breath: "See, I'm worried sick about her. Why would anybody want to kill her? What could she have done?"

Giselle squeezed a packet of Meg's coffee sweetener onto her spoon and licked it thoughtfully: "Dawn always got money. She always spends guys' money. That's how she got in the fight with Armand."

"The way he explained it," Rachel lied, "it was hard to follow."

"All I know's she was gonna give him the pictures, then she didn't and kept the money anyways."

"What pictures?" I wondered. "Porn videos she made?"

"All I know's what I heard upstairs one weekend I was there."

"You were there together?"

"Not that time."

"You mean he paid for the videos she made, but she never turned them over to him."

"That's how I heard it. He was on the phone to her, and you could hear him all over the whole house. Which, like for Armand, that's heavy." Giselle's eyes twinkled. Her long tongue licked the spoon clean. She reached for another packet of sweetener.

"You're sure the money was for the videos?"

"What else would it — oh, you mean — "

"He usually pay you okay? No trouble?"

She hesitated, unsure of how much I knew. "He buys me good clothes — these ones, for instance — and these nice earrings. He gave me this glass whale once — got a tiny Pinocchio inside. Steuben glass, like. Not some trashy glitz. That's how Armand is. Treat him right, he's okay. Go along to get along."

"Never any rough stuff."

"Armand? The most he does, he likes to fool around in the bathroom — you know, that sunken tub and the nice towels and you can take soap and slide around on the floor. Maybe he'll chase you around, you know, or spank your ass. Nothing much. You got to put up with stuff. The most he does, sometimes he likes to pee on you and then get it on in that tub."

A queasy smile dragged at Rachel's mouth. I shrugged: "Armand doesn't like women?"

"He likes his women fine."

"Bit of a racist."

She waved her hand — waved off the thought. "He's just this bad boy sometimes. You know? Be an animal, that's what he really gets off on."

"An animal."

"Sure. All that fancy art stuff, the gorgeous paintings and like that, it's great but it's unreal. So you got to get down, get basic. Like an animal. On all fours."

"Animals bite."

"They mate," she said, "like they mean it."

"And they bite."

Giselle touched her long fingers coyly to her upper arm. Look closely and her dark lustrous skin was bruised. She said: "It's like play. No real blood." Her tongue dabbed the spoonful of sweetener and the tip curled back into her mouth frosted white. "The weird one's that Nicholas. Sometimes you wonder, would he dig a hole in the grass out by those watchdogs and stuff you into it? Hey. Usually he's so-o-o nice. But then, like tonight, I close my eyes and I just hear that shovel scootching up the dirt."

Another entry for my notebook.

On the front steps Rachel nabbed my sleeve and pointed at an invisible shooting star in the hazy black heavens. "Ryan's promised to phone," she murmured. It was such a stage whisper, I smiled in the darkness. "He may do the black-and-white publicity stills for *La Ronde*. Maybe I'll get something out of him or Frank."

"Watch your step with Frank. He has a soft spot for starlets."

"*Dun-can*."

"Not that Ryan's the most reliable —"

"Hey, give me a break."

"And let me know how Amy is."

Giselle leaned out the Volvo to see what was keeping us.

Rachel said: "What about Armand Fixler's guy Nicholas? And you said we could file a missing persons report on Dawn."

"Whoa. Let's see if Dawn surfaces when Lynne Dresser passes on the warning. Why waste energy?"

Now Giselle was out of the Volvo and staring at the pointless heavens.

"You know why," Rachel warned. "And you'll feel just as guilty and rotten as me if it happens too."

▽

1 2

ON THE MAP NEW YORK is below Boston. At 3:00 A.M. it's a spin down a dark rabbit hole. The lights of New Haven flare up in the misty coastal darkness and die away. Then as dawn lightens the sky, the tunnel of streetlights opens up and spills you among the million cryptic windows of the Bronx. Beside me Giselle stirred and rubbed her eyes: "I went to school out there once."

At 104th Street, a few blocks down Broadway from my place, Giselle slipped one of my business cards into her yellow Esprit bag and glided into the subway entrance: a ghost in the shadowless gray dawn.

Vera's apartment on Ninety-sixth Street has old-fashioned door-knobs, high ceilings, a coffee grinder, and a genuine Miro lithograph that evokes a roller derby in a Spanish barnyard. In the eerie minutes before sunup the skylight over her bed gave Vera the delicate bluish skin of a a mermaid, as if I were nosing through some underwater grotto to her. She stirred enough to murmur: "Is that you, Reggie?"

Twitting me.

I apologized: "I took a chance and let myself in."

"You drive all the way down here without any clothes on?"

Vera arrived from Huddersfield, England, a dozen years ago with some kind of exam certificate, a change of underwear, and a British sense of humor. When we met she was working her way through CUNY by taming computer programs for businessmen who'd bought more power than they knew how to handle. When we met, I had moved out of the house in Natick and quit a criminally boring job in a Boston law office. Vera replaced my blown fuses. For a few years now we'd shared a letterhead as security analysts.

"Mmm," I said. "You henna'd your hair."

"You like it?"

I snuggled into her warm behind and kissed her neck: "Mmmm."

"Good," she yawned, rolling over. "What's up?"

"I'm trying to find a classy prostitute."

"I thought you liked my hair this way."

"It's conceivable she's already dead."

"That's a nipple you're licking so delicately."

"Aha. I thought so."

"Are you here to consult about a missing person or to get close to a person you miss? Are you coming or going?"

56

"Keep stroking my weary flesh and we'll see."

"Oh, is this thing yours?" She ducked down for a closer look. From under the sheet she crooned: "Hul-lo. You brought your pet ferret. Is he tame?"

"You've got him eating out of your hand."

"Oh my, he's cute."

"It's mating season."

"Isn't science lovely?" She sat up, stretching, with a deep breath that showed her ribs. "Well, Mr. Ames," she said gravely, "I'm afraid I'm going to have to investigate you."

When I looked up again, the skylight had filled with delicious morning sun and I could smell the automatic coffeemaker. Vee was sticking words in my ear one by one with her tongue: "Good. Morning. Sleepy. Head. That was glorious, but some of us have to get to the office."

Since Vera's kitchen is essentially a phone booth with running water, we set the coffeepot and croissants on the coffee table and had a nudist breakfast lying at opposite ends of her sofa in Granny Ames's big afghan, bare feet tucked under each other's warm behind. Vee's big living room looks like the League of Women Voters' book sale, with titles stuffing the shelves and stacked against the walls. Nearest me were czarist Russia in old photos and a biography of Ronald Reagan: *The Millionaire Movie President*. Vera said:

"I thought Rachel was coming down here with you."

"She's just taken a part in a play, so she has to learn her lines in a hurry."

"Good training. Maybe Rachel will be your first woman president. Government's all stage magic now. Sexy photo ops. Woo the voters. Kiss the rich. Bugger the hungry."

"Not Rachel. She roots for the underdogs."

"Silly sot. She'll end up working for a living. Like us." Vee wiggled her toes under me. "Speaking of which. You really must move your aircraft out of Phil's loft. The poor man's frantic to clear the place out."

"I came back today to arrange things."

"You didn't come back here for your damned pistol?"

"I'm trying to keep my distance from that mess. Somebody wants the kid bad enough to break into her apartment. Two guys beat up her boyfriend. Her sister's unconscious in intensive care with her skull cracked, courtesy of the same duo. It's likely they also tried to snatch her friend Lynne off the street right in front of me yesterday. One of them may be a Latino, possibly South American."

"Meaning what, drugs?"

"You tell me. Why would a couple bananas risk kidnapping a woman in Copley Square in broad daylight?"

Vera's toes tickled my coccyx. She popped in the last morsel of croissant and, chewing, said: "No offense, love, but I'm not sure you have the right personality to take on the drug cartels."

"It's only one wild guess."

"There are others?" She poured more coffee.

"It's possible Dawn's hiding from a jealous lover," I said. "Armand Fixler. Some kind of antiquities broker."

"Perfect name. He made it up?"

"Anything's possible. But whatever's between them, it ain't love. Maybe not even sex."

"What's left? Money?"

"Money and dirty pictures."

Vera blinked: "Oh lovely."

"More exactly, Dawn wants to make erotic videos that play out a woman's point of view. So I'm told."

"If you're teasing, Duncan, nice try. But we really don't have time for another roll in the hay. Drink your coffee."

"Her friend the broker sugar daddy bankrolled one of these videos, but evidently she took his money and never handed over the film."

"And what's the connection between this and the drug blokes?"

"You got me."

"Do I now." Vera climbed over my knees for a smooch, her breasts swaying sweetly against my chest: "Ah, your hair tickles." She got up, slipping on her bra and pleated blouse. Vee dresses European: what she owns wouldn't fill half a closet, but every hem and button is distinctive. Over her shoulder she said: "So the girl stole something. Maybe money or videos or drugs. Now she's deadly popular. Let's hope she's the tough gutter rat we think."

"You're a hard-hearted woman, Vee."

With her toe she nudged her briefcase around the corner into the hall: "I have to be. I'm the one in this firm who works for a living. Remember?"

$\bigtriangledown$

13

I DROVE US DOWN to our attic office on Houston Street in the Village, where Vera began debriefing the answering machine and I phoned my friend Bill Dempsey at NYNEX. While I endorsed a couple of checks, Bill ran down Lynne Dresser's phone number. An address in Worcester, as it turned out. That freed me to smack a last kiss on Vee and shoot around the corner and upstairs to Phil's.

It was cool and gloomy in the loft, and a ripple of dreamy exhaustion washed over me. In the dirty light the plane's fuselage could have been the contraption Daedalus used in his escape: a flimsy, cunning contrivance of tubing and nylon fabric. A modified motorcycle engine would turn the aluminum propeller. The wing assembly, which Rachel had covered in blue nylon, leaned against the wall. One more nylon panel and the tail would be ready too. As usual the sight of the contraption fired my imagination and put butterflies in my stomach.

At his workbench Phil was replacing the pads in a bass clarinet. His name is Vladimir but everybody calls him Phil: burly, perfectly bald guy in his forties, with rimless glasses, baggy green sweatshirt, and a voice warm as a down comforter. He was an ex-priest who repaired wind instruments for a living and slept on a sofabed up here. Apart from a collection of a thousand opera records and a lover who wrote a book about Beowulf and didn't get tenure at a state college in the Midwest, Phil still lived a life as simple as any priest's. He also knew about prostitution, having run shelters for homeless kids in Chicago and New York.

"Hey," he called, "you got through."

"I did?"

"The President's campaigning in town. Tying up traffic and getting tough on crime."

"I hope he leaves a few small crimes for Vera and me."

"All he does is push the death penalty for drug lords."

"Good. That leaves ninety-nine percent of crime. And especially white-collar crime. That's where the real money is."

Phil gave the bass clarinet a honk, testing the new pads. "There's Dan Merriam insisting that drugs are a symptom not the disease. But nobody wants to hear about poverty and greed and violence — the media people edit all that boring stuff out of his speeches. So now the

President's sticking the needle in him every chance he gets. Coddling criminals. Weak on drugs. Sissy Liberal. It goes over big with all the ethnic Democrats who loved Reagan and hate niggers. And Merriam tries to shrug it off with urbane quips like he uses in the Senate."

The news usually made Merriam a silver-haired leprechaun with a merry glint in his eye. But since he'd written books and often resorted to facts in a hot argument, network anchors had accused him of lacking a killer instinct. Which is why I said to Phil:

"They'll skin him alive."

"Unless his wife saves his fanny." Phil's fingers ran a soft clacking scale up the keys. "Couple days ago on NPR they ran a mike past Caddy Merriam, and suddenly she just lets go. Quarter of black males in their twenties are in the prison system these days. Half of all our kids are growing up in poverty. The rich are getting bigger tax breaks than ever. Bang. Bang. Bang. 'If it was a movie,' she says, 'it would be X-rated.' That's when they cut her off." The clarinet gave a fierce wild-goose honk and Phil wiped his lips with his knuckles. "She was all there. Straight from the heart. No teleprompter. You can bet the PR pros are trying like crazy to snuff her opinions."

"Somebody up in Boston just told me the prison statistic."

"Glad somebody's listening. It didn't make the TV news or even the papers. It's gonna be a dirty campaign."

"Lot of money riding on the outcome."

"In the meantime money's bought this building and it wants me and your airplane out of here. Sooner the better."

"Next weekend," I promised, "Rachel and I will move the plane up to Connecticut. This weekend I got ambushed." Last year Phil's mother died and left him a house in Larchfield, Connecticut.

"Sorry for the pressure," he said, "but the landlord's really on my tail. Maybe heaven's telling you it's time to finish up and fly that crate."

"Are you insinuating that I'm putting it off?"

"I'd be scared too." He touched a drop of oil to one of the clarinet keys. For a minute the room seemed full of flimsy junk. The whole flight project — cutting, welding, stitching — suddenly seemed dangerously frivolous. I said:

"You told me once about a kid you took into the midtown shelter. She'd been hustling for a slick operation in Boston. Only she went on a drug binge and stole a john's car and his plastic. What were they calling the outfit?"

Phil ran silent scales on the clarinet, the keys plokking on the dense black wood: "That was four, five years ago. Andrea, her name was.

Somebody ran her down on the thruway, I heard." He blew a long low note, but the pad leaked and the horn gave a raucous shriek like a calf in a slaughterhouse. I pressed him:

"This outfit, they were supposed to be very businesslike. Order by phone. Out of a photo catalog. Pay by credit card."

"I remember the business card looked like a valentine," Phil said. He put the horn down on the bench: " – Cupid. Dan Cupid."

"I'm trying to find a woman who may have worked for them."

"They've been shut down. Or forced into a name change anyway. Isn't there an easier way to get a line on the woman?"

"The one that keeps coming up is the obits."

"I see. Son, you got a problem."

Tuesday morning in the office Vee was at the computer crunching serial numbers for an automotive parts wholesaler, trying to track down some doctored invoices, when Frank Fascelle called from Boston.

I told him that Dawn owed someone a lot of money. "Two hombres beat her boyfriend Ryan half to death, but Dawn escaped."

"That the Ryan who does photography?"

"Know him?"

"He's done some publicity stills for the theater. I'd use him again if I thought I could count on him. Nice kid – very bright. But off the wall. Total flake."

"Well, the debt looks like the problem."

"Pain in the ass. You want to help, but you know damned well if you bail her out, she's never gonna learn."

"You've tried."

"And if she thinks you're playing the parent with her she'll rip you up one end and down the other."

"I believe it. Stay in touch."

"I'm keeping my fingers crossed."

The next few hours I spent in an electronics supply house on Long Island looking for missing computer microchips with a manager who kept throwing up his hands in helpless amazement, as if the little beasts had migrated like roaches through cracks in the foundation into the bagel bakery across the alley.

At two-thirty, with a take-out container of industrial-strength iced tea, I joined the first rush-hour cucarachas migrating home. Between sips of tea I summed up the day's work into the portable tape recorder. After some bumper to bumper, I lifted up mine eyes to the Manhattan skyline laid out in the August haze. The land of bilk and money.

When I barged into our stifling office, Vera nearly broke an arm trying to get her blouse back on. Every summer she develops a little strawberry heat rash where she cleaves. And every summer we debate whether the best treatment is a light dusting of cornstarch—as prescribed by Auntie Grace—or light licks of a tongue.

Bent over Vera's left shoulder, I was conducting medical research when the phone rang. Vera snagged it: "For you, Doctor."

Rachel.

"Hi, listen," she began. "I finished sewing the rudder panels for the plane."

"Good. Excellent. Thanks, kid."

"Want to come pick them up tonight?"

Something was wrong. I wasn't sure how I knew, but I did. It was like watching a navigator in an outrigger canoe read storm cues in the trackless Pacific. I echoed her: "Tonight?"

"Ryan—Dawn's friend?—we were supposed to meet at the museum this afternoon, and I waited two hours and he never showed up."

"Could be worse. I had an appointment with an unhappy electronics broker and he did show up."

"I've been phoning him all afternoon and it just rings and rings." Her voice was shrinking. "Tonight we were planning to do some printing in his darkroom, but I have a rehearsal and I wanted to let him know. What I think, really, I think he's in trouble."

"Call the cops."

"I did. An hour ago. They sent a police car by his house."

"Feel better?"

"They didn't go inside."

"Think he might've headed for the hills?"

"I'm going over there to see what's up."

"Not a great idea. Try the cops again."

"They won't do anything."

"Rachel, I don't like the idea of—"

"*I said no.* I want to see for myself. I want to talk to him."

"But what if—"

"Look," she said grimly. "I don't want to *fight* about this."

That was my usual line; hearing it used against me now, I wanted to laugh. Once dug in, she'd be impossible to budge. So I said. "Okay, okay. Listen. I've found Lynne Dresser's address. It's in Worcester. Suppose I come pick up the rudder panels. Then go round the mulberry bush one last time with Ryan and Lynne Dresser."

"I have a rehearsal tonight."

"I'll stop by."

"Duncan, you ever get this weird sense that just beyond everyday reality, if you weren't afraid to see it, there's, well—"

"Elves."

"Oh forget it."

"Sorry. I just meant you can scare yourself."

"You'll see what I mean."

"Good."

"If it's not too late."

14

HUNKERED DOWN IN HIS green *Amnesty* tee shirt and sandals, Frank Fascelle was onstage pep-talking his dozen actors: "Listen, it isn't how *much* sex there is in the play. It's that the sex works like money. A way of getting something out of other people. Not some great evil or some kind of religious experience, just an ordinary itchy greed for life. At the first performance they went nuts and wrecked the theater. Because the sex raises such creepy questions."

"Like death."

Half a dozen heads turned to look at Rachel. Frank pointed at her: "Exactly right. But hey—Rachel?"

She beamed. All eyes were on him now.

"Lighten up."

A good-natured laugh rippled through the group.

The rehearsal seemed destined to go on forever, and after the haul from Manhattan I was in no mood for the wait. So I phoned Ryan from the lobby and hummed along with the busy signal for a minute. Then I drove over to Medford for a closer look.

Ryan's lights were off and the shades were down—a darkroom precaution or maybe just his paranoia. The doorbell nagged to no end. In the dark I checked the front and back doors as the cops must have done earlier. No entry.

As I was marching off I remembered showing my driver's licence through the mail slot in the door the other night, so I grabbed my flashlight from the Volvo's trunk and doubled back.

Framed by the narrow brass mail slot, Ryan's living room was full of thick, tinted light like a murky aquarium. The flashlight beam skidded over objects. One by one details began to assemble into a sense the brain tried to fight off. He had set up his sparkling pearl drums but his high hat had toppled over. The flimsy legs under one end of the improvised door-table had given way, and the camera equipment had slid off onto the floor. Bloodshot haze of darkroom light in the kitchen doorway.

The tortoise's pen—four storm windowpanes taped together—had fallen apart. More exactly, Ryan had crashed into the pen. Shift your angle of vision and you couldn't miss the kid himself out cold on the green carpet in a scatter of broken glass. Focus and you noticed his hands together behind his back. If you stayed tuned, you also noticed something blank about his face: the word flicked into my mind so quietly it took me a second to catch the sickening implications. Duct tape. Metallic cloth duct tape. You see it holding rusty cars together. Strong, sticky duct tape. Over his mouth.

I beat on the neighbor's door till a fiftyish woman in curlers got up the nerve to come to her porch window. She peered at me over her air conditioner. I pantomimed dialing: *"Call the cops. Nine-one-one."*

She shooed me away.

"Call. The. Cops!"

She shooed me away with both hands.

"Call the cops, dammit!"

Then I saw it.

The new hearing aids can be very inconspicuous.

So I detoured to the Volvo for Messrs. Smith & Wesson, then mounted the porch again. This time I smashed Ryan's living-room window with my heel, snapped up his window shade, and carefully stepped through the daggers of glass.

The telephone dangled off the sofa, bleeping softly.

Ryan had his bloody nose in the pea-green rug next to a saucer of kibbly tortoise food. The cast was off his left forearm, which made it simpler for duct tape to bind his wrists behind his back. The ankles too were bound. His face looked battered, and his open eyes had the filmy dullness of cataracts. No respiration. No pulse. No reflexes. You didn't have to be a doctor to see that his next album would feature a choir of angels. So I left the duct tape on his mouth for the coroner and used his phone to dial 911.

Spatters of blood led from his busted nose across the rug to the kitchen. Gloomy red darkroom light choked the doorway. For a moment I held back, reluctant to meet Dawn Ashland on the floor in there.

But the kitchen was anticlimactic. There'd been a serious disagreement. A drumstick the size of a cop's riot club lay on the kitchen floor in a puddle with the stink of photographic fixer. A shoe had shattered a black plastic 35mm developing tank underfoot. The enlarger had toppled over into the sink. On the countertop half a dozen empty beer bottles lay at crazy angles as if someone had just bowled a strike. A fan roared in the window over the sink. No sight of the roll of duct tape.

I made myself go up the stairs, Smith & Wesson leading the way.

Empty rooms. No dead folks. No deadly folks.

In the bedroom three tall stacks of rock albums tilted crazily on a twin bed. On the floor was another mattress covered with photo mags and batches of dried, curling, black-and-white prints, at least one of

65

which was a female nude with the head of a red fox grafted onto her by some darkroom sleight of hand. Same creature as in Armand's print. There must have been fifty versions of the photo: different exposures, different croppings, different treatments of the boundaries between woman and vixen. Whatever it said about Ryan's fantasy life, it represented hours of work. I pocketed a sample.

Downstairs in the light I noticed I was tracking blood around, which wouldn't please the law.

A glance at the mess told you the apartment had been tossed, although Ryan was such a slob it was hard to tell how serious the search had been. Or what might have been stolen.

Downstairs, looking at Ryan again from the kitchen doorway, I realized that he had collapsed on top of the tortoise: you could see the smooth seagreen shell protruding from under his armpit, evidently crushed. In his panic to breath through his broken nose Ryan had sprayed blood in every direction.

The whole scene suggested a wild tantrum, a terrifying outbreak of rage. Hard to see it as a payoff for debts. Even shylocks have more professional restraint. I tried to picture my guy with the bitten ear in this room. But what I saw was Ryan reeling about suffocating on his own blood, and my stomach threatened to revolt, so I unlocked the front door and went out on the porch to welcome the law.

It was a long night. The first cops in the door took turns joking about drug dealers swapping assault rifles for duct tape. One of the cops wanted to peel Ryan's mouth free. He knelt for a fascinated closer look: "I know the guy can't feel anything, but I can't stand to see the tape over his mouth. I really can't stand it."

But they all knew that was the medical examiner's privilege.

The Medford detective in charge, a chain-smoking bony-jawed Irishman named Ed Riley, had to fend off the furiously helpful Mrs. Ohanion from next door. She'd definitely heard a commotion over here this afternoon—oh my god yes, men's voices of course. Not late, early—just after lunch maybe? Or a little later?

Ed Riley leaned into your face to talk, blowing his cigarette smoke out of the corner of his mouth, over his shoulder. When he got to me with his notebook, I went back to Saturday afternoon, when Rachel had dragged me over the back fence into Amy's yard. Afterward a suspicious Mrs. Ohanion let me use her phone to call the theater, but someone had already given Rachel a ride home.

At this point a state trooper showed up: Lt. Kerrigan, one of those ramrod joes who discovered the meaning of life in basic training and talks in clipped commands. He was courteous but firm with the city cops, as you'd be with a crew of retarded janitors.

With me Lt. K was disappointed but firm, as you'd be with a retarded janitor who'd murdered your wife and kids. He used hard words like *perpetrator*, but he used them a lot so a layman might be able to follow. He squeezed me for the meager facts about Dawn and Armand Fixler and the disputed pictures. When one of the local cops showed him one of the fox prints, his expression turned stony.

After that he joined Ed Riley in dusting for fingerprints, hoping for a hit on the AFIS computer system.

The medical examiner was close-mouthed and didn't remember that we'd met over a dead bookkeeper out in Newton the year before. He lifted the tape from the dead mouth with tweezers and put it in a plastic evidence bag. He picked through the victim's whitish blond hair looking for scalp wounds, then took Ryan's temperature to see how long he'd been cooling off. In the heat the kid was beginning to bloat.

While Ryan posed for a dozen snapshots, the medical examiner decided that a fist or other blunt object had broken the victim's septum, with resulting trauma that had blocked his nasal passages. Probable cause of death, asphyxia. Probable time of death, between noon and three this afternoon. The presence of duct tape made it difficult to ascertain at this time whether this was manslaughter or premeditated murder. The autopsy report might help.

When they lifted Ryan, the kid emitted an impolite belch that proved to be gas, not life. The crushed tortoise — Montezuma — came into view: in more ways than one. As we watched, the tortoise head slowly poked out into the light, bringing its black uncanny eye back from death. There was a ripple of surprise among us tantamount to a cheer.

Around eleven the landlord rolled in with a sheet of plywood in the back of his big station wagon. Bowlegged old gent in short pants, with less hair than the tortoise. As he nailed the plywood over the window to secure the apartment, he huffed and puffed at the cops under the misimpression that they'd smashed his window. He was so nervous that if they'd let him, he would have gone after the bloodstains with a toothbrush and a bucket of water right then and there.

As I was about to leave, the police radio reported that Worcester cops had just checked out Lynne Dresser's house and found it in darkness: no signs of forced entry. Which reassured me. But then I noticed that on the living-room wall Ryan's five exotic knives were still in their scabbards. Like the apartment's intact doorlocks, they argued that he hadn't recognized danger when it came knocking. For some reason it was the knives that cut through my weariness with a new worry: what if Ryan's open house had been — or was about to be — replayed tonight out in Worcester?

From a pay phone outside a twenty-four-hour Mini-Market I dialed Lynne's number and listened to the ring. Either she was keeping her head down or she'd moved to a safer address. Or she'd been visited by an ear with a bite out of it. The phone rang on and on like the pulse of an electronic heart monitor, making me aware of a certain tightness in my chest.

$$\triangledown$$

15

AT THE HOUSE RACHEL was in the side porch working at a piece of poster board with acrylic paints. Her light had insects whooping at the porch screens like crowds at a political convention. The window fan was roaring so loudly that I was looking over Rachel's shoulder at the tropical birds on her canvas before she finally heard my voice and yelped: "Jesus, Duncan!"

"You working the night shift?"

"You scared me!"

"Pretty birds. The acrylics really—"

"You dodo." She scolded the tip of my nose with a long paintbrush fledged in brilliant yellow. "How come you never picked me up?"

"I got held up."

"Great. Frank finally gave me a ride."

"All the way out here?"

"It's no big deal. He's a nice guy. And he wanted to talk about Dawn and if you're any closer to finding her."

"Where's your mother?"

"Out with Leon Sadler. She thinks he's going to offer her a real estate job."

Leon was a college roommate of mine. Back from Vietnam with a sudden wife and baby daughter announced to me by mail, I'd worked for Leon building up the real-estate and drugstore chain he'd inherited. He'd rescued me or used me for several crucial years: take your pick. After I quit and went to law school, Meg married him. The marriage lasted for a few miserable months.

"Hey," Rachel said. "I don't understand it either."

"I knew Meg was desperate for a decent job, but—"

"So what did Ryan say?"

"Ryan's dead."

"Oh shit." Rachel tossed the paintbrush onto her palette with a groan. "How?"

"Somebody beat him."

The fan threw stale heat at us. "What about Dawn?"

"Don't know."

When I told her what I did know, her eyes brimmed. She bit her lip and turned back toward the table. When she grabbed the posterboard

69

as if to tear it, I grabbed her lightly: "Whoa. What's the picture?"

"It's supposed to go on a wildlife fund poster — save the rain forests. Mom's friend Gina asked me to do it."

"I love the toucans."

"They're too cute."

"Come on, they're—"

"I mean, what's happening to the forests and the Indians, it's so — god, I should make the poster scream."

I shrugged: "Give people something to love."

"Then it's no different than some gorgeous stupid soda ad. Just another nice little blip of pleasure nobody'll even notice."

"There must be some kind of good feeling the ads haven't captured yet. You could—"

"Why did he have to die?" she blurted. The words fizzled in her throat. When I reached out she turned to her palette and picked up the brush. Crimson and yellow and flagrant cobalt blue smeared her fingers. Rather than take the hint I slipped an arm over her shoulder and across her chest, tucking my hand in her armpit. I squeezed her to me, casually and very tightly:

"On my way back to New York I think I'll look in on Lynne Dresser in Worcester, see if she's actually still there."

"Good."

"Want to give me the panels you sewed for the plane?"

"Sure."

She didn't move. She wanted me to think she was too old to need consolation, so she stood there hugging my hand in her hot armpit. I shifted my weight: "Love you, kid."

"Mmm." She stood there with the sloppy paintbrush in one clenched fist, eyes shut, stubbornly waiting for the sinister shadow of Ryan's death to blow past the humid moon.

16

PROGRESS HAS LIVENED UP the farmland out on Route 9 with promiscuous malls and colorful traffic lights, so even after midnight the ride to Worcester takes too long.

The Dressers' house sat on a hill overlooking the city. A working-class street of tenements and dinky singles, vinyl siding showing off the surface prosperity of the 1980s. Local square with one park bench named after a neighborhood kid killed on Guadalcanal back before the invention of Nintendo. Number 57 was a green clapboard box, its only bit of luxury an oval window in the front door. No sign of the red sports car. I pocketed my flashlight and my jolly juggler kit and went calling.

The doorbell didn't get results. With all the neighborhood's windows open, you have to be careful about inviting yourself in. Since the Dressers' porch window was open, I slit the screen and adjusted my bit of coat hanger to pop the spring tabs inside.

Hot in the house. Slipcovered sofa, Formica coffee table, tin pole lamps. Photos of kids at a backyard birthday and an amusement park, the girl presumably Lynne. A few screen mags and *Psychology Today*s on one end table, empty yogurt cup on the other. On a shelf behind the television sagged a row of supermarket encyclopedias and paperbacks: *How to Improve* this or that, plus assorted romances and a decrepit Dr. Spock. Nothing shocking, nothing you'd have to bury.

The TV set was warm.

This gave me such an unwelcome sensation that I felt the set several times trying not to believe my senses.

To be polite I called Lynne's name a couple times.

Nothing.

The cellar displayed an oil furnace, busted lawn chairs, a shelf of dusty mason jars, and a milk crate full of tools. No dead women with Lynne Dresser's clever dark eyes.

On the stairs to the second floor the old carpet was frayed enough at the bottom to be a hazard. But not the biggest hazard. I was halfway up the staircase when the darkness above me clattered—like a supermarket cart, I remember thinking: a clattery tinkle. And faked out, I tripped against the stairs just in time for the flashlight's beam to catch, coming at my head, a shiny chrome supermarket cart.

If it had caught me full square, it would have thrown me back down the stairs and broken my neck. As it was I dived under it. Or at least its wheels rebounded off my skull and shoulders before the thing overturned and dragged its metal cage down my back. My switchboard lit up like Broadway and pain flashed through me. I heard the cart crash into the hall below. The flashlight tumbled down the stairs in a series of wild somersaults. I let myself slip down a couple steps. Above me a woman's voice said:

"Come any closer and I'll blow your fucking brains out."

"Lynne?"

"I've got a gun, asshole."

"It's me," I croaked.

"Who?" In the silence I felt her calculating. Then a hush: "Oh shit. Is that you, Ames?"

"What's left of me." I let myself slide down a few more stairs and felt around for the flashlight.

"You broke in."

"Nobody answered the bell. I was afraid you—where's your car?"

"In a neighbor's driveway. After I told Dawn about the threats, and what happened in Copley Square—wouldn't you be looking for trouble? An hour ago the police were at the front door, so I've been keeping the lights off."

"You actually packing a gun?"

"I had to say something a man would understand."

My hand found the flashlight. Lying on my back I aimed it up at the voice. Lynne Dresser's pale face flared into focus. I said: "We need to talk."

She let out a huge breath: "Go on down. I'll come too. The bulb's gone in the hall."

In the living room she switched on one of the pole lamps and sucked in a breath: "Boy, nice gash on your forehead."

When I felt over my eye, my fingertips turned red. Lynne pressed me down onto the sofa, went into the kitchen, and came back with a folded paper towel and a twenty-dollar bottle of Oil of Teng, Herbal Healer. She swabbed the wound, refolded the reddened towel, then handed me a wad of tissues to stop the bleeding.

"I suppose that really hurts," she said.

"Last year I smashed my head on a bridge pier while someone was trying to drown me. The headache lasted for two weeks and I've had a nightmare or two."

"I hate being scared," she protested. "You hate everything when you're scared. You know?" Something about her voice, that low alto, almost a whisper, shifted the shadowy defenses between us. I said:

72

"For three hundred and sixty-five days I felt that."

"Huh?"

"In Vietnam."

"Oh. The trouble with Dawn is" — Lynne leaned back sideways on the sofa beside me — "she never panics. Even as a kid she was always in trouble because she wouldn't run away. Wouldn't hide. Wouldn't shut up. Not really a delinquent like they claimed. Just unscared."

"Rachel was feisty like that. My daughter."

"Well I wasn't. But see, Dawn grew up with a mother who needed Valium just for the nerve to get out bed in the morning. But that's the kind of world it was. I mean, here's this macho Joe Biondi keeping a grown woman in a mouse hole with a broom, sweeping up — no *tidying* up — Jesus, don't you *hate* that word? Eating Valiums and terrified to look out the door. Like her husband was Mighty Mouse, god on wheels, and as long as you obeyed him and kissed his tail, you'd never die. Ever see their wedding pictures?"

"Our backyard faced theirs."

"Maybe Dawn would remember you." Lynne got up to pull down the window shades, then settled beside me again. She lifted my hand to see if the paper towel had stanched the blood yet. All the time her voice rushed, low and urgent, as if we were running out of air:

"The thing is, back then families got their kids raised even though it drove the mothers crazy and the fathers had heart attacks. Now nobody has to stay married, but you see these young kids, they grow up in gangs and doing drugs, and all they care about's the excitement of a thing and —"

"Wait —"

"Where you take Dawn, now. She's been on her own since she was what? fifteen? She's seen the whole business fall apart and people trying to fill it up with sex, you know? That's why she wanted to make good sex flicks."

"Whoa, slow up. You're talking to a guy who just got run over by a shopping cart."

"Well, most X-rated films, they're really about who's on top, who sticks it to who, in how many unbelieveable ways. You know. Slaves. Dependency hang-ups. The usual."

"Power."

"Sure. Where Dawn now, she thinks bodies can have the power to focus you on another person. Like a movie projector, where the lens narrows down all this light and hey, suddenly there's a picture, a meaning nobody could see before."

I nodded solemnly: "Madam LaDawn. Secrets of the universe. Five bucks."

Lynne shrugged: "Okay, Dawn has her weirdo side. But she can be very down to earth. She's crazy about beautiful bodies. She'd spend hours studying fashion catalogs, loving the guys' squeezable asses and their hands and eyes. She'd be totally blown away by some girl's very sensitive mouth. Once she worked for this escort service, Dan Cupid — and even then the men she saw, the johns, they weren't enough. For most of them she was hired help, like a nurse. She liked them, but like the woman in Africa there, the way she loved the gorillas. Dawn wanted beautiful faces and closeness and words."

"Personal ecstasy."

"Sure. Whatever that is. What's the big rush to make fun of it? I mean, sex can be such a sad little thrill. Look at the people writing Dr. Ruth to find out what's wrong. People need to hang their lives on it, like religion. Ecstasy."

"And Dawn was working on the problem."

"In a way. Not just for the easy money — sex flicks don't pay that much. She really thought you could put ecstasy in a film so it would end up in someone's head."

"The X-rating board is going to be very confused."

"Sure. I mean, Dawn really believes porn hurts people. Except for her only sadistic stuff is porn."

"Nice distinction."

"They thought she was nuts. They so-called studio turned out to be this metal warehouse in East L.A., worse than an oven in the summer, with dumb sets made out of cardboard, like the bedroom walls ripple and shake when you bounce on the bed. And Dawn's there working on her ecstasy theory, trying for lines that make you feel alive. And instead it turns out to be this sicko flick called *Caspar Cuts Up*."

"I must have missed it."

She rolled her eyes: "It's supposed to be a weekend houseparty where this rich orphan guy screws all these fantastic women — that's the playing god part. But then to keep them all slaves he has to keep scaring them. So he shows each one the cut up bodies of other women so they become his sex slaves."

"Whoa."

"They've got these storewindow dummies strung up in dark corners of the set. Like meat on hooks. And the cute thing is, it's *supposed* to be fake — supposedly the guy's just scaring the women."

"And then?"

"Dawn never got that far."

"They sacked her?"

"Dawn couldn't make it in porn films. You know why? Because she talked too much. She'd get bored dry-humping these dumb hunks. Guys who couldn't even act interested in her—all they'd do is poke her boobs and drool in her earlobe and flex their muscles while the camera rolled. So Dawn would talk and talk. She'd invent lines for her character to say."

"Rewrite the script?"

"Mmm. Like she was supposed to play this virgin librarian who gets all hot and bothered when Joe Stud comes to her apartment to bring back some overdue car repair book. They're both overdue. Get it? Library book? Horny? That's the mental level of these things. Really simpleminded, like TV with pubic hair."

"So she rewrote the story?"

"In the shoot they're turning each other on, the librarian and the stud, and suddenly Dawn starts rapping to him about books, all the romance novels a librarian might've read. *The Flame and the Flower*, *The Proud Breed*, and whatever. And the director goes nuts. The men want humping and heavy breathing. They want the circus between the sheets. And here's Dawn, not a stitch on and all psyched, trying to show her character a little scared by this strange, exciting guy. She's going on about the romance novels, but really she's coming on to him in her shy librarian way, see. Licking his whistle, very tender, very *feeling*, because she's never been this close to a guy before."

"So they canned her for rewriting the script."

"It must have been a scream. Dawn trying to make the sex come out of feelings, and everybody else on the set trying to make the feelings come out of the sex. And they're all annoyed because they think it's just soft porn."

"Out on the coast," I said, "Dawn met a boyfriend who wanted to bankroll a sex film for her."

Lynne's eyebrows raised: "Who told you that?"

"Ryan."

"Ah. You've seen Ryan. Well, Dawn lived with the guy for months. Writing a screenplay."

"I know. I met him the other night."

"Armand?"

"He hints that Dawn was the great love of his life."

She shrugged: "Why not? Here's this guy in his fifties, he's got money, and he's nice looking if you like chins the shape of a catcher's mitt. And what's he got for excitement in his life but letters from dead people?"

75

"Only what was in it for Dawn?"

"If you can believe her, she fell for him. But if you ask me, she's always had this weak spot for father figures. Like the director she was blissed out on for so long."

"Frank Fascelle? He still misses her."

"Hey, Dawn loved the guy. Probably she still does. But you have to stop somewhere. You can't make love to the whole world. Except in films."

"Fascelle seems to think you and Dawn were lovers."

Lynne put her hand on my wrist with a complicated grin: "You believe him?"

"I think he's jealous. But he did offer me money to keep the investigation going."

"I bet he didn't tell his wife that."

"They're separated."

"I'm not surprised. Frank married her on the rebound from Dawn. He was pretty hurt when Dawn left. Later, when she was trying to break away from Armand, Frank wouldn't lift a finger."

"Armand's not your typical hairy brute. Why'd Dawn need help breaking away from him?"

"Maybe he has a mean streak. Maybe he has friends."

"Got another paper towel?"

Lynne took a closer look at my forehead: "Boy, you're still bleeding. Here, you need to press hard on it." She pushed my head back against the cushion and leaned on me so hard I got a close look at the Milky Way. I grabbed her wrists: "Hey! That hurts."

"Sorry. Ring the doorbell next time."

It was one straw too many, and the camel kicked her.

"Two things," I said. "One is, I'm not your flunky. So quit acting the wiseass. And the other is—"

"After my mother broke her hip," Lynne broke in, "she needed help getting around. But none of the walkers worked as good as an ordinary supermarket cart. So I grabbed one and lugged it upstairs for her to use. That's how—wait. You said two things. What's the other one?"

"Dawn's friend Ryan. He's dead."

76

∇

1 7

SHE FROZE, AS IF I were a snake that might strike. I felt her breathing stop. As she listened to the details she studied my face. Her pupils shifted a tiny bit once or twice, trying to see into me. One of her eyebrows was slightly wider than the other. Afterward she said: "So that's why the cops came by here earlier."

"What did Dawn say when you told her about the threatening phone call?"

"She was, oh, I don't know, annoyed. Flustered. Like, god I've got enough troubles."

"That's all?"

"She couldn't wait to get off the phone."

"You tell her Amy's in the hospital?"

"Somehow she already knew. I had the impression she'd even slipped into the hospital to see Amy once."

"Any chance our girl is free-lancing drugs? I keep wondering about the bananas who tried to grab you in Boston."

"Look. You never know for sure with Dawn, her mind's always going a hundred miles an hour. But she never did drugs around me."

"Then what went wrong between her and Armand?"

Lynne's shrug was no more than a subtle hitch. A twitch of her eyebrows gave the shrug a melancholy, anxious sense. "If you want my opinion, Armand loves what he hates. I mean, if she's a slut, she's not going to put him down. It's a turn-on, really exotic for him. The only problem is, deep down, if she's a slut, he'd really be disgusted."

"Which is why he fantasizes about how much talent she has?"

"He's not totally off base. You can be a slut and not be an idiot."

"You can also be too smart for your own good. I bet Dawn has some theories about who would want to beat Ryan to death."

Lynne bit her lower lip. Then she took the big breath that prepares you to dive headfirst into cold water: "Would you be willing—if I could get some sort of real story out of Dawn—would you be willing to talk to, you know, whoever's hassling her? She can pay you."

"Oh?"

"Would a couple of thousand be enough?"

"I stick my neck out while you watch?"

"I don't see why it should be so dangerous."

77

"Then why not do it yourself?"

That pulled her plug. "Look, you're a guy. You're an investigator, you know about stuff. Don't make me have to act helpless."

We watched each other. I said, "I need to talk to Dawn."

"I can arrange that."

"When?"

"Dawn's supposed to phone. Tonight or tomorrow. She owes me money. She owes everybody money. She's so damned irresponsible."

"When you hear from Dawn," I said, "phone this number in New York and wait two minutes for me to call you."

"Good." Her eyes suddenly filmed up: "I've got to be careful. You understand that, don't you? Please? If I don't protect her, somebody could walk up to her with a gun and—"

There were tears in her eyes. I watched them brim up then spill down her cheek when she blinked, left side first. You understand that, don't you?

Don't you?

I didn't like the odd mix of feelings that came over me.

Waiting in the Volvo, I could just make out a red Alfa Romeo Spider across the street in the Superette's lot. I couldn't watch the car and Lynne's front door at the same time: if she called a cab I might miss her.

I second-guessed myself for twenty minutes before a woman angled through a gap in the Superette's fence. The Alfa shot down the hill into the city like a cannonball going downstairs in the Washington monument.

Worcester is one of those New England cities whose redbrick factories invented the twentieth century—gauges, pumps, all kinds of gizmos—then slumped to sleep it off. Now urban renewal has been trying to wake up the town with dynamite.

The red Alfa aimed for the massive new Sheraton Hotel. Lynne knew where she was going. By the time I reached the hotel lobby she'd vanished.

As I hurried to see if the elevator would tell what floor it had just reached, the night manager called over from the desk: "Can I help?"

I waved my pocket notebook: "Lynne Dresser, woman that just came in—she left her notebook."

"Maybe you'd like to leave a message here at the desk?"

"You didn't happen to notice—?"

He stood self-consciously at attention in his blue suit and red necktie. Who could blame him. In the mirror behind him I could see my face, the gash in my forehead bold as an exclamation point. He lied with a smile: "Sorry. Are you a guest?"

"I'll see her in the morning."

He smiled hard.

"You have a guest named Dawn Ashland? or Biondi?"

He didn't even look at the guest register: "Afraid not."

Somewhere upstairs under one name or another, you could bet, Dawn Ashland was holed up. Short of provoking a midnight fire drill I had no way to draw her out. And I might not recognize her anyway. In the meantime I couldn't afford to scare off Lynne either.

If I stayed up all night staking out the premises, I'd be a zombie in the morning. So I went back to Meg's, put some neomycin on my forehead, aroused a tuna sandwich with hot salsa, gave five stars to a bottle of chilled Guinness, then mercifully passed out on the sofa we'd bought back when Rachel was in kindergarten and thought all sofas were trampolines, springboards to the moon.

In the never-never light just before dawn, Meg gave me a gentle shake, and out of long habit I rolled over to make room for her on the sofa, patting the cushion beside me. She shook me again: "No way, José. Wake up. Phone."

I gawked at the glory of creation, then slithered across the ghostly living room to the wall phone in the kitchen. Another irritable voice, Vera this time, reported: "We've got to find a better way to relay phone messages, love."

"Um."

"Call Lynne Dresser." Silence. "Duncan?"

"Um."

"You're walking in your sleep. Standing bare-bottomed in Meg's kitchen faking consciousness. I can picture it. Wake up!"

"Um. Thanks, I'll call her."

"For godsakes. Is that all you can say?"

"I'm dreaming I'm home in bed with you. You smell like warm croissants and I love it."

"Oh brother."

When I dialed Lynne, she sounded like I'd interrupted a noontime pool party. "I just talked to Dawn," she said. "I've got things to tell you. And money."

"What time is it?"

"Almost five. Can you come here at noon without anyone following you?"

"Why not now?"

"It's bedtime, Duncan. Don't you ever sleep?"

1 8

At SEVEN-THIRTY MEG and I shook some slivered almonds onto bran flakes and watched a girlish TV blond named Sara Jane Lee interview Senator Merriam's outspoken wife. Where campaign photos softened Candace Merriam's good looks, the studio lights emphasized her strong profile, the long jaw, and the impatient glint in her eye. She sat on the edge of her seat ready to thwart a hijacking: slim woman in her mid-forties, hands folded in her lap in a stilted knot—the pros had been coaching her. All in all, I couldn't see what had gotten Phil fired up about her.

The camera loved Sara Jane Lee's girlish strawberry mouth and blond halo. Her enthusiasm snapped, crackled, and popped—she'd never get old. With bossy familiarity she cracked a gentle whip. Some people, she said, thought Caddy Merriam was running for the White House harder than her genial husband. She wondered about the political risks of stirring up controversy.

Caddy Merriam started to say something about Eleanor Roosevelt visiting coal miners and their families during the Depression and speaking up for them. But Sara Jane wanted to talk about jailed blacks—the statement Phil had heard her make.

"You said that one out of four black American youths is in the prison system now and that's a national disgrace. Should the courts be more understanding toward black criminals?"

Caddy Merriam started to say something about kids growing up in poverty, but Sara Jane wanted to know what kind of special handling did Caddy think would work for black criminals? The candidate's wife said evenly: "I'll say it again. I think it's disgraceful that we let so many of our kids grow up in poverty. We can do better than that."

Which is where Sara Jane cut to an ad for an oat fiber cereal Meg and I were foolishly not eating. I began to see what Phil meant.

At eight-thirty I followed Meg out of the driveway. The air was cool but still saturated, and my shirt clung to my skin.

It took five minutes of brutal doorbell to shock Lynne out of bed. She slogged downstairs buttoning her jeans. "Boy, you're early," she complained. "I've been too stressed out to sleep much. I should do biofeedback to calm my alpha waves. You eaten?" She poked and prodded her wilting perm back into shape: "I feel like scrambled eggs."

"You look like scrambled eggs."

"Let's go out." She patted my arm. "I'll get my shoes."

Hard to know what to make of the element of playacting in all this. In the back of my mind I could hear Vera clucking: It's plain, i'n it? She wants something.

Next to the Superette in a lunchroom that hadn't seen fresh paint since Pearl Harbor, Lynne ordered scrambled eggs she didn't touch. The elderly waitress was assembling sandwiches by mashing scoops of egg salad onto white bread. Behind her was a Lucky Strike poster and a shelf of antique coffee cans. An air conditioner groaned over the door, but your skin felt coated with bear grease anyway. Lynne studied the haze on the surface of her coffee:

"My old man used to sneak over here for breakfast a lot. I only realized later that it was because he felt cooped up with my mother but he didn't want to hurt her feelings. They got along okay, but it was a job putting up with each other, you know? Were they, like, heroic for hanging in there? Or were they suckers?"

"I could ask myself that." She gave me a puzzled look, so I explained: "What's with the hotel last night?"

"You wanted me to talk to Dawn, so I did. Denny told me you followed me."

"You had on makeup, it was clear you had plans."

"Well what it is, Dawn's got a chance to make some new movies. Only she doesn't dare accept the offer yet. Till she finds a way to straighten out a misunderstanding."

"Which is?"

"She gave Armand some pictures to sell and took the money, but then the pictures didn't work out."

"She took money from Armand. Made some porn—erotic flicks. But they couldn't earn back the advance she took. That it?"

"Not exactly. She sold some pictures, but it turned out they couldn't be used so she took them back. And she kept the money."

"It's hot in here. You're losing me."

"Dawn, she sold some pictures through Armand. To some buyer—I don't know the name. That's where the money came from."

"How much?"

"She needed a car. And she owed people. And before she got too settled she wanted to see the world."

"So that's when she and Ryan winged off to London and South America for a month."

Lynne nodded: "She'll tell you she was happy for the first time in her life. No hustling, no schemes, no obsessions."

"A world tour might lighten me up too."

"Okay, okay. I'm not defending her. She's immature. Selfish. Impulsive. All that stuff." The elderly waitress shuffled over with the Silex coffeepot, and Lynne slid her cup over to meet it.

"So why couldn't they use the pictures she sold? Not dirty enough?"

"I didn't ask. All I know is, Dawn gave them to Armand and then took them back before he could deliver them."

"And kept the payment anyway. Which is theft."

"Maybe she thought Armand would make up the money as a, you know, like a gift."

"Then why'd she take off with Ryan for Timbuktu? Why's she still on the run?"

She thought about it: "If someone else paid out for the pictures and Armand's just a go-between, he may be in trouble too. Maybe that's why he wants so much to find her now."

"This happened while she was living with him?"

"Or just breaking up with him."

"Come on," I groaned. "This story's a bunch of soapsuds. Give me something solid."

Lynne opened the worn leather handbag next to her plate of dead eggs: "Duncan, look." She poked her finger into a rubber band-wrapped bundle of currency a couple of inches thick. From my angle the greenbacks could have been a baby crocodile eating her fingertip. She said: "What you do is, you ask Armand if he'll take back this much of the money. It's eighteen thousand. All that's left."

The wad helped explain why someone had tried to grab Lynne in Copley Square. I said: "They must be pretty interesting pictures to bring that kind of money."

She clapped the money on the table in a plastic Capezio bag and leaned toward me: "Ask Armand, will he let Dawn pay the rest in pieces."

"Installments."

"That's what I meant. Installments."

"How'd Dawn take the news about Ryan?"

Lynne glared: "She didn't say anything."

"What do you suppose that means?"

"Pain," she snapped. "It means she feels half dead herself." Her mouth hardened. She glared at me like a stern nurse in an old movie. I know how to glare too.

"Come on," I coaxed, "quit wrestling with me."

"Well use your brain. Dawn's in pain and she doesn't trust anyone enough to show it because the world is full of insensitive assholes like — oh forget it. Here — " She fiddled in her handbag and came up with a folded wad. Forty green portraits of President Grant. "She sent this. For you."

"For playing bodyguard."

"Armand will take you seriously. That's macho bullshit but it's true. He needs to be convinced that you're looking out for Dawn."

"I can't take the money."

"Because you think it's stolen."

"And because I think the kid's in a fix and I can't solve that for her."

"Then you won't talk to Armand."

"I didn't say that."

"Oh." She looked about to apologize. "Well, I'm glad."

"All this because Dawn made some porn flicks that couldn't make money."

She frowned: "So what's the big joke? You think it's funny?"

"Must have been one hell of a bad picture."

19

IN THE MOUNTING HEAT Concord's houses and lawns posed with the eerie perfection of a centerfold in a girlie magazine. In the middle of town, tourists with California plates rolled down their tinted windows to snap the local church. Not too many of these severe white spires in sunshine country. Lynne hopped out: "I'll meet you here on the common, okay?"

Armand's iron gates were open. Silver Porsche in the drive: no dogs. The lawn was so fine it could have been sprayed from a can. The Sandman was still operating on Armand when I arrived. He wasn't going to receive me at all until I told Nicholas how hard it was going to be for Ryan to get up this morning. I said, "I'm surprised the cops haven't been here already."

We ended up on hardwood stools in Armand's kitchen sipping amaretto-flavored coffee and eating designer toast while Nicholas heated the frying pan. Armand ate a no-cholesterol bacon substitute made from reprocessed Philippine mahogany. On his toast he preferred a generous layer of Snoote & Hogg's imported bongo-berry jam, by appointment to her Majesty the Queen. He preferred not to hear the details of Ryan's death, thank you, although questions kept popping out of his mouth. And out of mine:

"Where were you yesterday afternoon just after lunch?"

"Nowhere near the young man," he said smoothly.

"You might as well give me an answer. The cops will be here this morning asking the/same question."

"Well. Around lunchtime I had to appraise a 1786 Moses Henslowe grandfather clock for Daniel Skowman in Wayland. You've probably read about him, he's the —"

At which point I broke the news:

"Dawn Ashland's been in touch. She wants to give you eighteen thousand dollars and arrange terms to repay the rest."

To appeal to his appetite I placed the Capezio bag on the counter with the neck open just enough. Armand's voice sounded electric and unreal: "It's very late for this kind of talk."

"She's been too panicky to do anything."

"Who's problem is that?" In his clingy maroon silk robe and wire-rimmed glasses he advertised innocence.

"You're close to Dawn," I coaxed.

"I'd like to help. But I have bills to pay too."

"If you're not the actual buyer, who is?"

"Private party. This, what she did, it was very bad business. Very impetuous. People get hurt over this sort of thing."

"Look, we're talking dirty pictures, not stolen Rembrandts."

He was surprised: "She showed you the pictures?"

"No."

"I didn't think so. She's not a fool. She should hand over those pictures. Unless she's destroyed them."

"I don't know that."

"More likely she's resold them. Got greedy and tried to cut a better deal elsewhere. Maybe that deal's fallen through now."

"Hard to say. I'm only the messenger here."

"We're both in the middle on this one. Maybe you and I should turn that liability into an asset." In his left hand, like dice, Armand cupped the rubber earplugs he wore in his transactions with the Sandman. Nicholas went on frying mahogany. "Maybe you should secure the pictures for their rightful owner. For a fee, of course."

"Double-cross Dawn, you mean."

"My client's already *paid* for that property," he growled.

"And your client still wants them."

"For another couple of months the market will be very strong."

"But you never went to the police about the money she took."

"No. And something else. It's not good to have clients believing you may have cheated them. It's a risk. You must know how that works."

"One reason Dawn wants to settle is she's afraid of violence."

"It's about time."

"Among other things, she's worried about you being caught in the middle."

"She said that? I'm touched."

"Offer your client the eighteen thousand and call me."

"I'll pass it on." He waved a slice of fake bacon in the air to cool it. "But this is real money we're talking about. I suspect they'll want the pictures or a full refund." He gave a fastidious little snort: "This is America. We have rules for doing business."

"Mmm. The big dog eats the little dog."

"You'll have to excuse me while I telephone."

Meaning: get lost. I picked up the Capezio bag. Munching a stick of fake bacon, Armand actually saw me to the door. Just who was going to pick up the phone when Armand dialed?

* * *

In town Lynne dashed out of the drugstore and jumped into the Volvo. "I thought you'd never get back," she panted. "See the guy by the hydrant? In the Madras shirt? I walk around the corner, he's right behind me. I cross the common, he crosses. I run into the drugstore, and he hangs around outside."

Even as I turned to look, the Madras shirt was getting into a gray Mercury Sable parked by the pharmacy. Time to fly. Trouble is, Concord's not much of a maze. Though I circled through the streets as best I could, the Mercury kept nosing into my rearview mirror. Finally I gave up and continued on toward Concord's famous bridge.

At the site of the Revolutionary skirmish, I pulled into a parking lot next to a van unloading three crippled kids in wheelchairs. They all wore Disney World tee shirts. In unison they exchanged waves with Lynne. She squeezed my arm with both hands and said quietly: "I have this incredible urge to start running."

"It's too hot for athletics."

"I'm just praying you know what you're doing." Her hand was poking her curls into place.

The gray Mercury parked on the shoulder. Opening the Volvo's trunk I retrieved the Smith & Wesson and draped my sports coat over my arm to cover it. In the woodsy park across the street, we met a scatter of hungry ducks. No Minutemen. In this heat the shot heard round the world would have dribbled out of a musket barrel. Hot sun glazed the river surface, and even though the woods rattled with insects the air felt stupendously inert.

The Mercury's driver got out and drifted our way munching State Line potato chips. Hello Paul Revere. Square build: belly held in enough so that a pistol in his waistband might not show under the Madras shirt. In the sunlight his straight sandy hair and self-consciously tucked chin struck me as vaguely military. His chin hadn't matched wits with a razor blade this morning.

As he caught up to us on the rude bridge, Paul Revere began tossing potato chips to the ducks below. Lynne moved away, toward the granite monument farther along the path. Paul Revere leaned against the railing next to me. He sounded like Carolina, but I'm no expert: "Who's your friend?"

"My daughter."

"Where's Black Beauty?"

"Who?"

"The whore at Fixler's house the other night."

86

"Funny. I don't recall meeting you there."

He flipped open and shut a billfold with some sort of badge.

"Do that again," I said. "The hand is quicker than the eye."

"How's Armand today? He tell you where his girlfriend is?"

"What kind of badge is that? Not FBI."

"No, not FBI." He tossed some potato chips onto the river. "But if we felt you were obstructing justice – look at that, you'd think they were poison." The potato chips, he meant. On the current below, the ducks scouted the chips but wouldn't touch them. The wafers floated on the water, bigger than silver dollars. The man crushed the cellophane bag up small in his palm. I prompted him:

"If you felt what?"

"Give us a hard time and we can tie you up in legal knots."

"On what grounds?"

"You know what it costs to defend yourself from a prosecution? Even if the charges are dropped?"

"Excuse me while I turn on my pocket tape recorder."

"I'm only going to mention it once." The crushed cellophane bag fluttered down among the floating potato chips and began to uncrinkle in the water. I know there are federal agents out there working between the lines of the law, so to speak, but I don't like to think about it since it doesn't help my paranoia.

Paul Revere stood up: "Let's see what she says."

He made to go after Lynne. Turning, facing him now, I wiggled the sports coat on my forearm: "Stay away from her."

He stopped there, two feet from me, and caught on: "Jesus Christ. You threatening me?"

"You flash a little tin. Don't give me your name. Bullshit."

The three wheelchairs came across the bridge, the kids bobbing heads and waving wildly at Lynne.

"Tell you what," Paul Revere said. "It's hot. And we're getting off on the wrong foot. I don't like leaning on people. And believe me, the secrecy's better for both of us. All I'm saying is just give us a shot at the girl, okay? When it comes to immunity we can match any offer."

"You have a specific criminal charge in mind?"

"If you find this Dawn Ashland, put some glue on her shoes and tell Armand. Tell him she's ready to deal. He'll talk to people, and pretty soon the word will get to me. And we'll do the rest."

"Is Armand under surveillance?"

"Why should he be? You tell me."

"Got a phone number? An address?"

"Not for you."

"Why are you tailing me?"

"I don't want to hurt your feelings, you know?" Paul Revere eyed my sports coat irritably. "But for a ten-cent player, you want a lot of hundred-dollar answers."

The potato chips had disappeared beneath the water. For a tense moment we watched the shimmering surface, the sun blazing down on us. Then Paul Revere, whoever he was, gave the wooden railing a friendly slap and said, "Well, suit yourself."

He strolled back to the Mercury and drove off, without looking over his shoulder once.

Back in the Volvo, Lynne grazed—bumped—her cheek against my chest. "I don't mind telling you, I was scared shitless. You were great. We're still alive."

"Hey, take it easy."

"Bullshit." She squeezed my arm, my waist, then my crotch. She pressed her face into me, making soft kisses on my shirt. "I'm still alive. Jesus Christ. We're alive and I love it and nothing in the world matters like that. Nothing."

2 0

BUT SHE WAS SO rattled she insisted on a ride back to Worcester. So it was noon when I pulled up at Armand Acres to find Nicholas feeding the security dogs behind a locked gate.

This time Nicholas ushered me down the kitchen stairs to the office. A plate on the desk held a slice of rye cracker upholstered in jam and butter. While I waited in the Chippendale guest seat, Nicholas vacuumed the red carpet in short, angry strokes. When he noticed me watching, he said under his breath: "Shit stains."

Nicholas wasn't from the school of Jeeves. He seemed to be a combination of bodyguard and finicky aunt. You could tell he enjoyed fussing over Armand's loot. He liked dusting the display cases with the built-in halogen lights and the gilt picture frames. But there was something tough about Nicholas too, as if he was toting up the haul from a Viking raid.

When he finished vacuuming, my mind was starting to wander in the silence. Suddenly the portable phone cradle next to me on the desk said: "With you in a minute, Ames."

My skin crawled. Nicholas shifted his eyes to indicate the door in the rosewood paneling: the lavatory. Then Nicholas doubled up with a grimace that pantomimed a shotgun blast to the stomach. It took me a moment to catch on. He brushed his mustache in a way that masked either embarrassment or a rebellious smirk.

Armand came out carrying his cordless phone. In his clingy yellow jersey and wire-rimmed glasses he advertised innocence. He took a seat at the desk and fished out a Dutch cigar: "I've had full discussions of your proposal with the client."

His voice had the cheesy gentility of a banker or estate lawyer. I prompted him: "What gives?"

"The client would welcome an amicable settlement. There are two components to the proposed terms."

"What is this, the treaty of Versailles?"

"One," he said unfazed, "would be the delivery of the pictures contracted for. No further financial considerations need follow."

"Gotcha. And two?"

"No pictures. In that case she has two weeks to repay the money in full, plus fifty percent interest."

"That's loan-sharking."

"That's a modest penalty," he said prissily, "for stealing."

"Somebody really wants those pictures. What about the eighteen thou she's returning?"

"It's a nice gesture, but it's not enough."

"Then I'll keep it for her."

"Up to you."

"You may lose the whole works."

After twirling the cigar in his fingers like a drum majorette's baton, Armand lit it: "The client can't go to the police, neither can she. So I sense that the client is pursuing other remedies."

"What other remedies? Beating her to death?"

Worry liquefied Armand's eyes. The velvet slipped from his voice: "That was off the wall, the boyfriend's death. My client has no idea who did that. He's concerned. He thinks we're right to be concerned. Where does it stop, hmm?"

"Who's your client?"

He sucked on a cigar: "If I breach a trust, a client may feel let down. In my business reputation is everything."

I resisted the impulse to shake him like a cocktail: "Was your client planning to keep the pictures of Dawn or sell them to someone else?"

"I try not to know the details. Though I can tell you, we're not talking about photos of Dawn."

"Who or what then?"

"You should encourage her to—"

"Maybe I should encourage the cops to come see your etchings."

"I haven't broken any laws, Mr. Ames. If there's a thief, it's our friend Dawn. She can't go to the police and neither can my client. That's one reason the situation's so dangerous."

"And even your client's scared."

"Of course. I'm a little uneasy myself."

"Then there are other people involved."

"Of course. Which is why you should be a little scared too."

At a fast-food joint I ate a lifelike steak sandwich. Then at Roche Brothers' supermarket in Natick, I picked up cashier Rachel Ames. She had the afternoon off and wanted a lift into Boston to the hospital.

"Whoo, I'm tired," she sighed. "Work's really a bitch when it's so bo-o-ring." She slouched back in the seat dibbling a plastic spoon into a cup of raspberry yogurt. I said:

"Maybe you should've sacked out earlier."

"You still gonna be saying that to me when I'm forty? 'Rachel, you should get more sleep'? 'Quit painting all night'? No wonder Mom's afraid to tell you about getting back together with Leon Sadler."

"Oh?"

Rachel licked the spoon: "Sadler's asked her to run his real-estate business with him. She loves the money, it's a lot better than any job she's had since the divorce. I mean, she wouldn't have to be anyone's flunky."

"She ought to be able to handle Leon by now."

"Think she might have to marry him again?"

"Have to?"

"You know, as the price of this really great job?"

On Rachel's face slyness stands out like discount makeup. Meg's short-lived marriage to Leon had driven Rachel into a slow-motion teenage tantrum. Instead of playing along now I said, "Come on, give your mother a break."

"Like you did?"

That stung.

In the noonday heat, suddenly silent, we followed Route 9 past the grand competitive houses of Newton and the glitzy storewindows of Chestnut Hill. The trees were full of heat. Brookline Reservoir was brimming with tricky mirror sky. Rachel said, "Do you think it's possible Amy might — ?"

Her teeth caught between her bottom lip and the silence came back. Ahead of us Boston shimmered in the overheated air.

We were shimmying along on the trolley tracks on Huntington Avenue, almost to the hospital, when Rachel gave my knee a sudden pat and said, "Shit." And then, even more softly, "Sorry."

From the hospital I dialed Lynne Dresser, who wasn't picking up the phone, and Mrs. Daniel Skowman in Wayland, who confirmed that Armand Fixler had actually appraised her 1786 Moses Henslowe grandfather clock. Yes, he was at her house between twelve-thirty and two yesterday afternoon — about the time Ryan had discovered the high cost of living. That might account for Armand. I made a note to wonder about Nicholas.

Upstairs Amy was still in ICU, on a respirator, dreaming. From time to time she flinched and twitched, but all at random, responding to nothing the nurses did. Still, the medical staff kept hope flying while the patient, like the poisoned Snow White, made a mockery of life. A nurse trimmed Amy's nails and plugged and unplugged plastic tubing.

Everyone was careful to behave as if we had a person among us, not simply helpless skin and bones.

Kevin Hollings, the young Natick cop who'd introduced me to Red LeBeau, had driven Joan Biondi into Boston as a favor to Rachel. Joan greeted me with a jubilant hug. Kevin pumped my hand: "Good thing you found Dawn. You can see what a relief it's been for her mother."

"What are you talking about?"

"Dawn. She was just here. Gave her mother a big hug and—"

"Here? In this room?"

He nodded: "She's going off to make a movie."

"How long ago?"

"Ten minutes. She was sitting holding Amy's hand when I came in with her mother. They hugged and everything, and then Dawn took off down the hall. You don't look happy about it."

"She's running out on big trouble. Hang on a sec."

From a pay phone in the lobby, I rang Lynne Dresser's number: nothing. We should have agreed on a number of rings so she'd know it was safe to answer. Had she given Dawn a rosy picture of my talk with Armand? Or spooked her with the news that Paul Revere was trying to run her down? And in the meantime what was I doing with a Capezio bag full of hot cash? To Rachel I said: "Want to join me? Time for the last ride to Worcester."

21

LYNNE DRESSER'S HOUSE WAS shut up tight. While I tried doors and windows, Rachel wandered next door, where I found her consulting with the neighbors. Mr. Simosko was spending his vacation on a ladder stapling down strips of vinyl siding. Sure he knew the Dressers. Rachel handed him up some pieces of plastic clapboard. He was slapping the stuff over the window trim, fascia board, everything—as if wrapping the place in duct tape. "Stuff's maintenance free," he crowed. "Goes up easy too. That's the beauty of it."

"Did you happen to see Lynne Dresser this morning?"

"She's not back, is she?"

"I dropped her here just before noon. Now the place looks all sealed up. You didn't notice anything unusual?"

"Not really. Last night a drunk was prowling around their front porch. I would've called the cops, but I think he just wanted to relieve himself in the lilacs. There's a bar around the corner, Buster's."

When I asked him if Mrs. Simosko was home, he countered: "You in insurance?"

"No"—I flashed my business card—"Lynne was assisting in an inquiry involving a friend of hers."

Mr. S. called into the upstairs window, "Edna, hey. There's a man here wants to talk to you."

Husband and wife discussed matters for a minute before Edna finally came out onto their front porch. I presented my little white card and we danced around the block a few times. At last Edna said: "S'far's I know, Lynne's still out in Albuquerque. If she likes the job, she wants Mr. Simosko to help her sell the house. Mr. Simosko's willing to show it to people on Saturdays—not every day though."

"She's in Albu—?"

"That's New Mexico."

Clouds parted in the analytical mind: an arm reached down from heaven with a small wooden hammer and tapped the investigator on the cranium. Rachel said: "So Dawn Ashland was minding the house while Lynne was away?"

"Very nice person. Very clean," Edna added confidentially. "She hired a cleaning lady to come in once a week. Whether or not the place needed it. Frank and Mary Dresser, they both smoked their whole lives, and you know what a yellow film that leaves on everything."

"So you two got acquainted?"

"Somewhat. Dawn's always doing favors for you. Like Bobbi — that's my daughter, Bobbi — she's in travel consultation downtown here, and Dawn would go out of her way to buy her air fares through her. They get a commission, you know. That's how they earn their living."

"Has Dawn accepted the film offer she just got?"

"So that's not such a secret after all."

In Concord the mid-afternoon air wore a haze of warm shellac. This time, under protest, it was Rachel who waited for me in the pharmacy. "I don't want anyone thinking you know too much," I argued. "I'll tell you the whole story when I get back."

Armand's iron gate was hot to the touch. Nicholas sat me in the air-conditioned kitchen. The boss came up from his impregnable office with a drink in one hand and the portable phone in the other. "So," he breezed, "you have the pictures for me?"

"She's gone," I said. "Tell your client we need some time."

"Gone where?"

"She's accepted a movie offer. Apparently in L.A."

"How did you find out?"

"Footwork." I couldn't bring myself to admit to Armand that I'd been had. He wasn't impressed.

"It's an addiction with her, this playacting business. You want a drink? Nicholas makes something called a bongo-bongo. Very refreshing."

To mix a bongo-bongo you add lime, mango, and some other jungle juice to a Soviet ammunition dump and serve so cold the tongue sticks to the glass. Nicholas was straining out shreds of lime in his droopy mustache and beaming joy, so I decided to bongo too.

"I may go out to L.A. after her. But I need some idea where to start."

"I'm not in the dirty movie business," he said primly.

"Who'd she work for before? You were out there with her, you must remember something."

"Those were sleaze films she was — "

"Spare me your delicate feelings." I drained my glass and Nicholas refilled it. Rachel would have to drive to keep the state cops from discovering the recipe for bongo-bongos.

"I met Dawn almost by accident when — "

"Armand — "

His sigh could have inflated a truck tire: "Okay, okay. I can give you a couple of names, a couple of her girlfriends. But I can't guarantee any connections. Got a pencil?"

"Shoot.'

"I hope you find her. This so-called offer" — he spit a dainty puff of disbelief at me — "how bogus can you get?"

"You think she's making it all up?"

"I'd feel better if she was. What I think, personally, I wonder if it isn't a setup."

"A setup?"

"To trap her. Look at her friend Ryan."

"Murder her when she shows up."

"It crossed my mind. Or maybe this is a snuff film."

"As in — ?"

"I admit, it's a sickening thought. I'm ashamed to think it. But when I heard about the sadistic trick with the tape over the mouth and the broken nose, I had a very bad feeling."

22

A HOT SMOGGY BREEZE swept up the sidewalk outside the arrivals terminal at L.A. International. At Jerry Gold's Val-U-Rental on Lincoln Boulevard I had a choice of an open-cockpit Maserati or a Val-U Isuzu with Val-U air-conditioning. Then I phoned the first name on my list: Ben Bayer. A tape machine took charge: "Ben Bayer Enterprises, offering a full range of entertainment industry services. Wait for the tone and leave . . ."

It was 9:30 P.M. by now. There were two women on my list to try. But either nobody in L.A. is ever home, or these days only answering machines can afford to live there. In the end I took a Val-U trip to the twisted backstreets of Venice, half a mile from the ocean, where Ben Bayer lived in a mixed neighborhood of bungalows and beach shacks waiting for the next hurricane to export them to Mexico.

Under a yellow buglight on his tiny porch, Ben Bayer was reclining on a lawnchair. He was reading a chunk of typescript, wiggling his toes to the music in his headphones. Guy in his forties with a grizzle of beard and a jogger's sweatband, red elastic athletic shorts and knobby knees. Rather than look for a doorbell, I called out hello. He started, and when I introduced myself, joked about all the burglaries in the neighborhood:

"Quarter million I paid for this place. You believe that? Every putz and his brother wants to live in L.A. and touch the magic button."

"That includes Cyndy Field."

"Hey, you a friend of hers?"

"A friend of mine, Armand Fixler, told me to look her up."

"I know Armand. Deals in documents and like that."

"And Cyndy?"

"Cyndy's working for me again. Making videos. Soft videos. Kind of thing a trucker can bring home to the wife, or she could pick up at the local video store and surprise his ass off."

"Where you shooting?"

"Great studio. Part of the Metro spin-off over in East L.A. that got lost in the legal shuffle. Big warehouse. Very private, easy to rig for lights and shit. And here's the kick: it's full—I mean stuffed up the geeker—with sets. Damn near every sitcom living room and saloon you ever saw on TV is stacked up in there ready to go. No union carpenters, no guild writers, no nothing. The unions can stuff it."

96

"What's Cyndy's address?"

While I wrote in my notebook, he shot ahead in his enthusiasm: "All we got to get now is distribution. You follow? What good's quality if you can't move it out? We're into a quality product this time. Good acting. People who can make sex look, you know, sexy. Bliss can really look gross. Or dumb. I mean, we're talking moronic. You want good orgasms onscreen, you need people who can really fake."

"Cyndy likely to be around tonight?"

"If she's not out partying her tookas off, she's probably crashing."

They were on the other side of Inglewood, almost in Watts, in a concrete block bungalow the size of a roadside comfort station. On shadowy porches folks sat waiting for the next dirty midnight breeze. Heartbreak cowboy on somebody's radio. When I knocked, Cyndy demanded the secret password. I gave my name and a familiar voice said, "Oh shit." Then grudgingly: "Go on, let him in."

It was a boxy room still holding the day's heat and furnished with a kitchen table, a couple chairs, two mattresses, ashtrays, and a coat of green paint. The other room seemed choked with clothes. The open bathroom door showed enough cosmetics to paint a house. Cyndy was sitting on the mattress painting her toenails a venous purple.

Dawn Ashland sat at a table in undies and a UCLA tee shirt, bare feet up on the chair seat. Her hair was nearly black. In one ear glinted a G clef earring—the mate to Ryan's. She was dipping a teaspoon into a jar of Moon Fruit ("All the Moon's Vital Energy with None of the Calories.") and thumbing through *Unlock Your Past Lives: Getting the Most Out of Reincarnation* by Sheena Clarky, Ph.D. Judging from the dried remains, somebody had enjoyed a half-gallon of Rhine wine and a pizza here in a previous incarnation.

"Lynne," I said. "Am I glad to see you."

"How'd you find me?"

"It wasn't easy." I took the other chair.

When she spoke her voice had a caressing sort of intimacy that gave me goosebumps. "My god, Duncan. You're such a caring man. I feel so guilty. You came all the way out here for me."

"To warn you."

"Cyndy," she said. "This is Duncan. Remember I told you? He saved my life." Cyndy looked up from her toenails and gave me a friendly little wave. In the meantime Dawn's hand stroked the back of mine. "God, I'm so happy to see you."

The way Dawn touched my hand, Sheena Clarky, Ph.D., would have seen that once upon a time in ancient Alexandria we'd been Antony and Cleo. I said: "Want to tell me why you bolted out here?"

"Thanks for caring so much" — the emotion was thinning out now — "but I'm okay. Really. When I see Dawn —"

"When you see Dawn it'll be in the mirror." I tossed Sheena Clarky, Ph.D., across the room onto the mattress.

"Hey, that's Cyndy's book!" she protested.

"Game's over. Let's get real, kid."

"What do you — ?"

"Look, I fell for it. You snookered me into being your bodyguard and your messenger boy. But it's over."

Cyndy said: "Uh-oh. Fight coming. Want I should call Big Lionell over?"

"No," Dawn said. And to me: "So what do you really want?"

"Did you kill Ryan over the pictures?"

"Of course not. We agreed about the pictures."

I watched her closely: "So who killed him?"

"I have no idea. Let's take a walk. We can talk."

"Might be too dangerous."

"Look," she muttered, "I just flew all the way out here to get away from that whole paranoid Boston scene."

"If Ryan's any indication, you shouldn't even have let me in here the way you did."

"So go already," Cyndy sniped. "You're not her father." Not a helpful comment. I tossed her my car keys and said:

"Here, Cyndy. Take a ride. Get lost."

Cyndy hesitated: "You gonna be okay, Dawn?"

Dawn stared at nothing.

Cyndy was desperately torn. Not too torn: "If you're gonna be all right, I'll just go down to the car-hop for half an hour." And to me, to make it clear she didn't need any favors: "My regular roommate Whitney's staying at her boyfriend's tonight with the car."

"I understand perfectly," I said.

And locked the door behind her.

With Cyndy gone the only sound was some kid outside in the dark swinging back and forth on a rusty metal gate. Dawn put on an impressive yawn: "We've got to be up early for tomorrow's shoot."

Another yawn: her splendid teeth made me rueful about the junk-yard of fillings in my own craw. She pushed it: "Some of this can wait till tomorrow night. I'll buy you dinner then."

"Horseshit."

Dawn's smile did a Mona Lisa number, ineffably sad. So I added: "Let's cut the theater. Tell me what this is all about."

"Just because I'm living here in this rat hole, like a rat, at this particular moment—"

"Save the speeches. Just spill the truth in my lap."

"You're pissing in the wind, Duncan."

"Nice talk."

"Hey, I'm not your fucking daughter. I'll say what I feel."

I changed tactics: "Your acting was brilliant back in Boston and the joke's on me. But something's out of control. Armand's convinced you've been lured out here to be killed in a snuff film."

"Armand's an old woman."

"If he's a correct old woman, then you're a candidate for Saint Mary's cemetery in Natick."

"Piss off, Duncan."

"You think yelling at me's going to change anything?"

"You're full of it." She jumped to her feet. Trying to pace in that cramped room, she more or less turned around in a circle. Still, you could feel her trying to hammer her emotions back into place: "The whole thing's ridiculous. I gave back the money."

"Some of it."

"Most of it. What was I supposed to live on? They'll get their stupid money."

"Some people prefer revenge. They live for it."

"I gave back the money," she insisted.

"Maybe they feel you and Ryan cheated once so now they're entitled to a turn."

"Besides, all that crap about snuff films that was in the papers a few years ago—you know, the mob hitting girls, like in Brazil—it was all trashy bullshit. Rumors. Like the alligators in the New York sewers. Nobody's ever seen one. There's nothing to see."

"Well, Ryan's not seeing anymore Coming Attractions."

"Oh shit." Her voice ached; her bravado faltered. Just as quickly she recovered, reached over, and poked my ribs. "And if you're so worried and everything, where's your gun?"

"Wasn't worth the legal hassle to pack it on the plane. Stay out of trouble and we won't need it."

"That's always bugged me. It's the worst kind of weirdness."

"What is?"

"The way men threaten you with all this violence so they can be Mr. God Almighty and save your ass."

"You got any idea what it cost me to fly out here today?"

"Oho! The last of the big spenders. I offered you two grand."

"That's hitting pretty low."

"You get what you ask for."

"Like Ryan?"

She groaned. The pacing stopped. She threw her arms around herself in a shivering hug.

I took out the photo of the vixenish nude I'd swiped from Ryan's bedroom. With its bushy sideburns the fox face appeared to be grinning, winking at you; the woman's lovely body touched your feelings from a strange angle. I said: "Tell me about the pictures Armand's looking for. Has this one got anything to do with them?"

"What makes you think that?"

"A hunch."

"Well, you're not totally screwy."

"Thanks."

She yanked her blue jeans off the mattress and skinned into them, then stepped into her sandals and headed for the door: "Let's go out. I'm going nuts in here."

When I grabbed her from behind, she exploded with frustrated rage, trying to kick, elbow, buck me off: "Let go, asshole!"

"Whoa. I need answers."

I wrapped her tighter in my arms. She snapped her head back trying to bash my face until I rapped my knuckles on top of her crown and she shouted "Ow!" and threw herself out of my arms. The momentum carried her, staggering, into the sink-refrigerator unit against the wall, which gave a hollow rattle when her knee slammed it. Without a pause she turned to the faucet and—like a kid saving face—filled a glass of water as if nothing had happened. She drank the water in three swallows then refilled it: "You thirsty?"

"Sure."

"It never cooled off in here today."

She brought the water over—me prepared to duck in case she tossed it in my face. But no, she handed it to me with a kind of easy intimacy. Only the grim set of her mouth told you she was struggling inside. She could have used a shower too.

"Poor fucking Ryan," she groaned. "He knew this would happen." She dropped cross-legged onto the mattress, facing into the corner to hide her face from me, to cry. To the dirty blue wall she said under her breath: "Poor fucking Ry."

"This photo," I said, "is it you?"

"What difference does it make?"

"Is it what the money's all about?"

"Yes and no."

"For christsake, Dawn."

"It was all so stupid. I mean, you think you make allowances for people's stupidity, you know, their greed and stuff. But—"

She shook her head. There were tears. I got down beside her on the mattress. We were still sitting there in silence when Cyndy rapped on the door. I let her in: "That was fast."

"Goddamned cops," she groaned. She tossed my car keys onto the table so they chinked against the wine bottle, then flipped her cigarette butt out the open door and lit a fresh one. "I get almost over to Century Boulevard on this little side street and they pull me over with the flashing red light in the window. And this guy, looks like a Mexican. Plainclothes. License and registration he wants. Where you going? So I show him my ID and he takes my whole purse and picks through it. He says: 'You live alone?' Like uh-oh, am I gonna have to give this guy a freebie? So I told him I live with my older brother. And he's leaning in the window, he's got like cloves on his breath, and his fingers get fooling with my nipple. Then he says: 'You tell other people's lies, it hurts. Like catching your tit in the door, eh?' And oh shit, he pinched me so hard I almost went through the roof of the car."

Dawn got up from the mattress: "You never know with cops."

"They got sexual harassment, they got all these laws. And none of it works."

"I shook my head: "What if they're not cops?"

"You mean it's just some retards with a red light stopping girls to pinch their tits?"

"I hope that's it."

Cyndy's mouth fell open.

"Duncan," Dawn growled, "you're being such an asshole."

I said: "It's possible they stopped Cyndy looking for someone else."

Question marks danced in Cyndy's eyes. Dawn was furious: "If that's true, then they followed you here. Jerk."

"If a jerk can find you, anybody can."

"God, you are so pushy. You've got the money. Why don't you just talk a walk."

"Take it easy."

"I want to go to bed," Cyndy complained.

"Look," I said to Dawn, "it's the wrong time to let go."

"Who says I'm giving up?"

I met her eye and held it. She rushed ahead, a plaintive edge to her voice now:

"And anyway, what do you expect me to do? There's nothing you or anybody else can do. Except maybe watch me get hurt."

"Don't let go."

"Take a walk."

"I'm afraid of what's coming."

"You don't know squat."

"Listen, goddamn it." I threw my forefinger in her face: "I came all the way out here to—"

"And you can keep right on going."

I said some unkind things. Dawn wrinkled up her nose:

"Take a walk."

"Keep your door locked," I said.

Infuriating woman.

$\triangledown$

2 3

I HAD TO DRIVE back toward the airport to find a motel. Coming out of the shower, on an impulse, I flipped a coin to decide if I should scram on the morning's first flight: and won. Good. So much for guilt. When you hit forty you feel very queasy about an impulse to protect young women who happen to be beautiful. I phoned the airline to reserve a seat for an early-morning flight. Trouble was, jetlag tossed me and turned me all night long, and after my wake-up call at seven I shot straight back to sleep.

At eight-thirty I slithered out of bed and at a corner shop mashed a couple of donuts against my teeth. The newspaper bucked me up. Medical garbage polluting beaches. Rumor that Senator Merriam needed a psychiatric overhaul a few years ago. Rumor that for years Candace Merriam had been lovers with a boyhood friend of her husband's. Savings and Loan industry still in trouble. Drought losses mounting in the Midwest. Rhino and elephant approaching extinction in Africa.

Repent: The End is Near.

But instead of repenting or even calling the airline, I ordered a drum of industrial-strength coffee to go and headed for East L.A.

Ben Bayer's warehouse stood in what I thought was a desolate industrial zone until I walked into a corrugated tin garage by mistake and found three scruffy families of Mexicans using a small propane torch to cook a panful of eggs. From cardboard boxes stamped THAILAND they were assembling el cheapo costume jewelry. Before I could open my mouth, they scattered without a sound.

Outside I went from gate to gate, the asphalt heating up underfoot. None of the truckers I stopped knew where I was going either.

As it turned out the warehouse could have doubled as an aircraft hangar. By ten-fifteen no actors had yet shown up. Thanks to my lifelong friendship with Ben Bayer, the lighting man let me inside to help them assemble a backdrop. I helped the crew erect a staircase that went nowhere beside a painted window that looked out on nothing. Half the warehouse was piled high with movie trappings—gay nineties lampposts, a throne, a Roman fountain, a "Gunsmoke" saloon, a full set of chain-gang irons—layer on layer of wild centuries and exotic lands, as far back into the shadows as the eye could see.

A few minutes later the two cameramen arrived: film students, they claimed, toting ordinary-looking camcorders. When Ben Bayer and a few male actors showed up, I made myself scarce by climbing a utility ladder and sitting up among the steel trusses overhead: not a padded loge but inconspicuous. The last thing I needed this morning was a public squabble with Dawn. If trouble was in the wings, the only hope would be to spot it in time to—what? What did I think I could do?

Around eleven, five women turned up in high spirits, including Dawn and Cyndy, and Ben Bayer began cracking the whip—or the shoestring. "Come on, people," he kept reciting, "this is costing."

They started into a skit about a guy who stumbles into a college sorority looking for a crack house. Searching for the crack provided dirty wordplay that drove the story from one raunchy scene to the next. There were no costumes: the women wore their streetclothes and nothing at all as the plot dictated.

The humor took me back to high school when we used to sneak into the last gasping burlesque show in the old Scollay Square, where the shiny-haired emcee sang "A Pretty Girl Is Like a Malady" and hawked boxes of candy supposed to contain, like Crackerjack prizes, a twenty-four carat gold watch. Where the last vaudeville comics on earth told imbecile dirty jokes and strippers named Candy Kane and Dee Lightful took it all off, more or less, while couples applauded, old duffers tickled themselves under the newspapers in their laps, and passionate sailors tried to swan-dive off the balcony into the arms of Gina the Jungle Woman. Erotic paradise, hokey as the amusement park at Nantasket.

But then the business below me was fake too: slow motion stripping and teasing followed by ingenious combinations of bodies. The last bed held the crack seeker and all five women in a version of the overstuffed clown car in the circus. Everybody wiggled and stuck out a tongue, but from up in the rafters it could have been a football scrimmage.

Between scenes I helped with set changes by rigging the several ropes that could winch heavy things off the floor from up in the rafters. Either the actors didn't notice me or they took me for granted. They passed the lunch break in horseplay or small talk or griping about the grease on the cement floor. They were bored, yet there was also an air of summer camp excitement, of escapism and showing off. Then Ben Bayer was grousing again: "Let's go, let's go. This is costing, people."

The second skit sketched the contest between a mildly macho junior executive and his woman rival, who happened to be Dawn. The plot consisted of nose-to-nose bantering resolved every few minutes by some inventive sexplay—she wins a bet, say, and he has to crouch in the cubbyhole of her desk and keep her inspired while she runs an executive meeting.

Dawn rollicked in the farce and gracefully humped her way through the genital ballet. Ben Bayer hadn't been kidding: in the midst of so much grotesque huffing and puffing, she was lovely. When the camera demanded tedious retakes or Bayer would nag — "Come one, come on. Spread it. Wider, wider" — Dawn would play through these indignities with eerie patience. When conquering males couldn't keep their scepters up, she was easygoing, even indulgent. I had the impression she'd been beyond the usual taboos so many times that she'd come to feel a kind of sympathy for the beautiful, ridiculous human body. Not completely. She was furious when one of the lovers, fooling around, got his chewing gum matted in her pubic hair. There were wisecracks about scissors and freezing the gum to remove it. When the guy started pulling on it, she swatted him.

However dead the material, however nasty, Dawn was right. A snuff film it wasn't. No sign of serious threat. Where did that leave me? The transcontinental voyeur. The dunce in the rafters.

She happened to look up.

She was standing behind the working backdrop during a scene change, still undressed, in a nearly private space. At first she looked away as if to see if I was an optical illusion. When I didn't disappear, she pulled on her slippers, took hold of the heavy rope dangling a couple of feet away from her, and began to climb. You could see she was trying to get the hang of it, trying different loops with her feet, pulling herself up hand over hand. Every so often she would kick and twist a bit, then recover. Maybe she was imitating or remembering some gym feat.

I watched her inch upward admiring her stamina, and how game she was. Then I began to worry that she'd fall. But after a while she found a way to anchor herself by snugging the rope between her feet, and by the time she was so close I could almost reach her, I was mentally down on the rope with her, cheering her on, in a sort of erotic, admiring rush.

Inch by inch she pulled herself up out of the white lights into the shadows. When I reached down to her, she hung on the rope, throwing her head back in mockery. Sweat gleamed on her face. The rope had rubbed patches of red on her skin, from her breasts to her knees. She tried not to grin: "Admit it. You were wrong. I'm still alive."

"I'll say. Here, grab my hand. And you should know the world's watching."

Below us all eyes were on her. One of the actors beat his bare chest and gave a Tarzan war cry. Yet for all the wisecracks down there, her climb excited them more than any striptease. Dawn paid no attention: "You really think you're saving me, don't you."

"You're one hell of a gymnast."

"I love to watch the Olympics on TV. I wish I had that kind of discipline."

"You're not exactly a wet noodle."

She couldn't hide her pleasure: "After that little AIDS scare, I began doing workouts. I'm not in such bad shape, am I?"

"You're beautiful."

She cracked a smile of self-mockery: "Apart from that."

"I mean it's beautiful to watch your body defy the odds. Beat gravity."

"We should work out together. I bet you have a pokey little middle-aged belly."

"How do you plan to get out of this mess you're in?"

"You should've been a loan officer in a bank."

"You want my hand or are you going to keep walking on air?"

"I can't believe you came—I mean, here you are, way the hell up here in this sweltering roof—you know, for me. Either I'm incredibly lucky or you are the world's greatest pain in the ass. Here, pull me up, will you? Only don't fall, whatever you do."

"Answer the question."

"What, my plans? Are you kidding? You'll have to buy me dinner after work. Or if you're too cheap, I'll treat you."

"Thanks."

With one hand on the truss and the other gripping her slippery wrist, I hauled her up onto the steel girder. We perched there on the cool I-beam, in the hot gloom, while she caught her breath. As she started toward the ladder she said: "Hey, Duncan?"

I couldn't keep my eyes off her.

She poked me in the gut: "Smile."

The afternoon heat finally tortured the action to a halt. As we milled about breaking down the equipment, I noticed Ben Bayer handing a chunk of typescript to Dawn. When I passed him a few minutes later I said: "What about it? Can she write?"

He shrugged: "Hey, she's got a talent. But it's good, not great, and it's hard to market good stories out there now."

"Not enough action?"

"Sure, and too much stuff about the characters. Who they are and what they want. Jesus. Lighten up, I tell her. I mean, this one's about a housewife who's scared of everything. Afraid to leave her house. Driving the husband bananas. Then the woman's old girlfriend, who's been a high-class hooker, she comes back. She tries to help. And the housewife's real hostile at first. But the friend starts teaching her all these deep, sexy moves. So the woman wins back the husband and gets on top of her life again, and like that. Upbeat type of a script. But not really strong enough for us."

"Interesting."

"Yeah, missing that indefinable thing that would make it great, you know?"

24

DAWN INVITED HERSELF TO my motel for a shower and took a quick scan of the cable TV channels hoping to find herself in some X-rated art. Then she guided us to a Mexican place in Santa Monica where the special was chicken in Yucatan black bean soup. Scooping up salsa in nachos, slurping down a salty margarita, she was full of manic sparkle.

"I called my mother this morning," she announced. "Something's going on with Amy." She let the suspense build a second: "If you're a pessimist, Amy's right arm's been twitching." Dawn's teeth delicately crunched a peppery chip: "And if you're an optimist, like me, you'd say she's moving her right arm a little."

"Hallelujah."

"You ever go to a black gospel church?"

I shook my head.

"Couple summers ago I got stranded in Chicago for a few weeks, on the South Side, next door to this tabernacle. It turned me on. They used to say Hallelujah. If I was really religious, that's the kind of religious I'd be. They live in their bodies, you know? With that music that lifts you right off your feet and shakes the dust out of you. Not like us kids going to Mass, where the boss talked down to you from up in a whatsit—"

"Pulpit."

"Yeah, a stage set of heaven."

"I hear you didn't make too many novenas as a teenager."

A smile tickled the corners of her mouth: "I was a devil."

"So Red LeBeau tells me."

"Good old Red. I was this fifteen-year-old, this teenie-bopper, and I thought I was going with Red. But what he did, he set me up to service his buddies. Then him and me, we'd have a good time on the proceeds."

"Meaning Red was more or less pimping."

"Yeah, I wouldn't admit it to myself. My own worst enemy, you know? What it was, I think I sensed what would happen if I faced up to it."

"Meaning?"

The waiter brought over her hot quesadilla and my Mayan soup, and a fresh bottle of Dos Equis. Dawn spotted my soup with a few drops of hot sauce. She said: "Meaning finally I dumped Red one day. So of course he had to knock me around a little." She swatted herself in the jaw. "After that, no way. No more boyfriends leaning on me. Ever."

"But you went back to him to buy the sports car."

"He gave me a deal." She gave a sheepish shrug. "And I wanted to show him I was somebody now. I wanted the satisfaction."

I groaned. She gave the subject a quick twist:

"That's what I liked about working for Dan Cupid. It was computerized. Nice clean electronic matchmaking, with credit cards and a cash payment every two weeks for the girls. Everything but social security deductions. No hassles, no regrets. Except it got to be a job. A fuck factory. Bad as punching the register at Burger King with french fry grease in your hair."

"Like being a servant."

"It's pricks stand up and beg," she shot back. "Not the girl. I made good bucks."

"Then how come you're hiding under a rock now?"

"If you're selling something," she countered irrelevantly, "you need a good attitude. Self-control. You have to be able to figure what people want, that's all." She looked at me with wide-open eyes, discreetly chewing a mouthful of quesadilla, and all at once I wondered if anyone had ever peered through the masks and makeup to the hidden face of the girl she had been. "Besides," she said, "if you're just a kid, and a girl, and a nobody, and a piece of shit, and your family's screwed up, you can't be too choosy."

"Do me a favor. Don't offer my daughter career counseling."

"Want to keep your little cookie all to yourself, huh?"

The sudden sarcasm jolted me. On a hunch I said, "You grew up with your old man messing with you?"

She winced and shifted the subject: "It was Lynne who finally talked me into giving up the night shift."

Something clicked: "When I first met you in the Copley Plaza, when you were coming on as Lynne, you knew half the staff there."

"Mmm, I did a lot of hotels while I was living in Boston. Even the Copley."

"You did the Sheraton the other night in Worcester, too."

"Yeah, you were right on my heels. Denny the deskman told me. I was panicky to make some money since I was giving Armand everything back. And afterward I realized, there was no way I could make enough hooking to get out from under that kind of debt. So I decided the hell with it, I might as well go back to the movies."

"I thought I was tailing Lynne."

"I tell you, it's what got me through the panic, laughing at the way you swallowed the Lynne bit."

"Where'd you learn Lynne's psychological lingo?"

"From her books."

"You read her psych books?"

"You won't believe this. But I've been able to read since first grade. You jerk."

"Sorry. I didn't mean it that way."

"Oh yes you did. In the back of your mind you're convinced. *She's just a slut who peddles her twat. She's just a woman.*"

"Stop picking a fight."

"Mmm, we don't have time."

"True, you need to tell me about the pictures."

"First you need to drive me back to the studio to talk to Ben about my screenplay. They're setting up for tomorrow's shoot, and he wants to see me at nine."

"Stop stalling, kid. There's time."

"Don't boss me, Duncan, I hate that. I've spent my whole life getting out from under that."

"There's plenty of time if you stop running away."

She nicked the last morsel of food off her plate — she must have been starving. Her eyes met mine and held on. Frustration and worry wrestled in her throat: "Did it ever occur to you that maybe I'm not too proud of what I did?"

25

IN THE CAR DAWN was exhausted, maybe depressed. Her head lolled against the headrest and her eyes closed. L.A.'s lights swarmed off to the horizon and turned into the squinting stars. In the darkness only an edgy rasp in your throat reminded you that the vanished smog still contaminated the air. At one point Dawn woke with a start and said dreamily: "God, this place is exciting." And drifted off again.

The warehouse had only one window, in a closet-sized office at one end, and it was dark. "Looks like we missed everybody," I suggested. "Ben's gone beddy-bye."

"Huh? Ben? No, he stays up all night working. Besides, I have a key. There's a phone in the office." As she hopped out, a car pulled up behind us. "See," she tooted, "there he is now."

With a click the warehouse padlock snapped open. Only there were two clicks, one behind me, and when I paid attention, there he was, not Ben but the purple shirt, holding a snubby revolver loosely tucked under his left arm. In the moonlight his nose floated between empty eyesockets. He had a friend behind him.

"Lynne," I prompted. She paid no attention.

"Come on," he said. "You ride."

"Up yours," Dawn said, giving the sliding door a heave and pushing into the dark interior.

She hadn't seen the gun.

But it was Dawn they wanted, and in that moment of hesitation I took my chances, ducked, and threw myself into the doorway hoping to hear any artillery go over my head. But we were all faked out. I wheeled to shove the door shut and on the smooth concrete slipped onto my knees. I heard Dawn's footsteps running inside. Maybe she'd seen the pistol after all. I rolled over and dragged myself around the edge of the current backdrop into the stage set.

In the doorway purple shirt stood outlined against a sky littered with stars. Then his friend reappeared: handed him something. One of them slid the heavy door shut and the space went totally black: "Where's the light switch?"

"Is there a watchman?"

Where had I heard that voice before?

One of them flicked on a flashlight. The beam raked slowly across the floor, toward me, over me. Back and forth: patient, logical. Either they weren't so flustered now or they enjoyed a systematic hunt. The rush of adrenaline made me queasy. The light came back. I found myself crouched behind a car seat — the crew had changed the set. The flashlight beam outlined a steering wheel on a wood post, crossed the seat, and then broke up in a scatter of folding chairs off the set. I tried to mark the chairs in my memory.

By the door the flashlight searched for the light switch. A voice said: "No lights. May be a watchman."

As I crawled across the stage area, my right hand bumped into a canvas bag — camera bag. I slipped out a camcorder battery the size of a hand grenade and pitched it toward the door as hard as I could. It crashed into the steel wall with a satisfying slam, and in a panicky reflex a pistol shot whacked the darkness. Do that often enough and they might shoot each other. On the other hand, pulling the trigger once breaks a taboo and makes it easier to fire again.

The sportsmen consulted in mutters, trying to cooperate.

I crawled between the folding chairs. Where the hell was Dawn? Behind me the flashlight probed in back of the canvas backdrop; the light flared and died and came out the other side. I felt my way into the heap of movie props in this corner of the warehouse: slithered past a British phone booth, behind a *Dr. Zhivago* sleigh, under a fake marble fountain. I felt safer in this briar patch of junk, but uneasy too, because in the dark there was no way of telling how hidden I actually was. And if the eye could find you, so could a bullet.

Footsteps broke out behind the stage. Hers. Then his. There was a soft sickening thump as flesh and reality collided. Then a string of obscenities. Male voice. He'd stumbled into something. The flashlight swept round and round. One of them cried in a sort of rising, childish tantrum: "Where — the — fuck's — the — light!"

The flashlight came into the stage area probing from side to side.

I kept groping around for something to swing: a detachable chair leg, an umbrella, anything. My hands played across the face and scales of a wooden Chinese dragon. I crawled under a buggy with tall wheels and twisted up to check out the driver's seat in hopes of a buggy whip. I shook hands with a cigar store Indian. Balanced on the lip of a table, I reached up to grab an ax handle and nearly pulled down a stack of round life preservers when the handle turned out to be the spoke of a ship's wheel. The flashlight began to play among the props. I hit the deck and slithered deeper into the heap.

Something rattled. Trunk handle maybe.

112

I froze. Behind me the purple shirt began shoving things aside to get a closer look. I backed into a crevice formed by back-to-back sofas, flexing my shoulders to widen the space. Only the flashlight reappeared ten feet away probing between the wheels of a steam locomotive that turned out to be a giant cutout. From that angle the light would catch me head on. Like shooting fish in a barrel. I pulled my head between my legs and tried to show the back of my shirt, fabric that might just be another swatch of upholstery. Dust tingled in my nose.

Don't breathe.

I heard him kick something close by: glass tinkled to the floor. He cursed. Kicked. Another thousand points of shattered glass. And again, under his breath, cold, enraged: "Fuck. Fuck. *Fuck!*" And another burst of glass.

When I raised my head, the blurry edge of light had moved on. I rubbed my nose in furious silence. My man squeezed past naked mannikins stacked up like firewood in a pile that went up into the darkness. Then he tripped, something tipped, glass shattered. He jumped: "Stupid fuck." He said it a few more times to make it stick.

As he backed away it struck me as the retreat of a man spooked by the close quarters. He kept darting the light back toward me as if he sensed he was missing something. Not without reason either. Get him within reach and I'd give him a whole new outlook on life. Only when did you ever meet a predator who didn't keep a gun or a lawyer between himself and his victim? From the doorway the other shouted: "Let's torch the goddamn place."

"Wait."

"All this garbage would go up like —"

In the course of which there was a scuffle at the door. Shoving, grunts: surprise, pain from sharp fingernails or a kick. Then running footsteps. Dawn's footsteps. The flashlight sprinted toward them, but she'd apparently ducked among the props again. She knew her way around in here.

With the commotion as cover, I sprinted back to the set and slid down behind the onstage bed just in time to escape a nervous pass of the light. I could feel myself losing patience and it scared me. Logic alone can't tell you when your headlong charge is seizing the moment or fluttering like a pigeon into the mouth of a shotgun.

The sportsmen were getting worked up, egging each other on. As they played the light over the wall again, trying to spot a light switch, they seemed to be arguing over who the flashlight belonged to. Only this time my man noticed the office in the corner where he'd probably find the light panel. Get to the light switch, and that's the match.

Groping around me I found throw pillows, a leather glove, either a model spaceship or an electric vibrator, a box of lipsticks, and a half-eaten sandwich. The vibrator had the most heft so I heaved it over the backdrop toward the office door. It rebounded off the wall and brought both hombres running. I scuttled around the other end of the set, backstage, and made my way between the flats toward the office door. If I could catch him at the edge, up close, there was a chance I might shake the pistol loose.

I made it halfway.

The flashlight stepped around the edge of the backdrop and flooded me. He came up the narrow corridor gloating softly: "You stupid fuck." Over and over under his breath, half disbelief, half magic: "You stupid fuck."

My legs froze. No room to step aside. I could only run in the line of fire. Fear spilled through me.

"Where is she." The mouth and nose hovered in darkness. Shades of Spanish in his words.

"In trouble."

"Call her. Tell her to come out."

"She won't pay any attention."

"The fuck she won't."

"I don't have any more power over her than you do."

"Too bad for you, stupid fuck."

"What do you want with her?"

"The pictures. The kiddy pictures."

"I don't think she has them."

He sneered: "But you don't know, right?"

"Right."

"Then you're in the way."

I pushed against the weight of my fear. Made myself breathe. "She dodges my questions."

"You know too much, and it's not enough."

"I get nowhere asking her."

He mimicked me, the pistol wagging like a finger pointing: "You get nowhere asking her."

"I'm guessing Ryan had the pictures."

"Who, the boyfriend? He don't have shit."

"Then I have no idea. Like I don't know who you are."

"You know I exist. That's too much."

Meaning he had plans for me. The fear was like fire, catching everywhere in my mind at once, no matter how I tried to snuff it. No room to move either. The canvas walls on either side of me might as well have been cement. My eye followed the winch ropes we'd used this morning up toward heaven. A spider monkey would have a chance.

White socks.

I tried to keep my eyes steady on him, afraid he'd see it in my expression.

White socks.

My tongue rattled on: "I've got nothing to do with you."

"You seen my face twice. I don't want to be famous."

In my peripheral vision, overhead, dimly: yes, white socks. Sneakers and white socks. She'd shimmied up the rope. I began talking with my hands, easing a step forward, trying to look unthreatening. He backed up a step. "The way I got into this," I rambled, "was by accident. Through Dawn's sister." Whose skull you smashed. "Who had no idea of any problems with pictures."

We moved in little steps, me gesturing, chattering, him not so much backing up as giving me room, maybe hoping I'd give away some bit of information he needed. Suddenly with a grunt of frustration he snapped: "Stop dancing around!"

His friend appeared behind him: "Where's the other one?"

My heart stalled. If he glanced up it was all over. I felt myself tensing to rush for the gun hand—kamikaze stunt but better than being dropped in my tracks. Purple shirt snapped at him: "Cuidaté por la Puerta. Ella se va alrededor."

"So once I met Ryan," I said, watching the other head back to the door, "I began to realize how much money was involved. Big big bucks." I waved my hands in big, big circles, crowding forward.

"Don' *move!*" he rasped. I went with the momentum:

"Big, big balloons. So much that any idiot could see—"

I kept pressing forward. He eased another step back, wagging the pistol at me, frustrated, furious. You could feel the rage exploding: "Listen to me, you dead fuck. Listen to me. You are one dead fuck, you know that? You know that?"

"You want to hear about the money or not?"

He backed up: "You—"

At which point Dawn kicked him in the back of the skull with dreamlike, soundless violence. Suddenly his head snapped forward and Dawn was spinning wildly around in the air above us, her legs flying. The flashlight crashed on the cement; my grip shook the pistol loose and it clattered along the floor. Then my elbow was in his mouth, which

115

gave way with sickening ease. False teeth. He choked and took his knee out of my soft parts. Dawn dropped to the floor, but on my knee. Her force flattened me and wrenched me to one side. I stifled a howl. The purple shirt rolled out of my grip. For an instant the three of us collided insanely in the dark.

Dawn said: "I've got the gun."

Twenty feet away I saw a muzzle flash, and the detonation cracked the darkness. My man cursed.

He was dragging himself along the floor. We heard him stumble to his feet, his hand whistling against the canvas backdrop as he groped for something to steady him. He gasped: *"It's me."*

Dawn said coldly: "I'm going to blow him away."

His footsteps rushed. It sounded as if he fell around the corner. The sliding steel door grated in its track. Dawn said:

"Where are you?"

I grunted.

"You hurt?"

"Twisted my leg when you landed on me. I'll live."

"Can you fix the flashlight?"

She handed it to me: I unscrewed the head. Her voice shook:

"My hands are trembling."

"Cheap flashlight. I think it's the bulb."

I was shaking too. We were both shivering like skiers stranded in an avalanche, in a wall of overwhelming ice. Dawn's teeth were chattering. She was shivering so hard she clamped her hand over her mouth. I pulled her against me, trying to squeeze the anxiety out of her. After a minute the shock subsided. She had her free hand on my knee. "Boy," she whispered, "you're really trembling."

"Pulled a muscle."

She felt around: "Your hands too."

"Nervous reflex."

"Uh-huh."

"You really know how to use that pistol?"

"That's why I want the flashlight," she whispered.

"The bulb's —"

"Because I can't find the pistol."

$$\triangledown$$

26

Wᴵᴛʜ ᴍʏ ᴋɴᴇᴇ ʙᴇɢɢɪɴɢ for mercy, Dawn had to drive the car. Out on Whittier Boulevard I said: "Slow down till the stoplight just turns red. Then jump the intersection."

"To see if anyone's following?"

"You got it."

"You have the pistol?"

"Don't worry." We'd gotten grubby nosing along the cement floor to locate the pistol. "Those the two who beat up Ryan in the parking lot last month?"

"Maybe. I moved pretty fast when that went down."

"One of them put Amy in the hospital, I'm pretty sure. Are they the ones who offered you the ride in Copley Square?"

"I don't know. Sure. Maybe. I'm a little shaky just now."

As a precaution Dawn picked up some clothes at Cyndy's, then at my motel we washed up and checked me out. Against the advice of my knee we drove into Venice, backed into the dead end where Ben Bayer lived, and parked facing out onto the street just in case.

Party at Ben's. Inhale sharply, one nostril at a time.

The porch was aflutter with movie butterflies and studs in chin stubble and cowboy boots. No purple shirts. A woman in a bead halter made from little macaronis slipped her rum and Coke between my lips murmuring: "Who, Ben? He's going wee-wee."

"Thanks for the tip."

"What a dead party, huh? Absolutely nobody here." She shifted position so her macaroni halter rustled and her very dark nipples would show.

"I'm not here either," I said.

"Are you somebody?"

"Just a shadow on the wall."

"Oh." She thought a minute. "Remember me when I'm famous."

She put her plastic glass in my face again, so generously I had to jump back to keep the sauce from trickling down my neck.

The bungalow was your basic pup tent design, with a bathroom the size of a porta-toilet. When I knocked, the door unlatched. Inside were four guys squeezed together with blissful faces and unconscious eyes as if buried upright in some cryogenic locker. Ben Bayer came alive first: "'Scuse me. If you don't get out of my way, I'm going to claim you as a tax deduction."

He roared at his joke.

"Right this way," I said.

I crowded him out the back door into the dark yard. By a single light bulb in the garage opposite, a neighbor was test firing a motorcycle. "Cut the crap," he suggested, wiping his nose on the sleeve of his golf shirt. "I hate walking backwards, people fall on their heads all the time."

I encouraged him to stand tall against the side of the house: "You were supposed to meet Dawn tonight."

"Oh, it's you," he enthused. "Where you been? Dawn here?"

"Question is, where were you?"

"What? At the set, only there was nobody there. I had people coming over here, what am I supposed to do? If I told you how much time I've blown waiting for her, she's unbelievable, you'll see, no shit, take my word—"

His voice raced down an invisible track, powered by Columbian hi-test, round and round, faster and faster. I interrupted him: "You got any plans to buy Dawn's screenplay?"

"Hey, well. It's got promise, but the way the market is right now, where you need a strong new handle to—" His voice swerved off the track into L.A. agent gibberish. I called to him:

"What were you snorting in the can?"

"What?" He gave me a cagey look: "Ah, nothing much. Little old-fashioned stuff. Want a sneeze?"

I began to think he was as irrelevant as he claimed.

Dawn wanted me to join the festivities, but my knee said nothing doing. After trying the stoplight trick a couple more times and stopping for a six-pack of Cerveza Bohemian, we ended up in a motel in Santa Monica, just up from the ocean. From the ice machine Dawn hauled in a plastic bag of cubes and packed it around my offended knee. "God," she sighed, "I feel scuzzy. Mind if I shower?"

She had, I began to see, a thing about getting clean. Thirty minutes later she came out wrapped in all the towels in the house and sat beside me on the bed mussing her hair dry: "Food?"

"Later."

"I could get some cheesy popcorn."

"Not for me. Tempt me with a beer."

"You're not exhausted?"

"Get me the beer." I was getting tired of evasions: "And tell me what you're doing peddling kiddie porn."

"Huh?"

"You heard our man tonight. He's after kiddie pictures he says you have."

She burst out laughing. I said:

"I never thought warping little kids was so much fun."

"For heaven's sake, Duncan." She patted my chest patronizingly in a way that didn't lighten my mood. Swaddled in white motel towels she could have been an Oriental princess – Scheherazade – or an escaped lunatic. But then as she began brushing out her hair she said "I'm laughing because if I wasn't here to straighten you out, you could spend months on that puzzle. Years. It'd never be solved."

"Oh?"

"Because he didn't say kiddie porn."

"Horseshit. I heard him. He had my full attention."

"You'd make a great police dog. What a bite."

"*Dawn*," I growled, "get serious."

"What he said was, 'Caddy pictures'."

"Caddy?"

"Yeah, as in the Senator's wife. Who wants to be the first lady of the White House and all that."

"You lost me."

"I can tell. Your mouth's hanging open." Her gown of towels was hanging open enough to account for it. I said:

"What the hell do they want with pictures of her?"

"Suppose during this presidential campaign someone turned up pictures of Candace Merriam as a college kid. Here she is, the daughter of a famous doctor in New York. She's impulsive. She's got this intense artistic-type personality. Full of herself. Sewer mouth when she loses her temper. Tears when things get to her. Somebody who drives people crazy by telling the truth. And they say she's been having an affair. A real pistol-type personality."

"Like you," I wisecracked. Dawn nodded, unfazed:

"People say I look a lot like her. That's what gave us the idea."

"What idea?"

She rested the hairbrush in her lap and cocked her head as if thinking out loud: "Suppose when Caddy went out to USC to college she got carried away. Suppose she got into the hippie rebellion thing in L.A., doing dope and – I mean, say she agreed to pose nude for a photographer who was going to make a movie career for her."

"This happened?"

"Hold your horses. Suppose—would you open this beer for me?" She handed me a Cerveza and resumed her brushing. The towels drooped artfully across her left breast and cocked hip. "See, Caddy jumped into a shaky marriage when she was twenty-one, so this photo session would have been three years before—1965, like." Dawn took a gulp from the beer: "Suppose the poses are typical sixties cheesecake—no crotch shots, but everything else. Lots of kittenish girl-next-door cutesy pie—the Hugh Heffner bag. Not doing anything dirty, just lounging around in the nude looking blissed out."

"In color?"

"Black-and-white glossies. Fairly low contrast natural light shots in this funky apartment. Sixties artsy. You can see she's on the make. Like, she knows it's image that counts. Project the right image and your face is worth a million dollars. People will buy anything you say. Except when you mix up your images. Like when that Miss America—Wilson or Williams—when it turned out she'd done some nude shots and they crucified her. Think what would happen if this was a woman almost in the White House and she turns up in the news cute to the last drop."

"Political meltdown."

"Well, that's what this is all about."

I could feel my imagination floundering: "Hang on. You met a photographer who wanted to sell devastating photos of—"

"Not exactly. It was me and Ryan."

"You and Ryan met a—"

"Uh-uh. Not met."

"You stole photos from—"

"Afraid not."

"You found photos, copied photos nobody else—"

She let the hairbrush and towel fall, shaking her head. With her forefinger she drew a line across her naked collar bone as if to signal cutting a throat or— And all at once, as in the flash of a riddle, I saw it:

"Well, what do you know."

"Mmm."

"Faked it."

"Good dog." She patted my shin.

"You and Ryan faked photos of Caddy Merriam."

"Basically. It was a pain, believe me. I had to try all these experiments with theater makeup to shade my jaw and pull in my cheeks like hers. I had to try and get that birdlike profile. And Ryan kept futzing with the lights, and then all the darkroom garbage took him forever. He did hundreds of prints. He even found some outdated print paper at a tag sale that's more like what they used then."

"So you produced some fakes and got Armand to peddle them."

"It wasn't that easy. I even went out to L.A. and cooked up a story about a photographer—got street addresses and went through yearbooks and like that. Julio Romano. Sixteen-twelve Stratford Avenue. I found the name in a business directory from 1964. Guy's been dead for ten years. No relatives that I could find. How they ever gonna prove what he did or didn't do in his studio years ago? Anyway, it would take longer than any political campaign lasts. We worked out a story for how the portfolio turned up."

"Such as?"

"Such as the landlady where Cyndy was staying two years ago, Mrs. Pauline. Her mind was going with that memory thing, Alzheimer's. And she had this shopping bag full of prints her friend Julio Romano had given her before he popped off. So I'm looking through the prints and I come across these nudes. And I'm like 'Who's this Candace Chapell?'—that's her maiden name. What do I know? Then when I'm living at Armand's, see, I come across the name in a feature on politicians' wives in *People* magazine. Bazzoom! I connect the names, Chapell and Merriam. Armand fronts me the airfare to check it out. By now the landlady's in a nursing home. So Ryan copies her signature from rent receipts onto a bill of sale for the bag of photos and I sign it. And bazzoom! I show up in Concord with this envelope full of shots that can rip off the country."

"What a liar," I muttered. Dawn was flattered:

"I know. Me and Ryan stayed up all night for a week inventing the details, getting high and laughing our asses off."

"And what? Armand swallowed it and agreed to sell the goods for you?"

"Oh at first he got all puffed up about his expert reputation. Big conscience trip. But when you get his pants off, he's a treasure hunter. He got the hots for the deal."

"Only at the last minute you took the purchase money and the pictures and scrammed. How come? Armand caught on?"

Dawn turned, trying to plant a shy, rueful smile on me. "I had second thoughts. Personally I think it would be fine, you know these pompous people, they have the power of life and death—everybody should get to see their droopy white asses sometimes."

"But?"

"But Caddy Merriam keeps telling the truth about things. Like how kids get treated like animals and how the rich people get away with murder. You know, with the Wall Street cheating and the banks and all that garbage. And there's the other thing too."

"Which?"

"I didn't want to hurt another woman." Dawn arched her back and stretched for the ceiling with a deep, shivering yawn. "The way they treat her in the news — I mean, after all that trouble getting into her life, I couldn't — it just — oh screw it."

"You identified with her."

She groaned into the mirror: "Who kno-o-ows."

"But you couldn't resist the bucks."

"It seemed dumb to go through with the deal. Some expert with a magnifying glass would spot the fakes. Then there'd be bad vibes — FBI and all those jerks."

"Only it left Armand in a jam."

"He can afford it better than I can. I bet he knew all along the photos were fakes. Besides, he was dealing through a middleman anyway." She was avoiding my eyes. Hooking her heels on the chair seat, she put her chin on her knees, hiding behind her legs. "I just figured since Armand had this middleman, he was protected. Like, if he was selling to the politicians, they'd be so scared of a blowup they wouldn't dare make a big stink."

"Who'd he use for the blind?"

"It may be this ex-con — a guy he once moved some stolen antiques for. You can't just fence fancy junk like you can a hot TV."

"So Armand's done naughty things."

She winced in disagreement: "Just guessing. Armand was great to me when I crashed at his place to write my screenplay."

"So you and Ryan took the payoff and winged off to London and Cairo and Timbuktu."

"I wanted to climb up the pyramids and go inside King Tut's tomb without having to peddle my ass to do it. I wanted to look at the world as a free person."

"Dead people make lousy tourists."

She came over to the bed, whirled once, and dropped dead on the mattress beside me. "See, idiot? I'm not dead."

"The point is, you and Ryan went around the world in eighty days and got stomped in a parking lot your first week back."

"That wasn't Armand's fault, was it?"

"Ryan thought it was."

"Ryan was so jealous. Like he's got to compete with the guy or something. I mean sure, Armand had these ideas about me. And sure he got possessive. One more reason to hit the road. I never minded putting out for him. You know what he likes to do afterward? Lie there with his and your legs snugged together eating a glob of peanut butter off a butter knife."

"Peanut butter and oysters. Powerful aphrodisiac."

"But you don't want the guy falling all over you, dogging you around—be home for supper, where you going *now*? That garbage. Down doggy, down."

"So when you split, it was adios Armando."

"Okay, yeah." The way she conceded, it was like she was trying out a scenario.

"And you were angry enough to take photos, money, the works."

"Later, when they pounded Ryan—I thought, oh shit, Armand's next." She stretched out now with her damp hair on my stomach. "Then I was sorry. Hey, give them what they want. If they're fake pictures, so what? By the time anybody checked them out, Caddy Merriam would be dead meat on TV. That's all they want. And the shots aren't bad likenesses. I did my hair just like hers. I—"

"You gave her your body."

"She could do worse." She took my wrist and slapped my hand against her bare hip. The mild, spontaneous vanity of this made me laugh in spite of myself.

"Tonight suggests to me they want the photos," I said. "And they want to be sure you can keep a secret."

"Like Ryan," she said gloomily.

"So how do they know you and Ryan are the source for the photos unless Armand's told them?"

She drew her knees up and played them like bongos. Nervous. I pushed on:

"Would Armand finger you because you walked out on him? Or is he giving them you and Ryan to save his own skin? Did he give me that snuff film jazz to warn you because they'd made him set you up?"

"Or did he tell you so they could whack us both out here?"

"That's what I've been trying to—"

"Get Armand to call it off," she said. "He could tell them the photos are gone."

"If they've killed Ryan, they have a lot invested now. They're afraid one of us can finger them."

"How could I? I just told you—"

"But they don't know that."

"Only, you know something? I think one of those bastards tonight was the guy you talked to at Concord Bridge the other afternoon. The guy you called Paul Revere."

"If so, these guys are go-getters."

I interrupted the kneecap calypso. Dawn shook her hand free and rolled away. Her dark hair splashed across the white pillow. In a burst of frustration she cried: "Who cares? Who the f—-"

"They might want to take you out of the picture."

"You're trying to scare me."

"I'm trying to make you more realistic."

She made scissors with two fingers. "Snip. Snip. Snuff. God, I wish I was dead."

27

AFTER BRUSHING HER TEETH for twenty minutes in front of the tube, Dawn nosed into the sack with me and backed her perky bottom firmly into my stomach. The perky bottom sported a butterfly tattoo the width of three fingers. She rubbed her feet against mine to warm them. "Look," I said, "I'm beat. But if you don't go put on some clothes we're going to wind up a lot closer than the handbook recommends."

"It's okay, I won't do anything."

"Well you may not, but I will."

"It's okay. Go ahead, pork me. I'm so blown away I won't notice a thing."

"Hey, this is no way to run a ball club. Go put something on."

She groaned: "I just got settled down. I just got comfortable."

"Tough."

"Squeeze me tight, like a pillow, real real hard. I like that."

"After."

"I really don't want to die, you know."

"Nobody ever dies from putting their undies on."

"I mean it. I love my life. As screwed up as it is. I'm glad I'm me. I admit it, I've done lots of stupid, bad things. Believe it or not, there was a time you couldn't leave me alone in a room with your wallet. Once I stuffed my underpants into a birthday present this guy bought for his wife so she'd smell me and know what a phony he was. One Christmas Eve in Winchester I went to midnight Mass with this corporation lawyer — he'd just done this big junk bond takeover thing and he owned the fucking world. He kept insisting he was going to dump his wife for me — his idea, not mine. And afterward we sat in his car outside a school and did a teeny bit of coke like you'd give your hamster — bi-i-ig deal. So I kissed him off and he paid me, and when I joked about a Christmas bonus for sitting through Mass with him, he went crazy with his fists, and biting me, god! I thought sure I was dead meat."

Tears blurred her eyes. Since I didn't feel much like punching or biting her, and in the back of my mind Vera was dialing my number and getting a busy signal, I cradled Dawn in my arms and tried to think about a neutral subject, like how to get out of Los Angeles alive. But before long her left nipple stood up honestly into the palm of my right hand, and I had an overwhelming urge to comfort her.

Just when I thought we were both on the skids to sleep, she sat bolt upright in bed. My hand started to slip from her breast but she snugged my wrist under her arm to hold me there. After the tears her eyes had a dreamy look, raw but uncalculating: as innocent perhaps as she ever got. Abruptly she jumped out of bed and began snatching at her clothes: "Come on, Duncan. Let's get some food."

"Do you know what time it is?"

"I'll be damned if I'm going to lie here just waiting to be killed."

"It's late. If you consider the jetlag, I'm—"

"Give me the car keys, then. I'll go myself."

Which is how my aching knee found itself riding with her up toward the thousand pointless lights of Hollywood. A thousand tantalizing doorways and tricky keyholes. In seedy neighborhoods people sat outside panting in the midnight air. Along the strip nightlife was throbbing. Passionflowers of all sexes were still pollinating the bars.

Dawn gave me the tour of her old haunts. She wanted me to know how flipped out she'd been her first time here: cruising among the swanky houses of Bel Air and dreaming of what you could do on a movie screen to make people see the deadness of sex in a box. The phrase came back again and again: sex in a box. It sounded like a fast-food franchise or a horror-story coffin—I never figured out exactly what she meant by it. Something lifeless. What stayed with me was a moment in Beverly Hills when she parked so we could look out over the brawling twinkle of L.A. lights, and as usual Dawn bent the conversation around to sex, in a rambling elegy:

"The way I justified hooking was I thought, what the hell, I make bodies feel good. Look at all the righteous types that have no use for bodies. All they want is to deodorize them. They think they live in perfect thoughts inside their heads. To them bodies are dirt. Sacks of shit that wear out and die. Look at the TV preachers ranting. Look at the Nazis. You ever see that documentary on PBS about finding the concentration camps, where they're dragging the dead people into pits? Thousands of corpses. Thousands and thousands. Heaped up like french fries in the garbage. Dragging them by the ankles and the wrists. Babies and women and anybody. All these sad pitiful knees and bellies and shrunken boobs and wobbly heads. You can't begin to get your mind around it. What kind of people would ever treat bodies in such a way? Never mind the souls."

Dawn sat hunched in the passenger's seat, chewing gum, her voice small and fierce in her throat. "It drives you crazy, people pretending they know exactly how to live because deep down they're scared shitless."

126

"You're not scared?"

"Sometimes. But I'm sort of different."

"You're sort of different all right."

"Okay, so I'm scared sometimes. Fuck you."

"What do you want?"

"The same thing you want. To do something that matters."

"Ah."

"Like if I'd been born a few hundred years ago—say there actually was reincarnation, even though it's a bunch of bullshit. Well, if I had, I could've been a nun. Because that mattered a lot then. Helping people get food, helping them not be scared, that sort of stuff. You see where I'm coming from?"

"We're getting there."

We watched the lights below. She spit her gum into a bush: "So what do we do now?"

"I hate to be the bearer of bad tidings, but this is your problem."

"They're after you too."

"If I don't get back to work, my partner will shoot me and save them the trouble."

"Then I'll have to take my chances."

"Go to the cops."

"What, and confess I ripped off that money? That'd go over big. And cops can't protect you anyways. What am I gonna get, a restraining order like a punched-up wife? These guys, shit. They could walk up to you and—*blip*, you're dead—and they're long gone."

"You have to do something."

Dawn twisted up her mouth to keep her composure. "I'll just keep making the videos. That's a few bucks anyway. To hell with them."

"You can't ignore this."

"What are you talking about? Of course I can, I have to. If you don't have any money or credit or rich friends, all you can do is keep pushing ahead and hope you're still alive at bedtime."

"Come to New York, find a job."

"Hide out, you mean." She thought about it, then: "Oh shit. I'd never know when it's safe to be myself again. Besides, I want to make movies. I don't want to be an office temp. I don't want to marry a rich surgeon and drive his Jag out to the Hamptons every weekend. At least I don't want to marry one forever."

"You don't want to be dead forever, either."

"Oh bull!" Suddenly she was furious, glaring at me: "Doesn't it even piss you off that I was tampering with the stupid election?"

127

"In my racket," I said lamely, "you see more dirt than you can sweep up in one lifetime."

She leaned into me now, nose to nose: "Whoever they are, they've killed Ryan. And they're going to screw around with everybody's desires and fuck up the vote."

"Dawn," I grumbled, "you're trying to manipulate me."

"I don't have a big choice."

We simmered in silence for a while, but the thousand lights scattered across the valley before us seemed meaningless as smashed glass, and finally I said, "Let's find a phone. I have to check in with the office."

Outside an all-night gas station in Santa Monica, I was leaving a message on Vera's answering machine when Vee herself cut in. She squeezed me for details as I described Dawn's photo scam and our night in the funhouse with the flashlight. "Time to get out of there," Vera said. "I hope you agree?"

When I tried to change the subject to Rachel, Vera said: "She called tonight looking for you. Her friend, the one in the hospital—"

"Amy."

"—she twitched some today. They can't tell if it's just reflexes, or if she's really responding. Rachel, of course, is convinced the kid will be waltzing down to breakfast. She's taking this pretty hard."

"Fingers crossed. I hope Amy doesn't wake up to find her sister hung out for the vultures."

"What's the sister doing to protect herself?"

"She's cornered. The cops won't give her much sympathy." I was groping: "From one angle this is a local scam. Chickenfeed. From another, it could tap into the election and all the power up for grabs in the country."

"That's a lot of temptation."

$\triangledown$

28

NOT LONG BEFORE SUNUP Dawn and I were lying side by side in our clothes on the spongy motel bed, twitching on the edge of sleep. The TV picture danced in the darkness, though I'd made her kill the sound. The air conditioner throbbed. My knee throbbed. When I closed my eyes a flashlight slashed through the dark in the back of my mind. Every so often Dawn's cinnamon gum crackled juicily, and finally I snarled: "Look, you're going to fall asleep and choke to death on that gum."

"That would solve problems."

"Quit it."

"Sorry."

"How'd you ever survive so long without a pimp grabbing you?"

"Fast feet."

"Other women have tried that."

"I stayed off the street. Worked through contacts. Hotels. Conventions. The escort service, Dan Cupid, they screened out a lot of evil guys."

In the silence I could hear a car or two outside grinding away at the new day. Dawn's voice came back: "I got slapped around sometimes. But when it got dangerous I'd slip into some kind of relationship. Take cover, like. Frank Fascelle or somebody would offer me a place. And when I was singing with Steam Thieves I had Ryan. I don't mind relationships. If the person's right."

"You're wide awake, aren't you?"

"Am I?" After a minute she murmured: "Do you like fresh strawberries?"

"Sure."

"Chocolate?"

"Mmm."

"Toasted almonds with just a little salt?"

"Hey, what the – ?"

"That gives us something to work with."

"I'm not ready for work."

"I don't mean work, I mean daydreaming."

"I don't want to daydream, I want to sleep."

"Daydreaming together's better than bad sleep."

"Look, daydreaming's what got you into this mess."

"I admit it." She plopped a pillow over her eyes. That lasted two minutes, then she rolled toward me: "Leg giving you a lot of pain?"

"It's fine. I don't feel anything."

"Can you feel this?"

"No."

"How about this?"

"Uh-uh."

"This?"

"No."

"Liar."

Against my better judgment, already rueful, we rolled into each other. I pulled her tightly into me, whoever she was, glad in turn to be squeezed for dear life. And one thing led to another, as things do when you find yourself off the usual maps, between fear and the hope of some new insight that can steer you away from death. She rushed toward the promised land so fast I had to slow her down to feel with her. It was a slow fall into happiness, as mild and sensitive as lovemaking in a long marriage. Only when the excitement reached her, she plunged into it with the urgency of a swimmer frantic to make the shore: and swam and swam with me. We crawled ashore in each other's arms, and holding her I had one of those moments where you want to fill someone with all the tenderness and life in your measly soul.

Panting and fanning herself with the cable TV schedule, she whispered: "You really get carried away, don't you?"

"You weren't exactly twiddling your thumbs."

"No, like I could feel you thinking how my body feels."

"Just keeping in touch."

"I like that." The TV schedule crinkled as she fanned herself. "I knew I could get you if I tried."

"What's that supposed to mean?"

"Oh, don't get all bent out of shape. Everybody's got their little hang-ups. I wanted you. I wanted you a lot. I want to give back to you."

"But I haven't giv—"

"Shh. That's for me to decide." She laughed under her breath: "Maybe we can get to sleep tonight after all."

She stretched out to drop her gum into the tin wastebasket. Then she snapped off the television and cut the air conditioner. I got up to open the window, but the casement was painted shut. We lay side by side, quietly alert, skin cool and dry again: holding hands like a couple of kids. The G clef earring was so close I touched my lips to her ear once or twice. You could smell the Pacific Ocean a few blocks away, or maybe mustiness in the corner of the room just made me think of summer cottages and toy sailboats and tadpoles and puppy love a million years ago. Finally I said:

"You still have the photos?"

"They're at Ryan's apartment. If nobody's found them."

"Where'd he stash them?"

"Upstairs in certain record albums. Why?"

"Maybe you should offer them for sale one last time."

"No way. Why make me even more of a target?"

"Unless—"

"Nothing doing."

"They'd make great bait."

"No way."

"Know your enemy."

"Go to sleep," she sighed irritably, "I'm getting all kinds of scared again."

"Think it over."

"You know me. I'm always thinking."

"Excellent."

Her mouth tasted of cinnamon.

29

Over the phone Ben Bayer released Dawn from the film with an Oscar-winning pledge to mail her a check. At the ticket counter at LAX, she made a point of paying for her ticket out of the Capezio bag. In a shop on the concourse she bought a book called *Dolls and Deities: Women Who Changed History*, and between Nevada and Ohio we discussed Amazons, Boadicea, Queen Elizabeth, Madame Pompadour, and Carrie Nation.

In Boston the July heat wave had broken. The skyline had shrugged off its sickly haze: gulls scavenged out over the harbor. We took the subway into the city.

Changing to the Riverside line at Government Center, I bought a newspaper: not for the tedious catastrophes — a highway pile-up, Florida mailman gone berserk with an assault rifle — but for a political item. MERRIAM CAMPAIGN DENIES CARD-BURNING CHARGES. Senator Steven Flood was claiming that during an antiwar protest in the sixties Caddy Merriam had been photographed setting fire to a hatful of draft cards.

When I showed the story to Dawn, she yawned: "Everybody's horning in on my idea."

"You and Ryan fake that photo too?"

She shot me a patronizing squint: "Don't you get it? There's no draft card–burning photo. It's just how they win elections now. Don't you remember Bush using that guy Willie Horton like Dukakis wanted to let all these bloodthirsty animals out of prison? It's all TV."

"Look. Frank Fascelle's got his *La Ronde* listed in the 'Arts Calendar.' "

"I was supposed to be in it. But it's all bitty parts. And things got too complicated between Frank and me. Too high powered."

"He's offered to help bail you out."

"Two cents' worth."

"Don't knock it. He's been trying to find you."

"Frank wants the best for you. He really does. But he's always the director, don't you forget it."

Grumble grumble.

At Riverside we collected the Volvo and bucked Friday commuter traffic into Medford. A yellow rental truck was backed up to Ryan's front door. In green chinos and a STEAM THIEVES tee shirt his side-burned brother Dave was clearing out the drums and cameras and careless furniture. Dawn gave him a melancholy hug and her key to the apartment, then headed upstairs. Across the street a junior high dare-devil was surfing a skateboard off the granite curb.

Ten minutes later Dawn was back in the Volvo with half a dozen rock albums in her lap. From them she pulled half a dozen eight-by-ten black-and-white photos. One shot framed a nude woman with a guitar in an apartment window at dusk. She gazed out dreamily at the rooftops, her knee on the windowsill, in a sweep of feminine curves. She was a brunette with a well-behaved coed haircut. In the declining light her skin looked so alive that a touch might give her goosebumps. In each shot she kept her face at an angle to the camera, which made the actual shape of her nose and jaw a little ambiguous and suggested not so much arrogance as a knowing shyness. In one pose she shrugged a little, gathering her breasts and belly to shape in a way that could pluck your lyre. But mostly the pictures aroused an ache like nostalgia—maybe it was the mix of homey hippie innocence and girlish showing off.

"Like them?" Dawn asked.

"They're not Candace Merriam, they're you."

"Of course. What I did, I used makeup to shape my jaw the—"

"But these prints look twenty, thirty years old."

"Sure. Ryan dried them under a special light, UV or infra-red or something. Then he covered them with this silica powder mixture for a few weeks."

"They look like 1965. Joan Baez. Dylan."

"Exactly. Caddy stood five-nine in her bare feet and weighed a hundred and twenty-seven pounds. In sixty-eight she left USC and married this army doctor on an impulse. He died in an accident in Vietnam. For the next ten years she worked in a family planning clinic and did some acting. Then she married Merriam just before he became ambassador to someplace near Africa. See, I really did my homework."

"But you couldn't prove the photos are authentic."

"Or prove they're fakes. I mean, look at the times you think you recognize someone in a crowd. It's all a question of what you want to believe. Put them on TV news and enough people will buy it."

Dawn slipped the prints into one jacket sleeve along with the forged bill of sale. "They're intelligent fakes," I said. "Take good care of them. They're bait. Ryan's brother know about them?"

"Uh-uh. Nothing. Dave's bummed out right now about what to do with the tortoise. They're sort of extinct."

"How about a zoo?"

"That's like a prison. Think there's some way we could, like, mail it back to nature somewhere? You know, in a box with food and air holes?"

I didn't think so.

At the Alewife MTA station Dawn grabbed a train into Boston to see Amy at Brigham & Women's. I let the rush hour carry me on out to Concord, where Armand was exhaustingly cautious about answering the door. Turned out the help had the day off and Armand was on a stool at the kitchen counter eating a frozen macaroni and cheese dinner and a steak that must have been a whole steer with the head and hoofs knocked off. Apparently it was undercooked, because he was cutting all around the edges toward the bloody middle. He motioned me to the stool opposite him.

"You're limping."

"Dawn fell on me."

"Oh?" Armand pushed a glass and a bottle of first-rate California merlot across the counter to me and said, "Help yourself." Without looking up from his plate he added: "Good news or bad?"

"I found Dawn. And the photos of Caddy Merriam."

His eyebrows shot up like a window shade on a spring roller: "Has she changed her mind? If she releases them to the purchaser, probably all this misunderstanding can be — I'd hoped that we'd —"

His hand filled in the missing verb with a dismissive wave fit for a king. He was feeling better already. I said: "She'll give up the photos, but for a price."

Disapproval dragged at Armand's mouth: "For heaven's sake. She's been paid once. She absconded with —"

"She wants the debt written off. Plus ten thousand cash. And I need at least a preliminary decision right away or she'll bolt."

"I'll phone you tomor —"

"Too late. Phone your contact now. I'll wait."

"He may be out."

"Then I can tell her to be patient. If she bolts, that's the breaks."

Armand chewed the cow. After another slug of wine he went downstairs to his office to telephone. A few minutes later someone called him back. He came upstairs looking pleased with himself. "I think we can do business," he said gravely. "Tentative but promising."

"Good. I'll tell Dawn. Or do you want to?"

"Me? Is she here?"

"She's parked a little way up the street. She'd love to see you but she's afraid."

"Well maybe I will just — "

Palms up, his hands made a gesture of raising the dead. I said: "Go say hello."

When he stepped out I shot down to the office and hit the redial button on his phone. A woman answered.

"This is NYNEX Customer Service," I began. "We have a repair order for your number." The woman expressed surprise. I kept on, making up a phone number: "Is this 555-0879?"

"No." Helpful babe. I tried to sound bored and bureaucratic:

"What number is this please?"

She was reluctant, but she knew better than to defy the phone company. I jotted down her number, thanked her, and signed off. As I stepped into the kitchen Armand came around the corner, so I detoured to the nearest sink and wet my whistle. Armand had a long face: "No sign of anybody out there."

"As I told you, she's jittery."

He sighed bitterly: "That's not all she is."

$\triangledown$

30

FROM THE LOBBY OF Brigham & Women's Hospital I dialed Bill Dempsey, my friend at NYNEX, at home in Queens. He agreed to match the phone number I'd just called to an address. Then I went upstairs to Amy's room.

Nothing had changed. Amy lay there in peaceful, maddening slumber. She looked thinner than before, with a recurring tremor in her right hand as if she were tapping out Morse code we couldn't decipher: alive yet ghostly, beyond human reach.

Dawn and her mother, Joan, sat silently on opposite sides of the bed looking up at the TV screen, where black kids threw stones at South African cops. The women weren't talking. They gaped at the TV screen, glad for the escape, as if the paralyzed body in the bed summed up all the helpless living feeling between them.

Oddly enough, Joan was eager to chat. She let me know—wanted me to know, though she was too shy to admit it—that she'd decided to put her car back on the road. Soon. Amy's catastrophe seemed to give the woman a real enemy to fight, real pain to hate. The wound she couldn't talk about now was the renegade daughter sitting across from her, dead silent, wearing skintight rose slacks and a pair of plastic earrings as big as garden trowels.

Preparing to leave, Joan put a timid kiss on Amy's forehead. Dawn gave her sister a big theatrical smooch that tacitly criticized her mother's restraint. To look at them they were perfectly ordinary bipeds, mother and daughter. Only the kisses told you that in each other's eyes they had become bizarre freaks from totally alien mental worlds. Dawn walked out to fetch the car with me: "Did you see Armand? Is it go?"

"Looks that way. And I think I can trace his middleman."

"Great." She kicked a soda can so savagely it rose off the sidewalk and clattered into the fancy wheelcover of a parked Honda. On Huntington Ave a trolley clanked past flicking sparks off the overhead wire. It was that moment of dusk in which windows seem either brimming with electric light or darker than outer space.

I unlocked the passenger door of the Volvo for Dawn, and she reached across to open my door for me: "Can you give me a lift to Worcester?"

"I'm going to drop your mother in Natick. You might be safer there."

"At my mother's? No way."

"It's a roof. A bed."

"Did you see the way she pecked at Amy?"

"She's frozen up. You're the one who brags about being good to bodies. Turn her on a little bit."

She snorted: "Make it with my own mother."

"You know what I mean."

"Kiss her on the lips? Tickle her nipples?"

"Hug her. Cuddle her."

"In case you forgot. She's the mother, I'm the kid."

"Sometimes the play calls for you to swap roles for a scene."

"You're a pervert, Duncan."

"What have you got to lose?"

"My pride," she shot back.

"Your anger?"

"My freedom."

"How free can you get?"

"Okay, then. My fucking nerve, all right?"

When we pulled up to the hospital entrance, Joan darted out to the car as if the street were full of snipers.

We drove to Natick in silence. Parked under the streetlights, we could hear the cicadas fanning themselves in the maples above us. Along the street TV sets divided the darkness into cells of bluish living-room light. In the backseat Joan said softly: "You're not married to Meg anymore."

"We're excellent friends."

"I haven't seen Meg for ages." The words shook free in her throat. "I should make some time. It's hard for women to be friends in a suburb, I think. And when you have this anxiety business — this illness — it's like you're frozen in time."

She was pushing out of the car, careful, trying not to race into the house and hide under the bed. Actually it was the first time I'd heard her acknowledge her illness. And she was calling her daughter Dawn now, not Donna. Maybe she was coming back into the world. Dawn let out a dramatic sigh. I reached across and unlatched her door. She said: "Want to go to a motel?"

"Can't afford it. Either of us."

"You won't give me a lift to Worcester?"

"I didn't say that."

"But you're not offering."

"That's right."

Dawn muttered something obscene. But she got out.

Twenty minutes later Rachel was coaxing Meg and me to watch a video with her, *Roger and Me*. As I was taking recycled pizza out of Meg's new microwave, the phone rang. Dawn's voice. "Jesus, Duncan. You and your bright ideas. Hear that?"

She held the phone away from her ear and I heard a distant rapping noise. Come to think of it, I could hear the same noise through Meg's open kitchen windows. "Somebody building a birdhouse?"

"It's Red LeBeau, the guy I bought the Alfa from? He's after the license plate I borrowed."

"I don't blame him."

"He's threatening to maul me."

"Call the cops."

"Great. Just what I need. Cops asking me questions. My mother says they've already been here two, three times trying to talk to me about Ryan."

"How long you think you can avoid them?"

"Can't you come talk to Red?"

Pizza microwaved twice will stop a bullet, so I crossed the yard carrying one slice and stuffing the other between my teeth. The neighbor's beagle was blowing his bugle over the ruckus at the Biondis'.

Red LeBeau's tongue was loose. His right foot was vicious. When I came around the corner, his workboot was kicking Joan Biondi's screen door to smithereens.

"Give me the repair plate! I gotta pay the fucking registry an arm and a leg for it." The voice stopped, then tried purring: "Come on, Donna. Give me the repair plate and I can fix us up like new. All you gotta do is, don't come on like a fucking movie star, like I'm some piece of—" He tried to think what.

"Red," she coaxed through the screen, "I can't talk now."

"You respect me," he countered, "and I'll respect you."

"Okay," Dawn offered. "Meet me for lunch tomorrow."

"It's night now."

"You have this beautiful soft tenor voice," Dawn crooned. "I really love it when you talk soft."

"You're not pissed at me? I been worried about that. Because I couldn't help all that shit back then, that's how it is with two people who have this special thing going between them—"

"It's okay," she soothed.

"We knew how to have a real good time, didn't we? Shit."

"It's true. And I'll get you the plate tomor—"

"Never mind the plate. — You remember the time in the canoe, with whatsisname there, the college kid? I put him off on that little island and he lost his glasses in the water and he freaked out. You could hear him all over town. Afraid to swim ashore in the dark."

"He was my date."

"He had no business asking you. Big college man. He's gonna go to the cops, he's gonna press charges. Afraid to get his feet wet. Jesus, that was funny."

"You were pretty wild."

"Come on, open up, for christsake."

"I can't. My mother's upstairs, she's sick. You're scaring her half to—"

"Then come out with me. We can go over the lake with a six-pack and build a fire. I can get a canoe, I got—"

"Tomorrow. Lunch."

"Tomorrow my ass!" Red's workboot blasted the aluminum door. "Stuck-up cunt!"

I stepped up to the porch: "Red. Come here."

"Who are you?"

"A neighbor."

"Mind your fucking business."

I decided not to use philosophy on him. I said: "Here, have some of this."

When he bent over to look at my hand, I smashed the pizza into his eyes. The textbooks don't tell you much about the stopping power of pizza, so I played it safe and jumped him. After a short flurry of fists and workboots and snapping teeth he stumbled into a chokehold. His breath smelled fermented.

I walked him off the brick steps and over to the tow truck across the street. While he leaned against the fender I patted him down. "How many times you waited out here for Dawn?"

Mutter.

"Ever hear of a band called Steam Thieves?"

Grunt.

"You know a kid named Ryan, hung out with Dawn?"

"Fuck you."

"Here's a secret. Kid was murdered a few days ago, and the cops are looking for an angry male, not too bright, with a jealous interest in Ryan's girlfriend, Dawn. Even if you didn't kill him, you better stay away from Dawn before you find yourself rattling the bars at Walpole. Got me?"

He clawed at his cheesy eyes, grunting. The logo on the truck door said GLOSS AUTO BODY. The keys were in the ignition. I said:

"Time to go, lover."

From Meg's I phoned the Natick police. Kevin Hollings was off. I reported a drunk driver and described a particular pickup truck. Meg saved me the last slice of vulcanized pizza.

Saturday morning Bill Dempsey called me at Meg's: "The address you want is K. Klotze, 132 Bullock Street, Boston. If that means anything."

"It's pure music."

"You and Vera want to play cards one of these evenings?"

"Soon as they let me off the chain gang."

"What are you pushing for, a coronary?"

Bill had suffered a bad heart scare during the winter. I said, "I'm not complaining."

Half an hour later I dropped Rachel at a rehearsal and got out my street map.

Bullock Street sits off the Arborway a few minutes from the hallucinatory greenery of the Arnold Arboretum. It emerges from the once-posh Jamaica Plain of Boston's great, crooked Mayor Curley and stretches toward Franklin Park and suffering black Roxbury. On that end the two-family houses start jamming together and looking discouraged.

At 132 Bullock Street a small air conditioner roared in a window beside the front door. On the porch next door, a family was cooking animal legs on a charcoal grill, and greasy blue smoke sagged in the still air. I sang a cheerful salesman's hello: "Hi there. Anybody home at one thirty-two?"

The chef prodded one of the body parts on the grill: "The boyfriend's gone out. But Kathy's home, I think."

"What's his name again?"

"Who, Mitch?"

"Yeah, Mitch's last name."

"Barshack. Something like that."

"Thanks."

On Kathy Klotze's mailbox a couple of pieces of duct tape held her nametag in place—I was seeing the stuff everywhere lately. But a boy of ten or so opened the door a crack. "It's too hot," he said. "She's laying down."

"Mitch in?"

The kid was used to challenging people with his eyes: "Who are you?"

From my wallet I lifted one of the fifties Dawn had given me to cover my ticket to L.A.: "I got Mitch's money for the Red Sox tickets."

"Fenway tickets?"

"Look, if it's a surprise, don't tell him I spilled it."

"Mitch's out and she's sleeping. She don't want nobody bothering her. It's too hot. I'm putting the ice thing on her forehead, only if it's too cold her eyes ache and she gets mad. Like it's my fault."

I showed him the admirable face of President Grant: "So how do I get the money to Mitch before the ticket office closes? When's he coming home?"

"Whenever he's done at the Bowl-A-Rama—oh shoot."

In the whine of the air conditioner, somewhere inside the apartment, a woman's voice was griping. The boy straightened up as if kicked: "She wants the ice thing again."

He threw the door shut. The smell of burning skin from the grill next door stuck in my throat.

How many Bowl-A-Ramas can there be in Boston? The phone book showed only one, Neponset Bowl-A-Rama: as it turned out, twenty minutes away. The parking lot had a scenic view of triple decker tenements and storage tanks that had a scenic view of Boston Harbor.

With my jacket over my arm and the Smith & Wesson, I went inside hoping for a strike.

The place had tenpins, arcade games, billiards, trophy sales, a snack counter, and Siberian air-conditioning. Inside a murky lounge wall-papered in dark circus stripes, a bowling ball bag at his feet and a tumbler of Four Roses in his hand, it had Mitchell Barshack.

The bartender pointed him out. Sport in his mid-thirties wearing not a purple shirt but a silky green item off the rack at K-Mart with aviator sunglasses tucked in the pocket. Handsome face with a thin blade of a nose and a slicked wave of hair on top. His eyes—the lids—managed to look both sleepy and suspicious.

Total disappointment: no Spanish in the face and no bite out of either droopy-lobed ear.

He was talking to a dirty blond kid so fat his yellow knit shirt rode up around his waist exposing a band of hairy skin. A belt kept up chino pants that didn't quite button. The huge belly seemed to balloon up out of small hands and bowling shoes, as if he were getting an enema from a tire pump.

I said to the silky green shirt:

"You're Mitchell Barshack."

"You buying or selling?"

"Armand Fixler tells me you're interested in photography."

"Who are you?"

"I can get you the prints you want."

"That's what the bitch said the first time."

"She admits that was stupid. She wants to straighten it out."

"Plus ten big ones, I heard. She's a saint, she's gonna end up onna altar at Sacred Heart."

"The photos' value keeps going up." I shrugged. "That's the free market for you."

"This is all very un-fucking-usual." He stood up, drained his glass, and said: "Let's go somewhere, have a little privacy."

When the fat friend got up too, Barshack said, "This here's Jerry."

Jerry led us out of the bar to the lanes. We followed him down the gutter closest to the wall, through a service door that opened into the gallery where the pin-setting machines stood. Intense smell of paste-wax back here. No air-conditioning. The din of bowling could have been Vietnam. Incoming rounds rumbled down the lanes and exploded against the pins, the noise magnified by the raw cinder-block walls. I raised my voice:

"Noisy."

"We're not cutting a record, who gives a shit." Meaning Mitch didn't want the conversation bugged. He added: "So who are you?"

"A negotiator."

"You got a name or a number?"

"Duncan."

Wrong answer. Mitch's eyes twitched and Fat Jerry swept a meaty arm around my neck, his left foot tapdanced, his right fist rattled my kidneys, and I went down. I went down thinking it was impossible a rhino could move so fast. The pistol clunked softly to the floor in my jacket. By then Jerry was looming over me, his left foot on my groin: "Move and I'll crack you like a fucking walnut."

Anger flashed through me and fizzled in a puddle of pain. In a lane close to us pins exploded and dropped. Softly, almost caressingly, Mitch asked, "So who are you?"

I told him my name and he made a face: "Doesn't mean squat. Who you work for?"

I tried to get my breath back: "This the way you usually do business?"

From the rack behind him he handed Jerry a black bowling ball and said, "See if the holes fit your fingers."

"Jerry dangled the ball over my face: "How'd you like a bite of this." Not a question.

"Take it easy," I said. The concrete floor felt cool against the back of my head. My voice rattled.

"Maybe you want to inhale your teeth," Jerry suggested.

"The idea is to keep the body count down."

"If you mean the boyfriend," Barshack said, "let's get one thing straight. I don't know who hit him. That's why you have rules to do business. That's why you don't jerk people around the way the girl did. Because everybody tightens up on the trigger. And then there's accidents, and I'm right in the bull's-eye middle and I don't like it one fucking bit."

"That's why I'm here."

"I can make you eat this fucking bowling ball."

"Look. Armand tells me you want the photos. But I'm guessing you want them for another buyer. And I want guarantees nobody gets whacked over the deal. You want to tell me who the — "

Mitch turned to Jerry: "Don't drop that ball or there'll be shit-for-brains to mop up. What we got here's a total moron."

"Let's move the photos to the original buyer. But with an agreement we can all trust."

"Where's the bitch?"

"I don't know."

Mitch took back the bowling ball. Hefted it. Let it slip. I wrenched my face away. He caught the ball an inch from my eye: "Where's the douchebag?"

"She checks in from a pay phone."

Mitch snorted for Jerry's benefit: "Let him up before he shits his pants."

On cue the rhino lifted his foot. I sat up slowly, trying for a little dignity. "You and Armand," I said, "all the middlemen in this business — I gather you wanted to make the photos harder to trace."

"Deniability," Mitch said.

"So you don't want to identify your buyer to me either."

"Use your head. I get sloppy about names now, I can kiss my ass good-bye."

I got to my feet: "So what've you got going? A political connection? A mob investment?"

"What did I just tell you, asshole? You deaf?"

"I have to ask questions. In L.A. a couple of days ago I had a gun barrel in my ear."

"Then you must be doing something wrong. If you're hanging out with that bitch, you're lucky you lasted this long."

"Somebody's got to talk to your buyer. Who's it going to be, you or me?"

"Look, this situation, I told you, it's gotten weird. The boyfriend gets whacked. Off the wall. Guys start hitting each other, nobody knows why, nobody knows who. Fucking jungle."

"Somebody's got to ask your buyer what he wants."

Mitch dropped the bowling ball back in the rack. From the strain on his face he could've been doing calculus: "And what if she's diddling another scumbag right this minute? I mean, these pictures could bend a lot of minds, like the ad with the pretty face job there, Michael Jackson, worth a billion fucking Pepsis. If she's cutting another deal while I'm promising someone the photos—I get burned."

"You want me to talk to him?"

"What, and cut out my chop? Just bring me the pictures."

"And Armand?"

"Armand's better off out of the loop."

"That's fine with me."

"Just get me the goddamned photos." Slight whine in his voice now: the harassed executive having a hard day. "And don't fuck with me no more. I see right through that shit."

32

THE ANIMAL CONTROL TRUCK parked in front of the Natick police station could have been the Good Humor wagon. The station itself is a flat-roofed, sandy brick affair, windows and doors fortified like the Bastille. It stands across the street from a brick gothic church nearly as tall as a television broadcast tower, and Casey's Diner, which used to fork over the classic American hotdog before it became a parking lot a few years ago.

As a rookie cop Kevin Hollings had drawn a weekend shift again. He shook me down for news, and slaked my thirst for knowledge by tapping the computer in Boston for data on Mitchell Barshack.

Who, as it turned out, had just done three years in Concord for arson and extortion. In my notebook I logged in the data. I kept Kevin busy on the phone, feeding him questions for Barshack's parole officer and trying to run down the detective who'd handled the arson case. After half an hour the shift commander began trying to send Kevin out in the dog mobile — it took me a moment to realize that the boss resented the kid taking the initiative.

"Last night," Kevin said, "we grabbed Red LeBeau's license for drunk driving."

"He was on the Biondis' front steps courting Dawn at the top of his lungs. Trying to kick her door down. When you get a chance, ask him where he was the night Ryan died. Just for the record."

"You think he has the hots for her?"

"The guy's got his demons."

"I'll have a talk with him."

"I've got to persuade Dawn to stop ducking the police investigation of Ryan's death."

Kevin agreed. Then I left him to bring mutts to justice and winged around the corner to Meg's house to phone a state police lieutenant I knew, Phil Auburn. A year ago we'd been thrown together by a murder in Newton. I tracked him down at the Framingham barracks:

"Christ," I said, "it's Saturday. Don't you ever go home?"

Silence. Instant regret. I'd forgotten that Phil Auburn was divorced, a workaholic in his fifties with an amputated sense of humor, a breast pocket full of spikey morality, and no reason to go home nights. His voice spit icicles: "Who's this?"

"Duncan Ames."

"What've you got for me." Not a question, an assumption forceful as a fact. I said:

"What can you find out for me about an ex-con named Mitchell Barshack? Just did three in Concord for arson and strong-arm stuff. He's trying to defraud a client of mine."

"Where are you? Meet me at the new Fishwitch over by Shopper's World in half an hour. We'll talk."

He made it sound like a sentencing hearing. Glad to hear from me.

Fishwitch proved to be a fish sandwich joint, a new fast-food chain whose logo is a witch riding a dolphin. Phil had the Norwegian deep-fried fillet with lettuce, fries, and Gelusil. I offered him the glad hand: "The old ulcer still picking on you?"

"This place," he shook his head. "They fry everything but the napkins. But it's fast. And no cholesterol in the fish."

"They fry it in hot cholesterol, for christsake."

His bushy white eyebrows barely twitched. His big shoulders closed in confidentially on the table: "Your friend Barshack. Six months he's out, he has a Ford Thunderbird with power everything, brand new. He takes his girlfriend and her kid to Florida for a week. Disney World. Interested?"

His sleeve mopped up some tartar sauce. He saw my eyes notice it. Without missing a beat he wiped the sleeve of his uniform:

"Where's an ex-con come up with that kind of scratch?"

"Disney World's not far from Miami. Was he lugging drugs?"

"You tell me."

"I will when I meet the man. Who'd he torch for?"

"He lit three tenements in Dorchester for the same landlord, but the plea bargain only hung one on him. And also, we can't prove it, a furniture store in Mattapan. Plus miscellaneous probables — you could fill a book."

"That's all he does, keep home fires burning?"

"Are you kidding? He's got priors for assault and receiving stolen goods."

"What kind of goods?"

"Miscellaneous, including antiques and paintings."

Hello Armand Fixler.

I bought two diet colas — no ice in Phil's: gives him hiccups. For the next fifteen minutes we crisscrossed over Mitchell Barshack's life, me jotting down names and popping more questions. Finally one answer jump-started my engine. When I asked if Barshack had any political

147

ties, Phil Auburn gave a sarcastic snort but then reconsidered: "Wait, now. He used to give his occupation as real-estate management. Because he works for an outfit, what do they call themselves — it's owned by Joe Mazey, the one who ran for something. Congress maybe."

"He's a realtor?"

"More a developer, I'd say. Or an investor. And a landlord. He owns a lot of units in Dorchester, Roxbury, in there."

"Where do I find Joe Mazey?"

"He's got an office near Boston City Hospital. Lives down in Randolph, I hear. He's got clout these days."

"Did he win?"

"The election? I don't think so. This state has so many hacks and flacks and sacks of crap on Beacon Hill — don't get me started."

"Heavy political contributor?"

"Dunno. Politics makes me sick. If it isn't killing the unborn, it's putting your cousin on the payroll. They screw up the finances, and so it comes to pay raises and they stiff cops. — Ah, you have to go? Get back to me."

$\triangledown$

33

JOE MAZEY HAD BOUGHT one of the last patches of woods in suburbia: the sort of bosky acres that made puritan hearts beat like tomtoms when God showed them how to kill Indians and build fences. Nice mix of oaks, sugar maples, and pines. You came out of the woodsy driveway onto a sweeping lawn, before a white colonial house with a pillared portico worthy of Thomas Jefferson — unless it struck you as an oversized garrison model with fat white poles holding up the porch. I was musing about house design when an arrow slicked across the clearing and thunked into a wooden birdhouse in a pine tree a few yards from my left ear.

As I was trying to calculate the trajectory, debating whether to hit the deck, a collegiate Robin Hood sauntered out of the woods with a hunting bow sporting a clever peep sight. Good-looking kid with razor-cut dark hair and dark brows that made him look older than he probably was. With his pleated slacks and Banana Republic shirt he had a preppy sort of primness about him. And poise, or at least impressive overconfidence.

The arrow in the pine tree had a razor-sharp head that could pin a polar bear like a butterfly. In the pine tree the birdhouse was still swaying back and forth, the arrow so deeply embedded that it broke when I pulled it. The kid grinned approvingly: "You didn't even run."

I didn't take him over my knee either: "Nice hacienda you got here. Where do you keep your peasants?"

"We own all this," he said with a careless wave of the hand.

"Which makes you—"

"Yeah, I'm Joe Mazey—"

"Junior?"

"Huh? Yeah. I know this woods like—"

"Kit Carson." The name went over his head. He fell in step beside me:

"You know what happens to a squirrel when one of these arrows hits it?"

"Shish kebab." While he was thinking about that I added: "Your old man running for office this year?"

"Nah, he's helping other candidates."

"How come?"

"If they get in, they pay you back."

"No, I mean how come he's not running himself?"

"Face it, he got creamed trying for Congress. You gotta have millions to win. It's all name recognition and media and stickers and phone banks and technology. So first you have to build up IOUs from other guys with more money. If they like you, you're in."

"Too bad."

"Oh he's still moving. He's right on schedule." A defensive note stiffened the kid's voice. "Mel Grable boosts him on his talk show— they golf together. And the *Herald* says goods things. He's spreading his ideas on less taxes and more jails. I mean, he's a delegate to the national convention this week. That counts."

"He want to help in the campaign?"

"Sure. But the President has his own campaign people?" He gave the sentence an interrogative twist, as if saying *Right? See?* It was a habit: "You have to put up really big money to get noticed?"

"But your old man's trying."

"Of course." Jr. stopped in the driveway. "You're wasting your time, you know. He never does any business here at the house. He really believes in keeping private separate. Besides, they won't be back from Texas till tonight."

"I thought your mother might—"

"Nah, she's down at the convention with him. She's dying to meet the President in person. I'm staying here with my brother." We headed back toward the trees and the street.

"You know a lot about politics."

"Sure. I'm, like, a poli sci major? I'll do law school, then maybe run for something. I've been working for my father."

"Speech writing?"

He was flattered. The questioning note came into his voice: "More like property management? Investment?"

"Oh? Out here in the suburbs?"

"In Boston. One of the properties we have up there? This big housing project? It's doing downhill? Well, there's junkies and blacks and slobs in all the buildings. So, like, I work with the management picking which units we board up next. Once they're evicted you seal them up with plywood. It's the law. Attractive nuisance. You nail the doors shut. Just pound spikes right into the door frame. *Pow. Pow. Pow.*"

"Makes them hard to get open again, doesn't it?"

"Who wants them open again? Once the buildings go completely to shit, Washington lets you scrape them. One morning of bulldozers, then you can start over with condos and a better class of clients. See, there's a point of diminishing returns where it's more cost effective to blow the whole place away."

"And a better class of profit."

"Sure. Nobody works for nothing."

"What I hear."

He turned to eyeball me: "Who are you anyway?"

"I work with Mitch Barshack."

"He used to work for my father."

"He's been away."

Joe Jr.'s eyes wandered: *Does not compute.*

"When did you say your father gets back from the convention?"

"Nine-fifteen tonight. We're going to a victory fund-raiser at the Four Loaf Cleaver." He shrugged: "What's your name again?"

"Don. Don Segreti."

He shook my hand: "Here, Don. Watch this." From his quiver he drew an arrow and aimed through the pines toward the street. For a moment I was afraid he saw an animal.

"The street's out there," I warned.

"Watch."

The arrow slicked into the branches at chest height and hit something with a solid wooden *pok*. We strolled. A minute later the roadside mailbox came into view, an arrow embedded in the cedar support post.

"Nice shot, eh?" Jr. worked the arrow loose. "The ultimate mailman, huh? Wrap your letter around the shaft and take aim. Great way to deliver eviction notices. Shoot 'em right past the junkies and the psychos and all the pissed-off welfare mothers."

"Nice," I said. "Great boon to mankind."

$\triangledown$

34

$\mathbf{W}$ITH AN ADDRESS COAXED out of Jr. I drove from Randolph back into Boston, to Joe Mazey's Belfrey Street housing project not far from Columbia Point. Turn a corner and wooden triple-deckers give way to a cluster of brick boxes typical of postwar public housing: flat roofs and asphalt lawns and soviet-style utility. A few clothespoles leaned in the yards like trees after a hurricane. Jr. had told the truth: half the units had doors and windows spiked shut with plywood sheets.

Out front three half-naked kids were playing at manslaughter, bopping each other with empty plastic soda bottles, and one six- or seven-year-old with large red ears sat on somebody's steps. He slouched forward in red gym shorts, nose running, eyes so dull they might have been daubed on with a blue Magic Marker. He looked so sick when I said hello that I felt his forehead.

Hot.

The on-site manager was a braless fat man in his sixties wearing green chinos and a string undershirt. As he inhaled his Camels, his emphysema hissed like a can of roach spray. Edgar. I gave him the glad hand:

"Who's the kid? He's got a fever."

"That's just Moke; he's always like that."

"He's sick. Where's his folks?"

"She's working." He sucked smoke out of his cigarette, sizing me up: "Who needs to know anyway?"

"I'm looking for Mitch."

"Why? We putting somebody out today? I thought the skinny one paid her rent."

"Maybe I'm early."

"Besides, you don't need the roughhouse. I get good results just talking to them. . . ." His voice trailed off into discretion.

"I won't let Mitch throw his weight around."

"Help me move a door."

With a crowbar we visited an empty apartment to take a bedroom door off its hinges. The smell of the interior reminded me of the taste flu leaves in your nose. The door was hollow, so light you could have blown it next door with a sneeze. Edgar wanted it to replace a door another tenant had burned with a faulty kerosene heater last winter.

The hinges didn't quite line up, so he installed the new door approximately with two loops of coat-hanger wire instead of hinge pins.

"This'll do you for now," he explained to the tenant. Heavyset woman with fat bare feet and a handful of dry white dough. She started to protest the door hinges so Edgar rushed to add: "I'll be back with my tools soon's I have my break."

"The little kid outside on the steps," I said, "he —"

"I give him orange juice," the woman said. "Every hour, like I promise his mama. I tell her he needs the clinic, but she only got but so many hours since she's working."

"Suppose we go in my car?"

"They got particular hours."

"When the particular hours come," I said giving her a ten, "take him in a cab. Okay?"

When we got outside again Edgar said: "All they want's a little privacy from the kids so they can hump their boyfriend in peace."

"I understand they're about to scrape this place."

Edgar rushed to reassure me: "It's getting run down. But Mr. Mazey says he's got a place for me over in Charlestown I can have for the same rent. Or else at my age, hell, I'd be up the creek."

"How long has Joe Mazey owned this project?"

"Five, six years. Government sold it to him."

"Washington? HUD?"

"Yeah, Washington. Hell of a risk, if you ask me. You got working people pay their rent. But you also got these gang kids, they're wild animals, and then the drugs and the loafers. And the colored guys these days, they're falling apart left and right. One bad apple after another. Maybe it's drugs."

"That's what they keep telling us."

"Yeah, it don't seem possible. It's more like all the colored guys are eating some kind of prison and they fall apart." Edgar stopped walking to catch his breath and light up. He gave a soft smoky sigh of sympathy: "I can see how the place gets Mr. Mazey down sometimes."

On the other hand, put a seven-story building where we stood and you'd have a grand view of harbor and skyline. You could probably see the JFK Library from here. Call it Anchor Estates, do a color brochure. I said: "You know Mitch before he got sent up?"

"Hell yes. All his damn life, just about. Him and the brother Nicky."

"Where is Nicky these days? Still in town?"

"Hell no. Got a job, chief cook and bottle washer for a guy deals in antiques."

"Antiques?"

"Yeah, paintings. Autographs. Like that."

Well hello. I tried to slip my butterfly net over this pretty detail: "Hey that's right. I forgot. The guy out in Concord. Fixler. He's been with him awhile, hasn't he?"

"It's perfect for him. I could use a job like that myself. Nice house, all you can eat. You got the cable. You got a dispose-all under the sink. Vacuum built into the wall. Tile shower. And I'm not even soft in the head."

"Soft?"

"Don't get me wrong, Nicky's not a total feeb or anything. He just must of ate lead paint as a kid—that's what Mitch says. Hey, the pipes in these old buildings are full of lead, never mind the paint. That's why they took the lead out of gasoline, because these kids today, look at 'em, especially the colored, they're all a little, you know, backwards. It's done something to their brain. Nicky's a real good-hearted kid. Give you the shirt—"

"Not like his brother."

"Well, Mitch's always been one for the fast track."

"He stayed on good terms with Joe Mazey?"

"Yeah, well—" A little red light went on in Edgar's head. "You work for Mr. Mazey too?"

"I'm Don Segreti," I said. Handshaking Edgar was like squeezing a chunk of warm beef liver. "I'm doing some legal work for Joe. It's safe for me to talk to Mitch? He's on our side?"

"Sure, I suppose. He's worked for Mr. Mazey for years. From before Mitch did time, when Mr. Mazey bought a building over near Mission Hill, and the rent needed to go up, but there was all these leases they already had."

I had to smile: "And Mitch helped the rent go up."

"Well you know Mitch. He went in there and scared the living daylights out of those tenants. The old people were out of there overnight. And the couple college kids, these wiseguys that refused to budge, he leaned on them and got his first record for that."

"He what, roughed them up?"

"All those years of growing up over on Blue Hills Ave. No moderation. They don't know the meaning of the word." Edgar sucked fire into his Camel: "Well—you—know what—they say."

He wheezed like an automatic door closer, blowing smoke out his nose and ears:

"All good things must come to an end."

35

In THE NORTH END I treated myself to a couple slices of pizza. Today's *Globe* quoted Senator Merriam's denial that he had ever been treated for severe mental depression. That called for a swig of Cinzano. Which required a double espresso.

After that I phoned Vera to arouse her curiosity about Joe Mazey and federally funded real estate. Vera was balky, but her game-player's instinct won out: "Okay, look. I'll make a few calls. My choosing. If I hit something, fine. If not, we drop it. Fair enough? And I can't do much before Monday morning anyway."

I signed on the dotted line. Afterward I strolled along the waterfront relishing a fresh canoli and waiting for Joe Mazey's nine-fifteen flight from Dallas–Fort Worth to descend across the harbor on East Boston. Over my shoulder the city's new high-rise skyline twinkled like a pinball arcade racking up out-of-this-world numbers.

As dusk comes on in the North End, the old Italian groceries keep their doors open, selling snappy cheeses, fruit, olive oil, and pornographic-looking peppers. For a second among the dimly lit wooden display cases and pungent shadows I was the kid off a train from St. Johnsbury, Vermont, who'd missed his folks on the platform at North Station and wandered into these narrow brick streets, among the vendors' carts and the sounds of Italiano, a few days before Christmas back in nineteen-fifty-what? Too long ago.

I bought Meg a pound of espresso coffee and a wedge of fontina. Then I steered the Volvo through the Callahan Tunnel, under the harbor, to the airport.

In the arrivals terminal Jr. was waiting with one hand around a girlfriend as if she were a travel bag he'd just claimed. Her conspicuous lungs held up a strapless dress that was less formal than a gown in every way but the price. Jr. had traded in his Robin Hood threads for a respectable blue dinner jacket and banker's tie. I was chagrined to see how mature and responsible this getup made him look to me.

By comparison, Joe Mazey, Sr., bounded out of the luggage zone with a Texas tan and a jet-black Ronald Reagan pompadour. His luggage still had Republican convention tags on it. He and Mrs. Joe exchanged handshakes with the strapless girlfriend. Mr. Mazey was very impressed with her robust rib cage. They looked conspicuously well-heeled, Mr. and Mrs. Joe, with enough suitcases between them to colonize Mars. Mrs. Joe stood solidly by, watching her husband for cues — the candidate's knowing wife. She struck me as a golden coed who'd married comfortably and never passed up dessert again.

With his deep tan and silver longhorn string tie, on the other hand, Joe Sr. radiated healthy enjoyment. Out from under his pants cuffs peeked exotic leather shoes like two baby alligators. His large hands patted his own elbows, then steered Mrs. Joe down the concourse. The hands squeezed the girlfriend's arm, pinched Jr.'s left cheek, and left the heftiest suitcases for Jr. to carry. One of the hands produced the gleaming car key that took them into the city to the GOP Victory Fund-raiser at the Four Loaf Cleaver.

These days the Cleaver is more a religious experience than a restaurant, and I wasn't dressed for worship. My slacks didn't match the jacket and tie I had in the car, and the head tux screening guests could tell I hadn't offered up a hundred bucks for a plate of nouvelle cuisine rubber chicken. On the other hand, my tongue and my ID said *Security*, so he tried to be a good sport about it.

In the car Joe Mazey had ditched the longhorn string tie for a striped banker's special.

In the new banquet room the triumph was already in progress. You tread a carpet as blue and deep as the ocean, into a room with majestic woodwork and gilt-framed Americana — paintings of buggies and red barns and gilded age Fifth Avenue — tasteful mix of Disney World and the Oval Office. The microphone at the head table called attention to the entry of "our friend Joe Mazey, a real fighter."

Joe Mazey clenched his hands over his head, playing along. But the place cards seated the family away from the head table. When Mr. M. began to fight reality for a better seat, the usher hit him with a smile that would have stopped a heavyweight. The family sat down. I took up a spot by the bussing station where I could keep Jr.'s back to me, hear the speeches, and watch the forks tear the American chickens to shreds.

The diners toasted a parade of leaders, including the millionaire inventor Jay Jason, who was trying again to unseat Ted Kennedy. He recommended genius, success, and tax breaks for investors, and scorned big government, losers, and taxes.

The next speaker, who wasn't Joe Mazey, urged us to get out the vote and give generously to the GOP. The next, who also wasn't Joe Mazey, stomped Senator Merriam for letting murderers go free and shoving his universal health insurance plan down the businessman's throat.

My mind wandered.

As the podium was praying for a healthy economy, Joe Mazey took a stroll.

With its sumptuous tiles and ornate gold faucets, the men's room at the Four Loaf Cleaver gives you the excitement of Rome without the jetlag and traffic. Joe Mazey and I lined up against the wall and took aim. His several glasses of Chateauneuf du Pape outlasted my demi-tasse of espresso.

"So now the nomination's over," I said, "you think they'll really hit Dan Merriam between the eyes?"

Joe Mazey stared at the lovely marble urinal: "What Merriam wants—health insurance, education—that stuff's all abstract. What's real to the slob in the street is taxes. So we use the Reagan trick, tar him with taxes. We already got Mel Grable calling Merriam the Tax Maniac on his talk show. We got Mel and the *Herald* in our pocket." This bit of gruff joviality couldn't totally disguise Joe Mazey's shy nature. "The polls are turning around."

"You have to keep kicking him in the teeth."

"You don't think they'd do the same thing to us if they were smart enough to get away with it?"

"Wouldn't take much to drop Merriam. One real slipup. Some skeleton in his closet."

Joe Mazey zipped up. For the first time he looked at me.

The gold-plated faucets took the shape of voluptuous spouting mermaids. "Everybody's got skeletons," Mr. M. said, rinsing his hands briskly. "His poor wife's just about admitted to having an affair."

The hands plucked a white towel from the stack by the sink. They whisked the towel over Mr. M.'s gator-skin shoes, then tossed it at the laundry chute. He watched it miss and fall on the marble floor. I'd worked for enough tycoons to know that God provides clean linen.

In the vestibule to the men's room, between doors, I stopped short and Joe Mazey almost walked into me. I apologized: "By the way, I have the cheesecake you're looking for."

"Cheese—?"

"Photos."

Caution pasted his tongue to the roof of his mouth. He was stalling: "What kind of photos?"

I egged him on: "Tits and glitz."

"I don't know what you're—" He waved his hand at me, warding off a vampire.

"Caddy."

"What the—"

I played my hand: "I have a direct line to the photos. We can cut out Mitch. No middlemen."

"You know Mitch," he said softly.

"Ten thousand, cash, and Caddy's youthful indiscretions are yours. Do with her what you please."

"That's too much. After all the—"

"I'll phone you to talk details. Home or office?"

"Who are you anyway?"

I stuck out my hand: "Don Segreti. Finder of lost nudists."

"This is no way to do things."

"You're not interested anymore?" I made as if to walk.

He hesitated: "Just a second."

"Think it over. Check your piggybank. I'll phone you tomorrow."

"I'm playing golf."

"Where?"

"Glen Firth, out in Wayland. Till one."

"Let's have a drink at the clubhouse."

"How'd you get my name? Mitch? I don't need . . ."

His voice trailed off. As I pushed out the door the dreamy light from the lobby showed Joe Mazey leaning slightly forward, his clean hands knotted up into prominent fists.

A real fighter.

$\triangledown$

36

For SOME REASON GOLF has always reminded me of prayer. Maybe it's the reverent address to the ball. Or the attempt to escape from sand traps through one miraculous stroke.

Lovely day for golf: sun in the sky and a river of martinis flowing gently in the Glen Firth clubhouse. To preserve the occasion for posterity, I asked Rachel to keep me company. We put my mini-cassette recorder in her straw handbag, loaded Vera's half-frame 35mm minicamera, and rehearsed various possibilities. I phoned Phil Auburn at the Framingham barracks, but somebody had given him Red Sox tickets.

In the pro shop Rachel hit me up for a Glen Firth tee shirt, then earned it at the scheduling desk by looking for her uncle — who was golfing with Mr. Mazey this morning. Which is how we found out that Joe Mazey had teed off with a banker named Houle, a lawyer friend of former Senator Brock, and somebody by the name of Mazzaro.

Passing the time, Rachel settled at a patio table and began reading her paperback *Dracula*. By a stroke of good luck the blond waiter had just read *Dracula* last semester at Dartmouth, so he leaned close to Rachel's cheek and struck up a lively conversation about predatory bloodsuckers. His theory was they were all psychological.

Rachel ordered a Coke.

When I found a free table, the waiter asked to see my membership card. As he and I were discussing my appetite and the spirit of the law, one of the women at the next table called over: "Oh give the man a sandwich, Damon. Be a sport."

Which is how I became the proud owner of a Glen Firth Charburger with convict-stripes seared into the meat and a golf-flag toothpick stuck in the bun.

I was still chewing, a manila envelope beside my plate, when Joe Mazey stepped out the french doors to scan the patio. I waved. If anything, the sun heightened the youthful effect of his tan. It deepened the dimple on his chin and picked out a tiny patch of hairs he'd missed shaving his jaw this morning. The stubble was grizzled, which meant — Vera would have spotted it right off — that the executive haircut was a rinse job. Mr. Mazey had a musky cologne in his hair and a couple ripe cheeses in his armpits. He also had Jr.'s habit of talking in declarative questions:

"So you're here like you said?"

Rachel did a professional job of not seeing us. In the corner of my eye I watched her take her glass over to Damon for a refill. With her back to us you couldn't see her hand dip into the straw handbag to start the recorder. Returning to her table she put down the handbag on the side nearest Joe Mazey, left her Coke beside *Dracula*, and skipped off expertly to the ladies' room.

Joe Mazey took his time. He twiddled a personalized golf tee – same shape as the blowgun darts that pygmies use to hunt giraffes. When Damon came for our orders, the giraffe hunter ordered a Michelob. Finally I teed up a mental golfball to see if he'd swing at it:

"So. What about Caddy?"

"Caddy?"

"About these." I opened the manila envelope with the photos in it. His delicacy allowed him to peer inside. His smile was pure altar boy. Looking me right in the eye he said, "Pretty. But I'm completely in the dark."

"Ten thousand dollars will buy you a candle."

"I don't know what you're talking about."

I was nonplussed. In fact I was about to close up shop when slyness complicated Joe Mazey's expression – something in the eyes – a boy scout in a liquor store. I closed up the envelope: "No problem. It's an election year. There are plenty of patriots with cash."

As I started to get up he said: "By rights I already own those."

I sat down again: "That was a misunderstanding. The owner of the photos regrets it." At which point Damon came over with a bottle of beer. Mr. Mazey raised his glass in the sunlight:

"Tell you what." In the course of a thirsty swallow he wagged his finger at the envelope. "I'll give you five hundred, cash. No questions asked."

"Maybe five thousand."

"Everybody wants to suck on the public tit." He grinned without pleasure, then took another swallow of his beer and thumbed the woman in the photograph. "What can I say? A nice set, but would you want them running the country?"

"Are you making an offer?"

"She's got those brown nipples that look like dog yummies."

"You have a dog?"

"And you can bet they don't look like that today."

"How much is she worth?"

"Five thousand dollars for a pair and a hole in one. That's a lot of money."

He grinned. Mr. Mazey was becoming the life of the party. Or stalling me. "As pieces of paper with pictures on them," I said, "they're nothing. Very tame. You can do better in a girlie mag for two bucks. Beaver patrol, wide-angle lens, in full color."

"You think I don't know that?"

"Or they could be used to knock over the White House."

"This could've been so simple." He was disgusted. "Now the pictures are compromised and I got people doubting my word. The least I gotta have, the girl has to make the sale in person. This time we gotta be sure she agrees."

"Not a problem."

"I'm serious. If you ripped off the photos from her and she raises a squawk, where does that leave us?"

"She may decide you're not serious."

"Shall we set something up then? Tonight, say? There's a motel I know on the Charles in Boston—"

"Let's make it more public."

"Whatever you say. This evening I'll be in my office on Albany Street, Puritan Development Corporation. Bring her along and we'll clear this thing up, Mr.—Your name. It's not really Don Segreti."

I shook my head.

"I didn't think so. Just as well." He emptied his glass, burped, and pocketed his golf tee.

After he left I reached into Rachel's handbag and stopped the recorder. Out in the lobby I looked around discreetly. No Rachel. I darted into the pro shop, peeked into the ladies' room, then blitzed the members' lounge. Where the hell was she? My stomach began to worry. I went out to the parking lot and scanned the cars and then the nearby fairway. She wasn't waiting in the Volvo. I headed back inside the clubhouse, trying not to run. This time I leaned into the ladies' room and called her name.

Nothing. Dripping faucet.

Panic seeped into me. When I turned and met Rachel coming through the kitchen door, I hugged her and snapped:

"Where the hell—?"

"Hey, take it easy."

"That's my heart you hear croaking."

"Hey, I'm sorry, but listen." She took her handbag from me and handed me the little camera. "I started to snap the two of you on the patio. But the film advance is very noisy."

"If you want a big budget operation, join the CIA. What I want to know is where the hell you disappeared to."

"Look out on the patio. See that window, it's open a crack?"

"It's the men's room."

"I know that. There was a guy watching you and Joe Mazey from in there."

Not good news. "Get a look at him?"

"No, but I went over and leaned up against the men's room door for a minute. And guess what?"

"It was Elvis."

"There were two voices in there."

"And?"

"They came out in such a hurry I had to duck into the ladies' room, so I didn't see their faces. And I didn't get any photos of you and Mazey."

"You weren't in the ladies' room when I looked."

"One of them may be the guy we saw at Dawn's apartment. Remember the bite out of his ear?"

"How close did you get?"

"I tried to snap a picture of them with the camera in the bag here. But who knows if I aimed straight."

"From the way Mazey was talking I sensed a setup."

"Want to call the cops?"

"On what evidence? Unless you can nail these guys to the wall you just expose yourself." I scanned the lobby. "Where are they now?"

"Down in the pro shop looking around. Why?"

"They may be looking to snatch the photos." We hustled through the kitchen, past a sweating black dishwasher. I made Rachel wait in the back entry while I sprinted out to the Volvo's trunk, where the Smith & Wesson was waiting. I brought the car up to the kitchen entrance and Rachel hopped in.

"Here," I said, "hide this envelope. Let me have your handbag. Lock the doors and give me five minutes."

With the camera and the Smith & Wesson in the straw handbag, I slipped back into the clubhouse. Starting in the pro shop, I hunted through the rooms.

Nobody.

I ended up in front of the ceremonial stone fireplace next to a bluish-haired retiree who was scrubbing her golfballs with foil-wrapped after-dinner wipes. Even there, in the humdrum idiotic lobby, I had the crazy sense that I was the one being hunted.

37

MEG WAS IN JEANS and an old Niagara Falls tee shirt painting the kitchen cabinets. She'd rigged a sort of bandana out of a checked handkerchief, and for a moment I was jolted back to the first months of our marriage when we were pregnant and spreading civilization with a paintbrush in a crummy apartment in Allston. She gave Rachel and me a quizzical look: "Want to join the chain gang?"

"Hot work," I sympathized.

"I'm drenched."

"Mmmm, like a wet tee shirt contest."

Meg snorted: "Macho oink oink."

"The magic of the moment."

"It would be magic if you picked up a brush and helped."

"I have to go talk to Rachel's friend Dawn."

"Her mother phoned," Meg said. She wiped sweat from her nose and smeared a streak of sky blue warpaint on her face. "Joan wanted a ride into the hospital. Amy may be coming to." Rachel sprang on her mother with a ferocious hug. Meg yelped:

"Watch the paint!"

Rachel's sneaker thumped the paint can and a sky blue jet slurped over the edge. I grabbed a paint rag. Meg said:

"Want some of that French roast coffee you brought me?"

"Back in a minute," I promised. With Rachel on my heels I shot out the back door, across the fence to the Biondis' yard.

Joan Biondi was literally trembling over the news about Amy, and frantic to get into Boston. We cried a few hallelujahs together, and Joan survived one of Rachel's hugs. "I promised the Lord," she said softly. "If Amy recovered, I'd make myself go to the registry and get my driver's license renewed. But I don't know."

"I'll give you a lift," I offered. "Where's Dawn?"

"She's been, well, I won't say wonderful. But a big help. She's gone out and gotten things we needed for the house. A new vacuum cleaner, cooking things. She bought me a lovely new silk blouse and a handbag. We hardly fight about anything."

"She's at the hospital?"

"I hope so." Something guarded, even evasive in her voice worried me. "She didn't come home last night."

I felt myself flinch: "The guy who was here the other night come back? Red?"

"Once. During the day. He was very polite."

"He talk to Dawn?"

"She wasn't here then."

"If you see her, have her phone me."

"All those presents," Joan said, "all those nice feelings. You ever get the sense that things are too good to be true?"

One more question with sharp claws. I felt them circling overhead, dozens of questions, ready to swoop down and pluck your eyes out the minute you stopped paying attention. It struck me that Joan's newfound strength came partly from having a stricken kid to take all her concern. If Amy recovered, there'd be a temptation to turn her into her mother's mother again. So I lied:

"Nothing to worry about. Dawn takes care of herself."

In the end Rachel and Meg had tunafish sandwiches with low-cal mayonnaise and sky blue fingerprints on the bread. I ate tuna with hot salsa and agreed totally when Meg gave me blazes for putting Rachel at risk this afternoon. As I confessed to Vera over the phone, "I went into the country club as a hunter and came out a scared fox."

Vera listened.

"Mazey wants Dawn there when they buy the photos. To reassure his people she's on the level this time."

"Which she isn't."

"Hell no. It's a trap. If he touches the photos and we can prove it we may be able to squeeze him about the boyfriend's murder."

"But if it's actually his trap, not yours—"

"I'm worried. Joe Mazey wants the photos tonight."

"That's not much time."

I lowered my voice: "And I can't just bug out. Now that I've traced the chain up to Joe Mazey, they'll want my scalp too."

"These aren't good odds. Cut your losses."

"We could be only a step or two away from some political dirty—"

"Duncan, listen. You need the cops."

"I'm trying to draw Phil Auburn in, but he'll say the logical thing: unless you can prove they killed Ryan, there's no crime. He's as likely to turn on Dawn for the phony smut."

"What can I do?"

"Help me establish a chain of evidence that leads to the murder. At least help me think this through."

The phone circuit hissed softly like a leaking rubber raft.

164

Then Vera said: "Why don't I drive up there this evening. Make me a reservation at the Koala-T Inn. Make it a double, okay? And for heaven's sake, if you must do something rash, love, do it with me."

$\triangledown$

38

AT THE HOSPITAL JOAN rushed in the door ahead of Rachel and me. Rather than risk leaving the photos out in the Volvo, I tucked the envelope under my arm. You never know who's watching.

Upstairs we found Dawn working on her sister, coaxing and prodding. Looking up as if from the bottom of a well, Amy recognized the face hovering over her. She drifted beneath the surface, but you could reach her now. Her eyes responded, her lips tried to answer.

Joan was jubilant. Out in the corridor she took me aside with shimmering eyes. There was an excited hush in her voice, as if she had to downplay this miraculous good fortune to keep from attracting some cosmic punishment. "When Amy comes home," she panted softly, "I want to give her, I want her to have more of a future. I mean, I'm going to speak to her father. But I — Duncan, would you — ?"

"Would I — ?"

"Sometime would you be willing to talk to Joe about helping Amy get to college? Joe might listen to a man. With me, he just . . . "

Her voice crumbled away. She knew it was impossible. We could both hear the competitive growl in Joe's Biondi's voice. For a while we stared out the window. The afternoon was gone now, and the sun cut harshly across the houses stacked on Mission Hill. Grasping for some encouragement I said, "Maybe Dawn can talk to Joe. She could give him a run for his money."

"If he doesn't break her neck."

In the tremor of her lip, I saw the hint of a smile.

Dawn had no smiles for me. She came out into the corridor demanding under her breath: "Rachel just told me you found the guy who's hot for the photos."

"His name's Mazey. He runs the Puritan Development Corporation over on Albany Street. I think he wants to use the photos to win political favors in Washington."

"He the one who murdered Ryan?"

"It's possible. We need proof."

"Where's the money?"

"How'd you get here anyway?"

"I hitched out to Worcester for my car. If you sold the pictures, where's the money?" The muscles of her jaw cracked chewing gum, but she was wearing a sedate summer dress—one of Lynne Dresser's outfits maybe. I tried to stall her:

"What's the big rush?"

"I'm broke. I have expenses."

"What expenses?"

"What are you, the secret police?"

"You in trouble?"

"I came close."

"Close to what?"

"Court trouble."

"Court—?"

"Look. I was shopping—my mother's house looks like the Salvation Army. She hasn't bought a thing for the place since she got sick. So she needs stuff. New frying pan, a VCR. Some underwear. So I went looking over at Shopper's World, and of course I don't have all kinds of money, and—"

"Oh for—"

"So they almost busted me. I had to turn track star to get out of there and it spooked me, and I'm not going through that again."

"Listen, shoplif—"

"Zip it up, Duncan. You have your opinions and I have mine. And it's a free country, long as you've got the money to buy and sell other people."

I blew up at her: "You have eighteen thousand goddamned stolen dollars, for—"

"Hey," she said coolly, scanning the corridor, "why don't you tell the world?"

"You lose the eighteen thou?"

"I was afraid I'd have to give it back. And I'll need money to get out of my mother's house. I'm going nuts there. I wanted to give her some things."

"It's not exactly giving when you steal the gift. That's more than just love."

"Bullshit. What about the photos? You're going behind my back."

"I found the buyer—"

"That's what Rachel tells me."

"And I used the photos as bait. The deal was for five thousand."

"Five! That's giving them away!"

"The idea wasn't to make a killing, remember? It was to find out who killed Ryan, and if there happened to be some change left over—"

"So where's the five?"

"The guy balked. He wanted you to deliver the goods in person. Supposedly to check you out."

"So when do we do it?"

"We were supposed to meet at his office this evening. But I want to talk to you about it. I don't trust him."

"Well it's not up to you. Those are my pictures."

"It may be a trap."

"They're my property!" she growled. "Not yours. Mine." She started to turn her back on me so I grabbed her shoulders.

"Will you listen? Show up with those photos and you'll get a tour of the cemetery."

She twisted out of my grip: "So we take precautions."

I lowered my voice: "Okay. State police or FBI. You choose. I know a state police lieutenant who might not be too hard-nosed."

"Are you kidding? The cops would confiscate the photographs. They'd hit on me, not him."

"We'll have to negotiate with them."

"Be real, Duncan." Her voice spit disgust. "You think they'd let me keep a nickel of the cash?" She glared at me with an ugly sneer: "No way. Maybe we could bring Armand or somebody along."

"The cops are safer."

"Safe!" When I reached out she shoved me away and stepped back: "What good is safe if you haven't got a life?"

"Let's talk about this tomorrow when we —"

"Do you know how old I am?"

Her eyes blazed: very beautiful. But I wasn't twenty-five anymore, and she sounded so theatrical I couldn't help grinding my teeth.

"Hold still," she said.

"What for?"

"I'm going to kick you."

"You're — ?"

She kicked me. She gave my shin a little kick as vicious as a cop's riot club against the bone. I gasped. My eyes watered. "Hey, what are you doing?"

Her eyes darted around the corridor with a kind of frantic impatience. "Look what you're making me do," she protested. "You drive me crazy then you blame me, and where does that get us?"

She was panting like a wrestler. A couple nurses gave us the evil eye. Dawn pressed close to me, her forehead almost touching my chin: "How did we get into this?"

"Hey you two," Rachel called from the door of Amy's room. "Come

168

here. Amy's awake. She wants lemonade. Anybody got any lemonade?"

Amy was parched. She sucked at a long curled straw with hollow cheeks. She recognized her mother and Rachel and was glad to be kissed, though she told the young doctor it was almost Halloween, and she heard water running under the bed. She had an itchy spot on her back she couldn't reach. Her feet were cold.

"It happens," the doctor shrugged. "Patients regaining consciousness after a long lapse are disoriented. We'll probably see a big improvement tomorrow."

Joan made him say it again ten different ways.

When I turned to draw Dawn into the circle, she was gone.

In the elevator, dropping silently toward the street, I tried to reassure Joan. "Dawn's been on her own for a long time," I said. "It'll take a while to domesticate her again."

"It's her father in her," Joan said bitterly. "She can read your mind. But she doesn't feel for you."

"Give her time," I coaxed.

Rachel nudged me: "Where's your envelope?"

"I left it in the room."

"Shall we go back and check?"

No envelope anywhere.

Rachel opened her mouth to speak and we had the same thought: "Did you happen to mention Joe Mazey's name to Dawn?"

I swore.

In the Volvo we zigzagged through Roxbury to Albany Street. Puritan Development held the second floor of a rehabbed brick building down the street from Boston City Hospital. The Cadillac parked out front had Puritan sales flyers on the front seat. No red Alfa Romeo Spiders tucked up to the curb. Had we missed it? I let the Messrs. Smith & Wesson out of the Volvo's trunk to keep me company.

The building was locked but the buzzer buzzed. Upstairs the executive suite was locked too, but when I knocked on the glass window the executive came over to let me in.

A little bird told me Joe Mazey was gambling on borrowed stakes. My impression was he'd furnished the executive suite from an office-leasing outfit the way a theater director would arrange a set: waiting room chairs in orange upholstery, file cabinets, an IBM PC fresh out of the box, and in the spotlight a desk so big the Unknown Soldier might've been buried in the bottom drawer.

On the desk stood a framed photo of Joe Mazey shaking hands with Ronald Reagan while a choir of angels sang hosannas. On his blotter stood several executive desk toys, including a shiny chrome acrobat who stood on a pyramid of other acrobats.

The man was still wearing his clingy yellow golf shirt and two ripe cheeses in his armpits. I kept my back to the wall to have a head start on any surprises. I popped the question: "Is she here?"

"Who? The girl? Not yet. You're early." I watched his expression as he played with the desk toy acrobats on his blotter. Every time his finger knocked the top acrobat off the pyramid, magnetism hiked him back up.

"If she shows up to deliver the goods, you have the cash for her?"

"Tonight? Sure. Though I'm going home in a few minutes. You positive she's coming here? That's not what we planned."

"I can't guarantee it. Tomorrow at the latest."

"Good."

Why hadn't I thought to bring the little cassette recorder up here with me?

I left the chrome acrobat infallibly going nowhere and back and rumbled down the stairs, muttering at my own stupidity.

We crisscrossed neighborhood streets empty of red sports cars.

I didn't know whether to be reassured or spooked. "She's home by now," Rachel insisted.

But Joan Biondi's house was full of summer dusk. Joan stood in the shadowy front hall calling Dawn's name, listening to a June bug clatter against a window screen and smelling somebody's freshly cut lawn in the timid breeze.

Joan scuttled to the stove and put on the teakettle. Searched the refrigerator. Offered us this. That. Some dietetic peaches. Didn't want to be left alone with her fears.

Making a lot of reassuring noises, I backed out the door.

I swung Rachel around the block to Meg's and with a sloppy hug shooed her into the house, arguing. Then I headed east again on Route 9 spitting curses I couldn't swallow.

$\triangledown$

39

THIS TIME THE PURITAN Development office was dark. No one answered the door buzzer.

I had plans. I was going to check in with Vera. I was going to try to reach Phil Auburn at the state police barracks again. If necessary, I was going to socialize with Mr. and Mrs. Joseph Mazey and their son Robin Hood at their bosky manse in Randolph.

In fact I found myself on Bullock Street in Jamaica Plain, skipping up Mitchell Barshack's front steps. If Dawn had phoned Joe Mazey, chances are he'd use Mitch to nail her.

An alien with blue-green pigment around her eyes answered the doorbell. She wore a terry-cloth Disney World shirt, red slacks, and metallic toenail polish. She said: "No one's here."

She meant Commander Barshack was not receiving visitors from earth. Over her shoulder, through a mysterious time warp, I could see him watching a TV screen. Cans of rocket propellant were lined up around his command console. A fan played on him. I said: "This won't take a minute."

"Mitch don't want to see anybody," she insisted. We were doing a fox-trot in the front hall when she tripped and sat down on the staircase.

One look at Commander Barshack's eyes told you he'd been in orbit awhile. Safe to say he hadn't seen Dawn tonight. I said: "Joe Mazey's looking for the Hispanic guy."

"I remember you."

"Where's he staying?"

"You're blocking the TV. It's a special. Get out of the — "

Onscreen, gunshots popping like the Fourth of July, a shootout was in progress in Saigon or maybe Miami. I twisted the volume knob: "The girl's got the photos and Mazey's meeting her tonight. Where?"

"What am I, his mother, I know all his moves?"

"Mitch, listen. I know a state cop named Phil Auburn who wonders about a new car, the trip to Florida. He knows you made a pitch for the photos."

"Anyone can buy pictures." He struggled to concentrate. "It's a free country."

"If the girl dies, you go down. Kiss the fresh air good-bye."

"I'm never going back in. Never."

171

"You think Mazey will take the rap? How about a Latino with a bite out of his earlobe? You think he'll offer to do the time for you?"

"I'm never going back inside. All I want, just let me make a living. I got a place to live, I got Kathy. Got this kid to look after. What do I need with screws and all that shit."

Since a quick reconnoiter turned up no friends with bowling balls, I levitated Commander Barshack out of his chair by his shirt collar. Beer cans scattered. Commander Barshack explained that he was unprepared, otherwise my life would be forfeit. I said:

"Where are —"

"Listen, dipshit. I gotta piss."

"Mitch," I coaxed. "Where are they? Joe Mazey and the girl."

"This beer, Jesus, it goes through you like — two, three times a night you wake up, you gotta get up and —"

I rapped his nose lightly a few times to take his mind off his bladder. This made him irritable and inspired his girlfriend to raise her voice. His hands flew up to protect his face, but my hand kept questioning his nose until finally he tasted the blood and stopped to think: "I told you. Leave me alone. Talk to Mazey, he's the one decides shit —"

"What's his phone number in Randolph?"

"You can't call him there, he has a bird."

"What's the number?"

"Lay off the face!" he bellowed. It came up out of his throat like the noise of a mental ward, along with two hammy fists.

Useless. I sat him down in the recliner again. He wiped his nose and his upper lip on his hairy forearm, swearing eternal vengeance. His actual words were: "I can get you, asshole. My brother knows who you are."

His brother. Nicholas. Employee of Armand Fixler. At which point I remembered Dawn's voice at the hospital. *Maybe we could bring Armand along.*

"Thanks," I said. "You're a good sport."

In the front hall his girlfriend gave me plenty of room to pass. I caught a glimpse of her son at the top of the staircase in his underpants, and the fear in his face gave me a flash of guilt. I had an insane urge to explain things to him, but there wasn't time.

No pay phones in the neighborhood. The first one I found had swallowed a wad of gum, the second was dead. By my watch it was nine-thirty. If Dawn had reached Joe Mazey in his office, they could be doing business anywhere by now.

At a Sunoco station in Forest Hills I finally got a dial tone. When Armand's voice came on the line, I asked him if Dawn had been there tonight. He echoed me:

"Been here?"

"Have you talked to her tonight?"

"Well."

A fussy lie. I kept my temper: "She's got a buyer for the photos. She wants you to go with her to meet the guy."

"I couldn't possibly."

"She's in danger."

"Well, it means absolutely nothing to me." The fastidious Mr. Fixler.

"Dawn doesn't realize how—"

"Absolutely nothing," Armand said firmly. "And I don't have all the time in the world."

Armand hung up so abruptly I hesitated for a moment with the silent receiver in my hand. Long enough for another voice to mutter: "She called. Half hour ago. He wouldn't go with her."

Nicholas. Listening on an extension. I said: "Where?"

"Housing project in the city. You know where Columbia Point is? What you do is, you go in—"

"Gotcha."

"Hey!" There was silence, then the raspy growl again, slow and tense: "She's a good kid. Don't let them mess with her."

I was on the far side of Franklin Park, racing the lights on Blue Hills Ave., before the connection sank in. The caller who'd warned Amy about her sister weeks ago: it was Nicholas.

$$\triangledown$$

4 0

ON BELFREY STREET, HALF a block from the housing project, I spotted a red Alfa Romeo Spider at the curb, and the telltale license plate: ACTRYST. The only other space on the street was in front of a hydrant. With my sports coat over my arm, Smith & Wesson in the pocket, I went for a cautious look at the Alfa. I felt the hood to see how long it had been cooling. Which is when a voice from the car parked behind the Alfa said: "Just don't move."

He held the pistol close to his body. If I'd been twenty years old and a jackrabbit, I might have tried my luck. But in the instant I hesitated, he was out of the car and the pistol was close enough to make my skin cringe. It was an ambush and I had the panicky feeling of Vietnam, of reality falling apart in my hands like a soggy map. He grabbed my sports coat and the Smith & Wesson.

In the dark he looked squat and round-shouldered. When I recognized him, I tried to take back some initiative: "It's okay, it's me. Duncan Ames."

"That's the problem."

"We talked at Concord Bridge the other day."

"I tried to warn you."

"Paul Revere."

He draped my coat discreetly over the pistol: "Why don't you shut up and move your ass."

"Where's the badge tonight?"

"Up your ass. Move."

"Is this an arrest? You want to read me my rights?"

"Keep moving."

"Where to?"

Party at Edgar's.

Party in Edgar's kitchen, to be exact. The old man rocked in a chrome-legged kitchen chair that was missing a screw or two. It creaked in sync with his breathing. He sucked on a stub of cigarette, and his emphysema whistled stickily. Dawn sat on the floor with her back against the refrigerator. A note in spidery handwriting on the refrigerator door said TOILET. They weren't alone.

Even from behind I recognized the bitten earlobe. He tilted back in the chair that wasn't broken, his moccasins up on the table. His black curls glistened and his chin sported a thin stain of beard. He was wearing a purplish, almost gauzy sport shirt and dude slacks with pleats. No socks. No sign of Joe Mazey.

They were watching Edgar's mini-TV—it sat on the stove with the envelope of photos on it. They could have been a family killing time, except for a few details. Edgar's eyes glittered with fear and excitement, and Dawn sat on the filthy pink linoleum, legs out straight, her peach skirt streaked with dirt. The wall by the refrigerator was mottled with black mold. At the sight of her confusion, my stomach turned—anger, relief, fear.

"You were right," Paul Revere said. "She didn't come alone."

The Ear turned lazily to look at me. "Where you been? You kept us waiting. Can't get shit on this TV. No baseball scores, nothing. Just a bunch of science shit. Look at that."

The little black-and-white screen was showing the microscopic time-lapse growth of a cluster of cells into an embryo: rat or maybe human—the Ear clicked off the TV before you could tell.

"Come on," I said to Dawn. "Time to go."

"They've got what they wanted," Dawn said. Fear strained her voice. I reached her a hand, feeling cornered and furious at her.

Paul Revere poked me: "Get down."

I kept moving, trying to make it seem natural. When I reached to pull her up, the Ear said: "Sit."

His forefinger pointed the direction.

"Don't mind me," I said, "I've been sitting all day."

The Ear shook his head in disappointment. Paul Revere, however, hammered my skull with his pistol and kicked me halfway to Canada. It took less than three seconds, and, unlike the movies, there was no merciful scene change. I ended up beside Dawn, licking the filthy linoleum. Pain splintered through my chest and flashed behind my eyes. I smelled Edgar's bathroom loud and clear. Paul Revere waved my Smith & Wesson in my face.

"Take that stupid gun out of his face," Dawn snapped. I felt her palms on my face trying to hold my skull together. Then with the same irritability she said: "Look, give us the fucking money and adios amigos."

The Ear was impressed: "See? This one has more balls than the Dodgers. And after all she stole."

"It wasn't that much," Dawn shot back. "What's his name, Mazey, why's he so cheap? He owns all kinds of buildings and shit. If you want the money back, fine."

"What are you, a terrorist?" The Ear was amused. "If I got a big house, you can steal it, it's okay? A million idiots with shit between their toes can eat off my plate? And the Jesuits say go ahead, steal from him, in the name of the blessed fucking Jesus, he has so much money he doesn't have to work under the hot sun—"

"Come on," Paul Revere said. "We got a problem."

"*Priests* say that—you ever see sweat on a priest? So now you need rich gringo friends to defend your house." The Ear took his feet off the table: "This is no place to talk. Look at her, that nice dress on the floor. We gotta go someplace, have negotiations." To Edgar he said: "You got a rope so we don't lose nobody?"

Edgar lumbered out of the rocking chair. He disappeared down the cellar stairs, and we heard boards and junk rattling. Beyond the walls somebody's little kid was wailing. Small silvery eels were swimming around inside my skull: hundreds of them, wriggling behind my eyes. For a moment I couldn't make my tongue move, and panic flashed over me. Dawn tried to sound decisive:

"Let's just give them the pictures and go. I can come up with the money."

Edgar pushed up the cellar steps. "No rope down there," he panted. "There's a clothesline outside—"

The Ear gave him the nod. Two minutes later Edgar was back with a hunk of plastic clothesline. The Ear gave the rope a sample twist: "This shit is plastic. It won't hold a knot."

He threw the tangled rope in Edgar's face. The old man backed up indignantly: "I got electrical tape."

"You got 'lectrical tape."

"Like for hockey sticks."

The Ear asked heaven: "How do the gringos get so much money with brains of shit?"

"Hold on, hold on." Edgar opened the cabinet under the sink next to me. Through swimming eyes I watched him reach into a toolbox for a roll of packing tape. The sight of it brought Ryan's bloody face back to me. Paul Revere snatched the tape and bound Dawn's wrists behind her.

I was climbing to my feet when Paul Revere's foot shoved me to the floor again and pinned me there, heel planted between my shoulder blades. Inside my skull the small silvery eels were swimming around.

Edgar wrapped my wrists and ankles. It was good packing tape: the kind with tough filaments in it. I kept my eyes closed, trying to focus on the thousand spikes of light to block the pain.

Dawn began rattling on about the photos: "This is a waste of—I gave back most of the money. Not just a rip-off — I had to pay out to get that stuff from the photographer, this guy Romano. He was retired, with bad kidney disease, and he needed money for dialysis or he'd die." On and on. She talked a blue streak, making it up fast and frantic, all cunning and nerve, looking for an exit hole.

The left moccasin flipped the hem of her dress over her knees and wiggled into her crotch. She smiled harder: rubbed her cheek against his pant leg. Told him what nice fabric it was. The moccasin prodded her legs apart. He tore off another swatch of tape.

Dawn's smile grew fixed. Her face seemed suddenly all muscle: false and scared, mechanical as a puppet. But I knew what she was thinking: she'd do anything for a chance to run.

From the cupboard over the sink Paul Revere pulled down two big black garbage bags. The Ear slapped the tape over Dawn's mouth.

Then my mouth was covered too. A wave of sickness bucked in my gut, and for a bad moment I pictured myself suffocating in my own vomit.

At the table, in Spanish, they discussed the meaning of life. I heard Edgar say stupidly: "Vacuum?"

Fear squeezed the wind out of me. As I was struggling to get a calming breath, Paul Revere fished out my keys and went for the cars. The Ear went rummaging in the other room with Edgar. In that short moment, hands working behind my back, I pried open the cabinet door and felt around under the sink, blind and frantic, for the toolbox. Screwdrivers. Nail set. Pliers. Wrench. Tape measure. Nails, screws, sticky something — soldering flux.

A blade.

Christ, yes. A single-edge razor blade.

I dragged myself out from under the sink, hiding the blade up between my wrists as Edgar crossed the kitchen carrying a vacuum cleaner hose over his shoulder.

I kept feeling for the razor blade, woozy, making myself wait. A car backed across the yard to the door. Just as I began slicing at the tape with the razor blade, Edgar came in with a thick, mustard gold drape. I held off. Edgar spread the drape over Dawn and the other two carted her out to their car. The fabric sagged almost to the ground, like a calf going bye-bye in a burlap sack when I was a kid on the farm. The adrenaline kept me from passing out.

I squeezed the razor blade between the heels of my hands. Then the drape came over me, and with my mouth taped and my eyes covered now, I had to fight back panic. When I squirmed for air, a palm ground the dusty fabric in my face. I felt the razor blade slipping away, but my body wrenched about frantic for air and I couldn't help myself. When they heaved me into the trunk, my fingers dug between the heels of my hands—I felt the sting of superficial cuts, but no blade anymore at all.

Son of a—

Dawn grunted beneath me, struggling for breath. I rolled against the wall of the trunk as best I could. My ear brushed her face and came away wet with tears. Then a lid came slamming down, crushing my shoulder, and we were buried together.

We moved across the city in stops and starts—probably letting the Volvo catch up. At traffic lights I tried kicking against the side of the trunk hoping to attract attention, but it was too cramped and the engine droned and nobody came.

In the dark we wrestled to get the drape off me. We groped for tools, a tire wrench, anything. My hands and feet strained against the tape—I thought it might stretch, and it did, but not enough. Dawn caught my hand in hers and squeezed hard. The smell of her sweat and her perfume filled my head and for a moment it seemed as if we were one person, one thought. One fear.

We struggled. After a while gravity shifted under me, and I guessed we were climbing a steep hill or maybe going up over a bridge: maybe the Mystic River bridge, headed north of Boston. At the likely stop for a toll booth, I kicked the side of the trunk.

Nothing.

I began chafing my cheek against the steel rim of the trunk, snagging the edge of the packing tape, peeling it off my mouth. When I could move my lips, I turned to Dawn. With the tape half hanging from my mouth I began nibbling at her skin, catching the tape in my teeth, pulling a tiny bit at a time to free her mouth. Eventually she did the same for me until we had worked each other's lips free. Heaped together, we lay there sucking air into our lungs.

"Tire's jabbing me in the back," she muttered.

Like a couple of kittens we licked each other's faces, tasting sweat and salt tears.

41

"HELP ME," I CROAKED.

"It's tight in here, I can't breathe."

"Roll over."

We did a contortionist number, twisting about so I could chew at the tape on her wrists. And I was beginning to make progress when the car stopped again. Doors slammed. I was sick with helplessness and fear. It seeped through me like poison. I tried to fumble the tape back onto Dawn's mouth.

At which point the lid opened. Hands slung me onto the ground. I heard Dawn slump into the dirt. There were stars marking the routes to heaven and the air smelled sweet with decay and waste and raw earth. A landfill. Dump. Distant city lights stained the sky off toward the horizon. I fought against the tape on my wrists. Somebody slapped fresh tape over my mouth. Then for good measure the same hand pasted a patch of tape over my eyes.

"Don' worry," the Ear crooned. "You'll feel better in the car."

I smelled Edgar very close. When hands grabbed my feet, I kicked furiously. I kept it up with all the violence I had in me, until the Ear intervened. "Watch," he complained to the others. "When they fuck with you, what you do is, you press the button. Like this."

He pinched my nostrils tight.

My body fought insanely for air. Finally on the edge of suffocation, I lost it, and after another while he let me breathe. "You gonna be good?"

I flung myself sideways. Rolled. But you don't win any sprints rolling to the finish line, and in a few seconds he was kneeling on my chest, his fingers cutting off my wind again. The Ear said: "You don' 'preciate the trouble I'm taking for you."

Pain fired through my body. This time he pinched until my thoughts scrambled and my bladder let go and my heart went berserk.

When he let go, the air gave me so much relief I lay perfectly still, in a block of ice, afraid to twitch. The wet was warm and then cold. I heard them set Dawn in the Volvo. The door chunked shut. I heard the distinctive rattle of the Volvo's exhaust pipe as something — what was it? "Peel the tape," a voice said, "and you got a couple of lovers, got carried away." And Edgar's wheeze: "But it's summer, who rolls up a window?"

179

The vacuum cleaner hose.

Then the Volvo was idling and they were slinging me into the backseat beside Dawn, cranking up the window to hold the hose nozzle in place. The door slammed and I had a crazy sense of the gas chamber, an execution. In the blackness I sucked in a last full breath and held it. Could I kick out the window? Could I kick —?

"Turn your face to me," Dawn said. "Move. Come on." Her tongue felt across my cheek for the edge of packing tape. Then her teeth nipped and tugged, the tape ripped loose, and my mouth was free. I breathed out, then ducked my head down toward the floor trying to find air to breathe. "Hurry," she said. "Come on."

Her tongue searched across my face. She nibbled the edge of the tape over my eyes until it began to rip across my eyelids.

"You okay?"

"No choice. Pull."

My right eye came free, and the bridge of my nose. The left eye hurt too much. To hell with it. I nudged her away:

"Cigarette lighter. Can you reach it?"

"Why?"

"Do it."

She rolled over the seat backs into the front seat. Hands bound behind me, I twisted around to grab the window crank. I forced the crank through another quarter turn, tight enough to constrict the flow of exhaust. Dawn jammed in the lighter to heat it up. I turned to shove my arms over the seat back. Dawn squeezed aside: "What do I —?"

"Burn the tape off my wrists."

"I'll burn you —" She began coughing.

"Do it! Go!"

Even with the hose pinched, the air was poison. We backed toward each other. Hands behind her, Dawn tried to aim the hot lighter at the tape between my wrists. She dabbed gently, then frantically. In the darkness I tried to guide her by the feel of the heat and a quick curse when she hit skin not tape. We were both coughing now.

The lighter cooled. As she plugged it in again she began to gag. This time she burned my wrist enough to make me bite my tongue, but she also weakened the tape enough for me to break it. I ripped at the tape around my ankles, then wrenched myself over the seat back into the driver's seat. As I was freeing Dawn, she gasped: "Oh Jesus! They're here! Lock the —"

I smashed the doorlock down just as Paul Revere's hand seized the handle. The latch clicked and clicked. He dived for the back door. I stomped the clutch and the gas pedal in one frantic motion.

The engine stalled.

As the back door swung open, I ducked my head expecting a bullet, twisting the ignition key.

We skidded into motion. I threw the wheel left, then right, and jammed the pedal to the floor. The tires screeched dirt. The hose clinked and thumped and then fell away.

He held on until I swerved into the chain link fence beside the road. It must have been a surprise to him too, because by then there was no room to let go and the fence fabric caught him and spun his body violently about. Arms, legs, smashed against the side of the car. The edge of the door chattered against the chain links.

Dirt road: fence on the left, behind it the moonscape of a city dump; on the right, an embankment — some kind of canal or stream. Dawn opened her window and we were greedy for the night air. Across the canal the headlights caught an enormous brick smokestack rising out of the gutted foundation of an old factory. The canal was full of darkness. The road narrowed. I didn't like the feel of it, but then I didn't have much choice.

There were headlights behind us. They sparked in the rearview mirror. Dawn let out a low howl.

We careened into the winding dark, my free hand blindly tugging at the tape on Dawn's wrists. "Please," she prayed. "Please."

Her hands came free.

She was peeling her ankles free when I saw the gate coming up. Back entrance to the dump. Closed. The embankment on the right dropped off into the dark. I sensed water down there. No room to turn around. We had escaped headlong into a dead end.

Crashing the gate without time for seatbelts seemed likely to put one of us through the windshield, so at the last second I braked hard and nosed into the chain links.

"Let's go," I said.

"I can't. My feet." Dawn was dragging herself out the door: dragging her bound feet. I dug at the tape, twisted, tried to tear it. The headlights behind us closed in.

"Here we go," I grunted, and heaved her onto my back. I eased her over the gate, then put a foot up on the Volvo's fender and vaulted over myself. The headlights came at us. Dawn was hunched down, digging at the tape with soft furious squeals of frustration.

"No time," I gasped. I crouched and came up with her slung across my shoulders and staggered ahead into the dark. The ruts and ridges kept tripping me. We passed a bunch of white washing machines and refrigerators like igloos in the black wastes of the Arctic. With my wet pant leg and her breath in my ear, it was as if I'd woken into childhood, into a kids' game whose aim I couldn't grasp.

To the right I could make out sheds. Behind us the gate rattled. The only chance was to lose them.

I staggered off the dirt road toward the sheds, and nearly broke my ankle against some sort of heavy axle. Pain grunted out of me. Dawn pulled her arm tighter around my neck and I choked, wrestling against her grip like a lifeguard. Over my shoulder I could hear footsteps in the dirt.

In the moonlight we passed a bulldozer and a dumpster the size of an armored car. I don't know what I expected to find under the flat shed roofs. An office, a watchman. A place to hide.

There were two buildings divided into bays like stables, open in front. The first housed a bulldozer blade, tools, a jumble of water heaters and pipes that rattled when I tried a closer look. His footsteps slowed up: reconnoitering. Somewhere a dog was barking.

"Hold tight," I whispered. Dragging Dawn, I crossed the open yard to the other shed. Heaps of broken glass glittered in the stalls. I felt around for a sharp shard. Then I lugged Dawn around back of the shed where the eave was so low I could boost her up onto my shoulders. She pulled herself onto the roof, and I passed her the blade of glass: "Here. Cut yourself free."

"Wait." She was a hoarse whisper in the moonlight. In the distance a dog barked.

"Shh. He won't look up there."

"What about you—"

At the far end of the shed the shadows moved and I knew it was the Ear. My skin cringed. I slid around the corner hugging the wall. On the other side I grabbed a couple bottles off the glass heap. He came out the opposite end, running. His momentum carried him a few steps into the yard, in the moonlight, and I saw the gun come up. I flattened back against the shed, and he saw his chance.

When the footsteps closed in I stepped out and pitched one of the jars at him with all my strength. It hit just under his chin and he let out a squawk, but I wasn't close enough to rush him. While he thought about it, I hurried around the rear of the shed, toward the mountains of refuse slumped under the distant moon. Maybe I could lead him into the wilds of the dump and lose him.

But I was running too fast, too free, too sure, and in the blackness a tangle of venetian blinds snared my foot and catapulted me sidelong and amazed toward the planet Neptune. The fall sucked my lungs flat. By the time I could breathe he was somewhere behind the shed, very still. Invisible.

The blinds crinkled and clacked under me so I tried not to move. My jaw rested against an empty paint can, a brush dried in the residue, the handle sticking out. I worked the rest of the tape off my left eye. The dog was still barking. Watchdog maybe. A rat scuttered over a pile of tin cans. As my eyes searched the dirty moonlight, shapes hovered on the edge of possibility. He could be anywhere: he might step in my face before I could spot him.

Then he moved, coming toward me.

As I tensed to run, I realized he was backing away from the shed, scanning the roof. The gun barrel winked in the moonlight.

I yelled.

Dawn scrambled on the roof. In the wilderness of trash the detonation was a feeble pop. Then she was gone. I grabbed at the darkness around me for something to heave at him. Threw the other jar. It exploded against the wall of the shed with a trivial plink.

Son of a bitch.

Even as I stumbled to my feet, the pistol went off again in the yard. I heard curses—her voice—and running feet. A figure darted into the moonlight, female shadow running with an unmistakable female gait. The pale skirt rippled. I waved.

He fired. He fired and the venetian blinds gave a comic twang that scared me down again. Dawn was limping. She sprinted toward me, arms pumping, body pitched forward at such an angle I was sure she'd fall on her face and he'd catch her, stand over her, put a leisurely bullet in her brain.

"Over here."

She was panting, hurt. "Landed. In glass. Here, feel."

She pulled up her shirt and I felt the warm skin just above her hip. A sticky wet patch and—christ—a ragged puncture.

Her breath hitched: "Hurts."

We were half running now. Without deciding, without planning, we were dodging among bedsprings and sinks and hulking stoves, past toilets and bathtubs ghostly white in the moonlight: blundering into a gutted armchair and a baby carriage. I tripped in the spokes of a bike. The pistol fired and an oil drum a few yards away grunted.

"Slow up," Dawn panted.

"How'd he find you on the roof?"

"Shoe. Came off when I yanked off the tape. Fell on him." I looked down: sure enough, one bare foot. "There's so much sharp stuff I don't dare take off the other one."

"You're fine."

"Damn glass," she gasped. "Couldn't even see it. Like one false move and the dark takes a bite out of you — hey, watch where you're going."

"Sorry."

"When you get hurt," she panted, "first you don't feel anything. Then you do." She sucked in air. "Boy, do you." She laughed but a groan came out of her. "Oh shit."

In the distance the dog was howling.

$\triangledown$

42

WHEN WE REACHED THE dirt road we cut left, and for a moment I was sure we could double back to the gate before him: wheel the Volvo around, get the hell away. With each stride I looked for the gate to appear. But then Dawn grabbed my arm: "No. This way."

Just in time.

He came scudding down the hill into the road ahead of us. The son of a bitch had a sense of direction.

Running at a crouch, we ducked off the road into a soft bed of ashy rubble. The whiff of ashes, acrid and invisible, hacked in my windpipe. It was as if we were going up in a cloud of poisonous smoke no eye could see. The ash sifted gritty into my shoes and clung to my sweaty skin.

She led us across a ridge, then through a ravine in which we sank to our ankles, almost to our knees, in ashes. Under her breath, in sync with her strides like some army drill, Dawn was muttering obscenities over and over. Keeping herself going. Pushing. The dog sounded closer: a raucous idiot yap.

We staggered up a steep slope of new trash. Tin cans, garbage bags, garbage smells. Even with one shoe gone, Dawn was light and agile. I kept slipping in the debris, digging my shoes in deep, wavering backward. A rag of cloud dragged across the moon, and I thought if we could just be quiet enough, invisible enough, we'd get to the other side; shake him off.

Near the top of the slope a dog came bounding over the wall of trash. He launched himself toward us, almost into my face, a long black snout and the body of a terrier. I dropped into the trash and he plunged past me, halfway down the slope, righting himself, turning. Then he was on our heels, barking. I warned him off with my foot, growling at him, hoping he'd get the message. But he kept after us: kept yapping.

At the top we found the road again, or another road. The bored moon drifted. Dawn was limping badly, slowing down. She kept cinching in the shirt around her waist, stanching the wound. The dog would run ahead a few yards, then stop, dig in, and bark. It was a low, irritable sound, almost a cough, just loud enough to get us killed.

As the road rose up over the depths of buried waste it silhouetted us against the moonlight, so we cut to the right, into fresh-smelling, freshly bulldozed earth. The dog stuck with us, advertising us to the world. A couple of times I scooped up stones, which he took for a game.

The next thing I knew, we were climbing up a slope of old paper. Weeks, months, years of newsprint and telephone books. We staggered from bale to bale of headlines. Loose pages slipped underfoot and twice I went down, clawing at the slick pages for a handhold. Toward the top it was all loose paper: ads, catalogs, trash, woozily unstable, impossible to climb. Dig with your feet and paper would skid greasily out from under you. Tomorrow the bulldozers would bury this spill of words under a thin skin of earth.

As we neared the crest of the hill he saw us. The bullet slapped into the mountain of waste-words under my feet. I grabbed Dawn and pulled. A smothered cry of pain burped out of her, but I drew her over the crest with me, and we went down. She tumbled forward in the darkness and her body slipped headfirst down the paper slope. The dog pranced beside us.

In a few places where the bales of paper had heaped up there were crevices. "In here," I whispered.

She balked.

"Look, there isn't time to discuss this."

"Let's keep on."

"You're hurt." I shoved a couple of bales to widen the opening and pushed her into the gap. She wiggled in deeper, twisting her head down. Layered with newsprint, she disappeared. He'd never find her. I was starting down the slope when she screamed. It was an unwilling, stifled yelp, and it brought me staggering back up the slope to claw her free.

She clutched my wrist with both hands and pulled with such terrified strength I fell on top of her. She was screeching under her breath, thrashing. "Dig me out."

"You're better off—"

"Rats. Underneath."

We worked her loose. She was panicky now, pushing me away:

"He's close. Hurry."

Toward the bottom of the slope there were big cardboard cartons: the sort of boxes that house people in dark corners of New York and Mexico City. Duck into one and he might miss us.

"Come on, kid."

"I can taste blood. Is that possible?"

"We're almost there."

The first couple of boxes reeked of garbage.

I shoved her into the next overturned carton as gently as I could, then piled in after her. When she groaned I hugged her tightly to me. "The dog," she croaked.

To my horror the dog nosed up to the opening of the box and growled at us. I groped for something to throw, but there was nothing, so I lunged at him. My fingers caught a hind leg, and in my sprawl I managed to wrench him off his feet. In a wild reflex his teeth raked my arm, but I got a grip on his chain collar.

The jaws flew at me, unbelievably fast, from another dimension of time. My face whipped aside in time to miss the incisors that scraped my ear. I dropped on him, covered him, crushing the air out of his lungs. It was my body thinking, hands wrenching at the chain collar to choke him. He flew into a survival rage: legs, spine, flexing wildly under me, teeth slashing at phantoms. In my own rage I gave the collar a last brutal twist.

Then his breathing died to squeaky whimpers. I dragged him twitching and heaving into the box and flattened him under my ribs. Gradually I eased up on the collar. We huddled there in the insane darkness, my left hand at his throat, right hand stroking the bony skull.

Someone was coming down the slope. At the sound the dog jolted into a frenzy again, struggling to get loose. Again I dropped on him: flattened him under me. The footsteps were closer now, so this time I twisted the collar and held it fast. The dog struggled less and less. The blood roared in my head. The burns on my wrists stung.

The Ear stood at the bottom of the newsprint mountain, a few yards from us. He stood there, silent, the moon on his shoulder, his head cocked: ruthlessly casual, just a teenager plinking rats in the town dump.

It was an uncanny moment, all possibility. He was too distant, yet my body tensed to rush him. Get it over with. It was as if the fist at the dog's throat was thinking: to hell with the risk, you can do anything. Nothing can stop you.

Get it over.

I took a full breath. But she had my ankle. Dawn had both hands wrapped tightly around my foot, her cheek pressing hard. The fact took a moment to sink in, like waking from a powerful dream into your own confused body, and I hesitated.

At which point the Ear moved. He came toward us in the filthy moonlight, the pistol at his side. His shoes kicked loose riffs of paper. I sucked in a final breath. Get it over with.

But she held fast to me, and I didn't dare loosen my grip on the dog. *Get it over.*

Then he was past us, above and behind us, out of sight.

When I crept out he was cutting diagonally back up the slope to the road.

"He's gone," I whispered.

Her hands let go. Her whole body let go, and she slumped in the darkness. Feeling above her hip, my fingers met blood. The soaked fabric scared me. The fear stung me, so sudden and so deep I felt tears start to my eyes. I let go the dog and twisted about to find her wrist. There was a pulse, but it was — or I convinced myself it was — unsteady.

"Come on, kid," I said. "Upsy-daisy."

She groaned: "It hurts everywhere."

"Let's go home."

"You go. I'll wait here."

"You need a Band-Aid."

"I'll wait here."

"This place goes on forever. You faint and I might never find you again."

"I hate this weak feeling."

"Everybody does. Come on. Upsy-daisy."

I pulled her into the moonlight. The dog's body twitched, the tail shivering in nervous spasms, more dead than alive. I scanned the ridge above us. No signs. We'd have to chance it.

When I hoisted Dawn onto my back, she let out a long slow sigh of pain. With an eye on the moon so I wouldn't get us lost, I staggered uphill, crossing sidewise to ease the angle of the slope. She was breathing in little hiccups and the hill kept throwing me off balance. It was like Vietnam, only I wasn't a kid anymore.

Near the gate I settled Dawn onto the ground. I heard a car start. The Volvo was still nosed up to the fence. I doubled back and collected Dawn.

"Where you been?" she murmured. "I was all alone."

As I was twisting around to lower Dawn onto the other side of the gate, I heard a throaty bark. By the time we reached the car, the dog was at the gate scolding at the top of his lungs.

I wrapped Dawn in Vera's plaid blanket and stripped off my own messy shirt.

Driving alongside the embankment I looked for the spot where the fence had scraped Paul Revere off the car door. My reward was to find in the Volvo's headlights not Paul Revere but the Messrs. Smith & Wesson. As I scrambled back into the car, Dawn said:

"What'd you find?"

"The key to the city."

"You're crazy."

"I'm not the idiot who damn near got us killed."

"If you'd only listened to me when—"

"Just shut up. Okay?"

"Whoo, that's right. Go ahead. Blame me. That'll do a lot of good."

$\triangledown$

43

COMING UP THE SOUTHEAST Expressway back into the city, Dawn passed out. Her head drooped and she slumped into the door, scaring the hell out of me. I couldn't drive much faster. Potholes jolted the car and knocked her skull against the window, so I pulled her toward me and finished the trip with my right hand holding her upright.

Even in Emergency at Brigham & Women's, the intake paperwork was brutally slow. Lying facedown on a stretcher, jiggling her lacerated foot, Dawn gave the admitting nurse her name and described a fictitious accident involving broken glass. Looking at my bloody tee shirt and grubbiness, the nurse drew quick conclusions that came to focus in a scowl.

As they wheeled her off for stitches Dawn saw me turn to go. "Hey," she cried, "aren't you going to wait?"

"I have to clean up some broken glass."

"Hospitals scare me to death."

"You won't feel a thing."

"That's what scares me."

Her cheek pressed flat against the crisp white sheet. I squeezed her shoulder, mussed her hair: "You'll be back on your pogo stick in no time."

"Duncan?"

"I'll pick you up. Or buzz Rachel and she'll swing by for you."

"Wait. Can you solve this thing for good? Or am I going to be scared to go outdoors for the rest of my life?"

"I'll see what I can do."

I skipped off to the pay phone and thumbed in coins. I chatted with Phil Auburn's answering machine. At Natick police headquarters Kevin Hollings was working the night shift and glad to hear from me:

"Duncan, I been trying to reach you. The autopsy report's in on the boyfriend, Ryan—"

"Good. But I just had my ass kicked by a couple Cubans in a municipal dump and I'm in a bit of a hurry."

"A couple what?"

"A couple salesmen from Miami."

"What are they after?"

"They want to fix the presidential election."

"But that's impos—"

"Look, I'm in Boston. Any way you can meet me?"

"I'm on duty. There's no one to cover for me. They'd have my head on a platter if I bugged out."

He was right of course, so I told him so and promised to get back to him.

At Meg's, luckily, Rachel answered. I tried to head off the thousand questions: "I found Dawn. We're okay."

"The way you say that—something's wrong."

"Dawn's in the emergency room at Brigham & Women's getting a stitch or two—cut herself on some broken glass. She may call in the morning for a ride."

"But I want to know what—"

"She'll tell you. And I'll fill in the truth at breakfast."

"Something's going on."

"Let's have those pancakes you make."

Rachel grumbled.

At the Koala-T Inn in Newton Lower Falls, Vera was already in bed with the late show and thrilled to hear from me: "Where have you been? I've been twiddling my thumbs here for hours. I thought you needed me."

"Have you got a jersey or a sweater that might fit me?"

"Oh my, Duncan. Am I going to have to start hiding my bras and frillies from you?"

"Can you meet me in fifteen minutes in Boston?" I described an intersection at Savin Hill, near Columbia Point. In the background I could hear Katherine Hepburn and Bogart plucking each other's leeches en route to torpedo the local Huns. Vera said:

"What are we supposed to be doing at Columbia Point?"

"I'll know better when we get there. Did you bring the video camera?"

"Yes, but you really should plan, love. It's a bad habit, this improvising all the time. I gather you expect trouble."

"Well—"

"Let me put it this way. Are you bringing a pistol?"

She felt me hesitate.

"Duncan, we're not the police."

But she didn't say no.

In fact Vera brought me a striped tank top that fit perfectly except for the elbow-length sleeves and a strip of bare skin around my waist. "Wait," she said, "what's wrong with your wrists?"

"Couple burns."

"How did — ?"

"Lock your car and hop in. I'll tell you on the way."

Belfrey Street was deserted. It bothered me that I might not recognize their Mercury — did it have Florida plates or had I dreamed that?

In one of the back apartments at the project there was a fight, a couple of overtired voices snarling by an open bedroom window. Vee and I strolled around behind to check out the ruckus and surprised four boys — all young enough to sit on Santa's lap — passing around a joint in the furtive summer darkness. They scattered under our noses like mice.

"Bloody hell," Vera gasped.

"Lucky none of them had a gun."

"They're tots," Vera fumed. "What are you Americans doing to yourselves?"

Edgar's front door was closed and locked. Through the open living-room window you could see him in his chair watching a bearded TV face in a shiny chrome army helmet and smoking a cigar. The face was recommending the Bible and demanding donations. An 800 telephone number was superimposed over the preacher's chest as in a police mug shot. Usual row of sheep manning the fund-raising telephones behind him. Vera said:

"Make yourself scarce, love. If anyone sees you in that ludicrous shirt, they'll have you arrested."

Vera hit Edgar's doorbell and, when nothing happened, knocked. Just when I began to think Edgar was as dead as his doorbell, he wheezed, "Who is it?"

"Jackie. You the one that called?"

The door cracked, revealing an Edgar eyeball.

Vera said: "Where's the Latino? He said to be here by midnight. Seventy-five bucks. No hassles."

"It's after midnight," Edgar said testily. Always sensitive to etiquette, our Edgar.

"Yeah, well you're not the guy."

"You talk funny," Edgar suggested. "You from down east?"

"Where's the Latino? He told me midnight."

"Felix is over at the motel. What'd he send you here for?"

"Nookie." Pause. "Do I gotta spell it out for you?"

"No, I mean — "

"Which motel?"

"He don't like — "

"Look, I'm late, he's gonna beat on me, okay? You want to make it harder for me?"

"You got a car?"

"Where's Felix at?"

"It's over in Allston. Off Storrow. You know where Sammy White's is? But see, the fastest way is you go around the Barney Street side and take a left up this narrow street, it's a one-way but you can hook around by the old—"

"Forget it," Vera said. "Just give me the name before he kills me."

"It's the Imperial. See, it's by the Charles River, near—"

"How do I find his room?"

"He don't like anyone giving out informa—"

"Cripes, you really want to see me get whacked around, don't you?" Vera pouted. The door opened a bit wider, revealing two Edgar eyes and the modish Edgar undershirt:

"It's number seventeen. It's under the name Rodriguez."

"Hey, you're a sweet guy. I won't forget this."

44

THE IMPERIAL MOTEL IS an average overpriced Boston hostelry on the Charles River across from the old redbrick Watertown arsenal. It was the place Joe Mazey had suggested for our meeting.

Just up the river the gothic stone rooflines of the Perkins School for the Blind nest among the trees. After midnight, instead of the scenic view, you get to admire out-of-state plates in the Imperial parking lot. Out front of room number 17, I admired a Florida plate. It was attached to a smoke gray Mercury Sable with aerodynamic styling and a trunk that will hold two bound and gagged adults, alive or dead.

"That's the car we were in," I said.

"Leased in Miami."

I made a note. In the window of number 17 on the second floor balcony there were slits of light.

Commandante Felix was in.

We trotted over to the pay phone in front of the liquor store next door, and Lt. Phil Auburn's answering machine gave me the brush-off again. I recited our location onto the tape.

"I suppose the show must go on," Vera grumbled. At the foot of the stairs she put her palm on my chest: "Wait here, love."

She rapped at number 17, and almost immediately I heard Felix the Ear. I took a firmer grip on the Smith & Wesson. Above me Vee sounded delicately flustered: "Oh, I'm sorry. I must have the wrong address."

"Maybe not. Who you looking for?"

"I'm supposed to meet Joe."

"Who's this lucky Joe?"

Vera gulped: "Joe Mazey?"

She sounded so vulnerable, so shy, I could barely catch her words. In the right mood our boy could purr too: "I gotta tell you. Joe, he's not here tonight."

"You know him?"

"Sure. You his girl?"

"Some nights."

"But not tonight it looks like, hey?"

"We never come here. Except tonight he told me this place."

"Maybe he wants you to meet me."

"He's a good guy. He treats me real good."

"He knows I'd treat you good too."

"What's your name?"

"Carlos."

"I'm Jackie."

"That's a good name. I like that name. Her husband was the President when my family came here from Cuba. My father was a brain surgeon in Havana. They want him to run the new government when we finally get Castro." He mused: "I like Jackie."

"I don't know what to do now. I don't want him to get mad at me."

"Not Joe Mazey, he's a pussycat."

"It's not like I can call him at his house."

Felix Carlos the Cuban Ear purred: "It's too bad I got to go meet somebody now." Then a brainstorm: "Why don' you wait for me? We got a little frigerator. We got stuff to eat. Nachos. Tequila. We got a couple roast beef grinders left. Tonight's the last night, we gotta eat it all up. When I come back, maybe we have a few laughs, do some snuff."

"Snuff?"

He sniffed loudly a few times to illustrate. Vera cooed:

"That sounds very interesting."

"You got an educated nose?"

"I like to feel happy."

"Or maybe we smoke. You ever smoke bazuco?"

"Bazooka?"

"Great mind tricks."

"Great mind tricks." A new, teasing note came into Vera's voice: "That sounds nicer than going home empty-handed. But I can't just party, you know? I got rent, people to pay."

"Whatever Joe Mazey gives—when I come back, I give you two times that. Three times."

"More than seventy-five?" She sounded so bashful Felix Carlos brayed a soft gloating laugh.

"After I come back, that's nothing. That's—"

He snapped his fingers. The clicks resonated in the cinder-block stairwell. *Nix. Nix.* Vera giggled. Felix Carlos crooned:

"Come inside. Wait for me."

The door closed. I crept to the head of the stairs and leaned against the cinder-block wall listening.

Five minutes passed in which I scared myself silly: one sloppy word in there and she . . .

But then El Commandante Felix was out the door and skiing down the stairs toward me so fast I dashed to the bottom and around the corner on tiptoe, in a wild, silent ballet. I flattened against the wall. If he took a wrong turn, I'd have to rub his nose with the gun barrel and take my chances.

In fact he skipped out to the Mercury on springy steps, swinging a leather attaché case. As he pulled out onto Storrow Drive, Vera clipped lightly down the stairs: "Quick, don't lose him. This little piggy's going to market."

We scrambled for the Volvo: "What's in his room?"

"His buddy. Out cold on a twin bed. All bandaged. He's had some kind of emergency treatment. His lights are really out. Either the medics shot him up with morphine or Carlos has him nodding on something more recreational."

"He was hanging on to the rear door of the Volvo, and I scraped him off against a fence."

I wheeled the car out of the parking lot and headed intown. "Any sign of the photographs?"

Vera shook her head: "Nothing. I gave the drawers and closets a glance, but the photos are probably in his briefcase. Things look packed to go, by the way. They've got a grocery bag full of opened junk food. Cheetos and cocktail pretzels and those Mexican corn things. And a half-eaten grinder in the wastebasket with ants working on it."

"Figure they got what they came for."

"The bloke just walked out and left me sitting there. Very careless."

"He's half street-smart punk, half cocky commandante."

"I bet any sensitive stuff's in the briefcase."

"I predict Carlos bolts for Miami before the sun comes up."

"I had the distinct impression he was hot to make it with me in order to humiliate Joe Mazey."

"Beat the competition and capture the market."

"He's rather nice looking. He tries to give the impression he grew up around money. What is he, Miami Cuban?"

"I wouldn't take his word for it. If Joe Mazey's peddling the photographs to honchos high up in the President's campaign, they may have hired this guy to do the dirty work."

"Like Emilio Whosis, the Watergate burglar."

"Sure. It's possible these guys were sent to erase any trail the photos might have left. It's possible they planned to kill Dawn and her boyfriend even if they got everything they wanted."

"So maybe he's about to turn over the photos to Joe Mazey in exchange for a big payoff."

Harvard Stadium, the Ivy League answer to the Roman Colosseum, slipped by on our right.

I caught up to the gray Mercury as we were passing BU, and gave a wave toward the theater where *La Ronde* was about to debut. But Vera wasn't having any: "For heaven's sake, Duncan. Stop acting so unconcerned. It makes me very nervous."

At North Station, Commandante Carlos peeled off onto the Southeast Expressway. On the radio WCRB was cranking up Schubert's *Death and the Maiden* quartet. Not the right moment for that twosome, so I searched out some Coltrane.

"If you're right," I said, "and our little piggy's going to market, then chances are we're headed either for Joe Mazey's office or for Edgar's.

The Mercury sailed past the towers and spires of official Boston, perfectly at home. Carlos slipped from lane to lane as if he owned the road. Vera said:

"I hope you realize that we're depriving some Boston cop of a chance at promotion."

"I called the two cops in this state who'll talk to me. Neither one could join the party."

"There's more than two."

"But not much time. And cops need hard evidence and search warrants to get excited."

"What are we supposed to do?"

I shrugged: "Put salt on his tail."

"I know stupid jokes are supposed to buck me up, but what I could use is some strategy."

We talked strategy. How to gather enough evidence to bust the son of a bitch or at least get some leverage — a guarantee of Dawn's safety, say. None of the possibilities looked irresistible.

As expected, Commandante Carlos slipped off the expressway into Dorchester, through a neighborhood spiced by immigrant businesses, from Oriental groceries to a Cape Verdean bar. To avoid unpleasant suspicions in his rearview mirror — there aren't that many hundred-year-old Volvos on the road anymore — I kept well behind him. Even so, we ended up on Belfrey Street as Felix Carlos was only half out of the Mercury, so I had to take a sudden detour up an alley to avoid him.

"Let's go. Got the video camera?"

We felt our way down the sidewalk toward the housing project, happy to have streetlights out. Felix Carlos bounced along with the briefcase lightly swinging by his side. The light from Edgar's window attracted him like a moth.

Vera whispered: "It'll be morning soon."

"Good hour for business. Easier to tell who the players are when the streets are empty."

He had to rap smartly on the door to wake Edgar. The door closed behind him. Vee said:

"Things may happen fast if Edgar tells him about the hooker who was here looking for him."

"He's likely to get spooked."

"Let me check the camera." She reached into the soft vinyl handbag in which she carried it. I went to the window.

The old man sat in his high-backed rattan chair smoking. On the tube some slickie was peddling *House of Lena* hair restorer with gusto that killed the real voices. Edgar said something like, "He's not here yet." Suddenly a hand appeared before my eyes and pulled down the shade. Vee and I backed around the corner.

With my ear to the window I could hear Edgar protesting: "Well I ain't no plumber." He began explaining the theory of drain maintenance, with emphasis on the superiority of the rubber force cup to caustic cleaners. "See, all that stuff in the ads, all it is is lye. I put tons of it down that toilet already, I'm surprised it don't eat right through the floor, and what good did it do. The thing's still all bound up. You need a plunger is what you need, and somebody stole mine. There's a vacant unit next door, where I can go."

The impatient Felix Carlos went to the kitchen door, opened the screen, unzipped, and watered the back step.

"See, I have to fix everything inna whole projeck myself," Edgar was saying. "It's on my list for tomorrow. Fix toilet."

Vera poked me: "Look out, headlights."

We slithered back against the brick.

A Cadillac slid up to the curb: one of those jobs with the spare tire streamlined into the trunk à la 1929. The streetlight gave a glimpse of Joe Mazey. Approaching Edgar's door he looked every which way: a man in unfamiliar territory, used to doing business behind a desk, where your fingers can do the walking. Vera said:

"Back door?"

She led the way. Carlos had left the screen ajar, and a pungent smell of urine.

In the front room the TV was blessedly dead. From the sound of it Edgar was greeting the boss on bended knee, calling him Mr. Mazey, kissing his ring and anointing his feet. Joe Mazey said:

"So you got the photos?"

I had to open the screen door an inch at a time, lifting it from the bottom to take the weight off the creaky aluminum hinge. Vera eased the door shut behind us, minirecorder in her free hand.

Edgar's kitchen smelled like Edgar. The bathroom smelled like latrines in Vietnam and supported many forms of life. Telephone on the Formica counter. I double-checked Smith & Wesson in the light, trying to follow the voices in the next room.

"I told him, I says, Mr. Mazey won't like no violence." Edgar the tattletale. "That's when he got the idea of the car exhaust."

"So where are they now?" Joe Mazey asked.

"All the time I'm thinking, if it was Mitch now, Mitch would handle this more—"

"Edgar," Mr. Mazey suggested, "shut up."

"They got loose," Carlos shrugged. "They ran."

"You screwed up."

"You're the one wanted it clean."

"Right. So now we got two near-misses running around out there totally pissed off. Why didn't you leave them alone?"

"You want peace of mind or not? Her boyfriend's dead, she was hinting things."

"But you said that's nothing to do with you. There's no proof."

"You get accused, you're useless. The pictures are useless."

"Right. So you what, you gas her?"

"You want this bitch squeezing you? Maybe selling her story to the TV or some shit?"

"So you half solve it, half screw it up royally."

"It's okay. They're too scared to breathe now."

"Is that a fact?"

"Anyway, what can they prove?"

"If one of them yells and it stirs up pity for Merriam, they win, we lose. His people are experts at pity. Tears for the niggers and the welfare sluts and fairies and every other freak in the circus."

"You got deniability. That's why we come up here."

"Only you screwed up."

"I been wasting my life up here for you people."

"You made up for any losses out of your suitcase. Don't give me the big investment line."

"It didn' cost you nothing."

"Except you screwed up."

An edge came into Carlos's voice. "You see any niggers here?" Pause. "You talk like you see a nigger."

The sort of growl that makes you reach for a stick. Joe Mazey protested: "Don't be so sensi—"

"Don't *tell* me."

"Take it *eea*sy." Joe Mazey's voice had a wobble in it.

"Don' *tell* me what to do!"

I looked at Vera and flicked the safety off the revolver. Time to dance.

▽

45

EDGAR SAT IN HIS undershirt on a blue velvet sofa that had a bad skin disease. Pile of old newspapers against the pale green wall, seashell ashtray on top. Plastic wastebasket. Picture of the Parthenon higher up on the wall, Day-Glo on black.

Joe Mazey sat in the rattan chair. His fingers pulled at a long loose strand of cane. The heels of his crocodile shoes dug into the tabloid newspaper on the green carpet. From where I stood the headline read

BABY DESCRIBES HEAVEN
BEFORE BIRTH

but the man in the chair saw only Smith & Wesson.

Felix Carlos had on a two-tone brown cowboy shirt and a look of pure danger. Not the eyes—they looked bleary—but the jaw, the disgusted mouth. When he spotted Vera behind me, the mouth produced a little grin: friendly, face-saving, cold-blooded. His right hand tensed over the briefcase on the television set behind him. Something inside there was drawing his trigger finger.

"Have a seat," I said.

Carlos ignored me. I wagged the pistol at the sofa:

"Sit down."

Carlos grazed his knuckles over the ribbon of beard along his jaw as if testing my reflexes. He was rocking subtly on the balls of his feet. Priming his reflexes. Testing. I said:

"What's in the briefcase?"

Smith & Wesson were casting a spell over Joe Mazey. Finally his tongue pushed words out: "Tonight, I have to say this, I wasn't responsible for what happened, I—"

"How about Ryan Kassiotis?"

"Who?" Anxiety clouded Joe Mazey's face.

"The dead boyfriend. Ring any bells?"

Joe Mazey pulled at the loose strand of rattan as if he could unweave the chair and himself and disappear into nothing. His voice was husky: "I didn't know."

"Somebody taped his hands and mouth and beat him to death. Same game your friend Carlos here prefers."

"Accident," Carlos said softly.

201

"That the kid died?"

"The tape. I never heard of the guy." His open hand hovered over the briefcase. Pressure was building in the room. I shifted to Joe Mazey:

"You want to tell me exactly how much you're not involved? Or would you rather tell it to the cops?"

Joe Mazey's eyes saw the wide arch of empire falling.

Carlos let his hand settle slowly onto the briefcase leather. Testing. Pushing me. "So," he smirked. "What we got here, bandits? A holdup? How much do you want? Five thousand?"

"The whole story."

"He's not a cop," Joe Mazey said. He was thinking out loud, in a trance. His words struggled to catch up to his mouth like amateur ventriloquism. "Mitch says he's some sort of investigator."

Carlos laughed: "You know what I think? I think he's not gonna kill anybody."

He patted the briefcase. "Get away from the briefcase," I said.

"You know what else? He don' know anything."

I took a chance: "I know you came up from Miami with a suitcase of coke that you peddled to pay for the photos. And then when Dawn stiffed you, you decided to kill her and her boyfriend. Make sure she wouldn't spoil your photo headlines."

"Your head's screwed up," Carlos said.

"Get away from the briefcase. Move."

"Put the pistol away."

"Horseshit."

He shrugged and reached for the twin chrome latches: "A pistol's no good, man. You can' use it."

Daring me.

The briefcase lid came up. Inside was the manila envelope with Dawn's photos. His hand hovered over the envelope. I said: "Step back."

"I show you something."

"Back off."

Slow, dreamlike, his hand settled toward the envelope, closing in. I raised the pistol. "You pull that trigger," he murmured, "and the cops got you by the balls. Shooting an unarmed man."

"Self-defense."

"An unarmed man."

"In the commission of a felony."

"An unarmed man," he repeated softly. "I know the law. I got witnesses. You gonna kill everybody in this room?"

The hand, the itchy fingers, closed on the envelope. Lifted it. Half a dozen little baggies of Colombian joy underneath: nested among them, his Beretta. Carlos rattled the envelope, daring me closer. Close enough and there'd be a scuffle. In a way he had me and he knew it. In moments like this cops clobber the guy and write it up as resisting arrest. I said: "Put it down."

"You got a warrant to be in here?" He grinned, giving the envelope a sarcastic little wiggle. In a sort of slow motion ballet he turned, keeping his other hand up, near the Beretta. To Joe Mazey he crooned: "Think about it. No warrant, no badge, nothing. You know how illegal this gringo is?"

"*Stop!*"

"This is bullshit. I got DEA connections. You gonna kill me in cold blood?"

When I closed in he tensed into a sort of gunfighter's crouch, teasing, ready to go for the Beretta or the pistol in my hand. I hesitated. Behind me Vera's voice murmured: "Nick him."

"Hand me the photos," I said.

His free hand slipped into his pocket. He smirked: "Gringos think all Latinos carry knives."

In slow motion the hand came up with a yellow object that suddenly sprouted a flame — butane lighter — and ignited the envelope.

Daring me.

Move on him and someone would go down.

For a split second I debated, then decided: let it burn. Let Dawn off the hook. Nail the bastard on the cocaine. We watched the envelope burn slow and smoky. When the slow curl of flame reached his fingers, Felix Carlos dropped the envelope into the wastebasket. It smoked and flickered there till the trash caught. Flames shot up. They curled and shrank the top of the wastebasket and gave off a poisonous stink. As they subsided the rim of the wastebasket shriveled in on itself.

With his hands away from the briefcase, I scooped up the Beretta. A trade: the photos for the pistol. To Vera I said: "Time to phone the cops."

"Don' rush," Felix Carlos said. He reached toward the briefcase and the bags of white powder.

"Hands off," I warned.

When he ignored me I pulled the trigger and put a .38 slug into the rug beside his right moccasin. That affected his sense of humor. For a moment, too late, Edgar covered his ears with his hands. "All I'm doing," Felix Carlos said, "I'm gonna put it down the toilet."

"Toilet's stopped up," Edgar croaked.

"The sink then," Felix Carlos shrugged. "Then we're even."

"Sit down," I said aiming at his right knee.

"Okay, okay." He backed up a step.

"Vera?" I glanced behind me to see what was holding up the phone call.

Mitch.

46

IN THE KITCHEN LIGHT his face looked puffy and yellow, his eyes bad. The pistol looked capable enough. Vera stood with her hands half raised, still holding the phone. Mitch waved the phone back to its cradle, then signaled me to drop the Smith & Wesson. He saw me calculate: "You want me to take your fucking head off?".

I put the two pistols beside the briefcase on the television. It made sense: Joe Mazey wasn't here to buy baggies of snuff. He was here to introduce Mitch.

"So what the hell's going on?" Mitch demanded. "I'm coming up the sidewalk, I hear fucking gunshots. I look in, it's this turkey and the little lady here. What gives?"

Joe Mazey bounced to his feet: "Where the hell have you been?"

"I got here on time," Mitch countered, "you'd be in deep shit." Six hours sleep had sobered him up a lot. He turned to me: "What're you doing here?"

"Plea bargaining," I said, "who takes the rap."

Mitch looked from one face to another: "Plea bargain?"

"Like who gets credit for dealing the coke in the briefcase."

"Which is?"

"Which is you," I said. "Didn't I tell you? Your friends here want you to go down as owner of record. In exchange for—"

"I'll take care of him," Carlos said.

"In a minute." Mitch waved Vera into the living room. She backed against the wall by the stack of newspapers. Carlos reached for the Beretta, but Mitch's gun hand waved him off. "Hey. In a fucking minute, okay?"

"Maybe this is old news to you," I said, "but Carlos here tells us he's got federal connections. Maybe DEA. Maybe CIA. If the local cops bag him, he says he's undercover. To prove it, all he has to do is give them a name, an easy collar."

"Me."

I shrugged. My mind was improvising so fast I felt a little crazy. Which is what Carlos said: "This guy's out of his mind. I almost dropped him a few hours ago, he walked right into it."

Mitch said: "Yeah, this asshole walks into anyplace."

Joe Mazey twitched his fingers nervously as if he couldn't decide

205

which button to push: "Like your place, did I hear?"

"Damn right. He busts into my house, I'm watching TV, I look up, there's Kathy knocked on her can in the hall and he's leaning over my fucking chair like a dentist grinding at me."

Carlos and Joe Mazey met my eye. I told the truth: "I was looking for you two."

They glanced at each other. I said:

"How else do I find you?"

"I threw him out on his ass," Mitch said.

"You should've warned me," Joe Mazey said.

"How'm I gonna warn you when you got an unlisted number? I call you, you have a hissy about wiretaps."

"You could've — "

"The fuck!" Mitch growled. "We been through this shit before."

I took a chance: "The other thing is, the cops will credit whoever owns the coke with killing Dawn's friend Ryan." I needed another lie to warp things the right way: "Because they turned up a baggie of coke in his apartment just like these."

"Anybody can do coke," Carlos said. His eyes clicked with Joe Mazey's: "Let's get the car."

Carlos had turned to the front door when Mitch said: "Hold it. Give Joe the keys. He can drive."

"What you worried about?" Carlos demanded.

"I don't want to be left with the cleanup on this one."

I noticed Vera's elbow moving slightly against the wall. Toward the light switch. "We take them into the woods and leave them," Carlos said. "By the time they get back I'm gone. No coca. No evidence. No case. Nada."

Mitch waved the pistol: "You're gonna just — ?"

At which point Carlos spotted Vera's move: "Watch the light-switch!"

Heads snapped toward Vera. Carlos's hand snapped toward the TV, the Beretta. I dived at his legs, carrying him backward until he slammed into the front door. Twice the Beretta went off in my ear. *Vera*. The impact of the door knocked the wind out of him, though he clipped the back of my head with the pistol barrel two, three times. In a rage of pain I drove my fist into his groin and heaved sideways to give Mitch less of a target. I broke the Beretta out of Carlos's hand and rolled against the wall flinching against gunshots Mitch would fire.

But I had time. When I wrenched around I saw that I had all the time in the world.

Mitch had sprawled into the pile of newspapers, scattering news over the rug. Blood from his chest dribbled down smooth pages of fashion-wear and comics and puddled where it met the floor. Later the cops would determine that he had gotten off one shot, which lodged in the ceiling next to the light fixture with the shade made from a plastic milk carton: trying to hit me or Carlos — I prefer to think Carlos. In the kitchen I heard the telephone dial whir, then Vera's voice inviting the cops over. In the corner of the living room Edgar took his hands off his ears and said very loudly:

"You saw it. I didn't do nothing."

47

SHIFTS HAD CHANGED BY the time we got to the hospital to pick up Dawn. The admitting nurse in Emergency was kind but firm:

"Dawn Ashland is not here."

"They were going to let her wait in a recovery cubicle till I could pick her up."

"They wanted to admit her, but she wouldn't hear of it. She's gone. She went out that door hobbling like a little old lady with her stitches."

"Could they have admitted her upstairs?"

"I'm sorry, but I saw her go out those doors maybe half an hour ago. With a man who I guess wasn't you."

"What did he look like?"

"He didn't come in. She was waiting in the foyer. When she saw him she took off. When a new shift comes on, we have too much paperwork to sit around minding other people's business."

"I signed the billing paperwork for her."

"I'm sorry, but your signature doesn't guarantee she'll sit and wait for you."

Outside the sun was just clearing the rooftops, splashing soft, clean light against the apartment houses across the street. As we walked to the Volvo, Vera said: "Who do you suppose it was? Taxi?"

"Nobody knew she was here."

"She must've phoned someone."

"Somebody who'd come to the rescue on a moment's notice."

"How many men could she know?"

I groaned. Vera stopped in her tracks:

"You mean you're not the only pliant boob out there."

I did what I could. I phoned Armand and Frank Fascelle — even Red LeBeau. I woke Rachel up. When I tried Joan Biondi, she shyly boasted that she was going to the registry to have her driver's license renewed today. Nobody had seen Dawn.

At the Koala-T Inn in Newton, Vera and I faked sleep till near noon. Then for an hour we clung to each other in bed, piecing the night together, talking about bad dreams and playing with each other: trying to put desire between us and the thought of death. "Every time a pin drops for the next few months," Vera murmured, "I'm going to freeze up and croak."

"Mmm. Me too."

"I hate it."

"Mmm."

Gently, roughly, no touch of the fingers, no touch of the tongue seemed to revive her. Her body seemed inert in my hands. And me too: none of the magic tricks brought the rabbit out of my hat. The burns on my wrists bothered me more now than last night.

"Come on," she coaxed swaying her breasts across my stomach, "we're turning this into a problem." She patted my thigh and reached for her bra. "Let's go have lunch and I'll fondle you under the table in the restaurant."

"If there's a cover-up, I'll go to the newspapers."

"Oh-oh," she groaned. "Here we go again. Hook me up."

My hands slipped under her arm and played with her breasts. She sat on the edge of the bed letting me sift through the details of the morning's police interrogation one more time. Once or twice she said something like "We'll see" or "Too soon to tell." Mostly she was patient and attentive, as if we might stumble on some crucial item that could change the whole case. Finally she tilted her shoulders forward to shrug off her loose bra and stretched:

"Sorry, love. But I'm tired of this. I'm going to turn around now, very slowly, and slide my hand up the inside of your leg, and take your sensitive dandelion in my fingers. Mmmm, like this. And then I'm going to do things to you that you'll remember for the rest of your life. Oh my, what have we here?"

When Vera snickers it sounds like potato chips crunching.

I pressed her down onto the pillow and whispered in her ear:

"When you snicker it sounds like a bag of potato chips."

She threw her legs around me and panted: "Oh God, I can't control myself any longer. Take me. Take me now, Reggie!"

Which, in a sweet roundabout sort of way, I did.

"Duncan," she whispered as our hips were urgently forgetting death together. "I know you're going to say you love me. And God knows, I love you. But last night — we really must stop taking idiot risks like that. Otherwise I — you — "

What could I say?

Afterward, while Vee was in the shower, a beautiful blur behind the pebbled glass, I remembered again what I'd been meaning to ask her. "At Edgar's," I called, "when you were against the wall like that. Your elbow started to hit the light switch. I saw it — Carlos did too. It's what triggered the gunfire."

"What?"

"Why didn't you put the lights out?"

Behind the frosted glass her breasts and shoulders rose in a shrug: "I tried. The damn switch was broke."

48

MAN FELLED IN
DRUG SHOOTOUT

That's how Mitch entered the history books with his story botched. The papers played up the melodrama. The *Herald* ran a photo of the housing project looking like an abandoned fish cannery on the Maine coast, and the caption:

FOUR HELD HOSTAGE DURING
DRUG ARREST GONE SOUR

Police say that Mr. Barshack was attempting to purchase cocaine with a street value of a quarter million dollars when he realized he was dealing with a DEA agent and tried to shoot his way out.

The ordeal began earlier in the evening when Edgar Simmons, 69, noticed signs of a drug deal in progress at the Belfrey St. housing project he has managed for two years. Mr. Simmons telephoned the building's owner, Mr. Joseph Mazey, to report his suspicions.

By the time Mr. Mazey arrived from his home in Randolph, he found Mr. Barshack holding at gunpoint Mr. Simmons and an agent of the Drug Enforcement Agency whose name has not been released.

Before the incident was over, two business investigators from New York City would also be taken hostage.

Further on, if you read carefully enough, there was a human interest element in the story.

After a wild melee that erupted a month ago during an eviction in which drugs were suspected of playing a role, the building's owner, Joseph Mazey, had vowed personally to investigate problems at the site. "These are mostly families with children," he said Monday. "They need a stable, secure atmosphere to grow up in. I felt a personal responsibility."

An anonymous caller from an anonymous phone at Meg's house tipped off a reporter that Mitchell Barshack had worked for Mazey's Puritan Development Corporation. The tip came out this way:

Mr. Barshack had worked off and on for Puritan Development Corp. as a property maintenance assistant. Puritan's president, Joseph Mazey, said, "I blame drugs for this tragedy. They just ate away his character."

The obituary was more fundamental:

Mr. Barshack leaves his wife, Katharine Klotze, a stepson, Brian Klotze, and a brother, Nicholas Barshack of Concord, as well as an uncle, Gerald Barshack, of Flint, Michigan.

Simons-Brahman Funeral Home, 222 Florence St., Jamaica Plain, is in charge of arrangements.

There will be no calling hours.

49

AT THE FISHWITCH IN Framingham, the Wednesday luncheon special was a deep-fried Icelandic fillet with Viking Sauce on a bun. Lt. Phil Auburn had three. He pushed one toward me when I sat down. "I ordered for you. What do you drink? My treat."

Sitting up straight in his crisp state police uniform, Phil Auburn looked not quite comfortable and perfectly at home here. He joined the queue at the cash register — shoppers and store clerks on their lunch hour.

In the newspaper open beside his brown tray was a page of campaign stories. Senator Merriam was hotly denying rumors that he had ever been treated for major psychiatric depression. But his wife was still catching attention too. Beneath the caption

CADDY TAKES ON WEALTHY

Caddy Merriam was quoted urging public opinion to pressure the rich to reinvest more in America. "No more take the money and run." Apparently she'd struck a nerve." A New York investment banker called her "charmingly irresponsible." Nevada's senior senator complained that she was "dishing up Communism." A spokesman for the President's campaign ridiculed her as "the same woman who favors child-care bills that would put preschoolers into the hands of homosexuals."

Phil Auburn brought us root beers. His he took neat: ice gave him hiccups. He scraped Viking Sauce off his fillet and squirted on a neat *S* of ketchup. "Where's your friend, the Natick cop?"

"Kevin? He'll be along."

"Where were you yesterday?"

"Manhattan. Rachel and I had to move some belongings out of a loft."

"Your ex didn't want to tell me your whereabouts."

"Meg worries."

"Doesn't want to lose her bread and butter?"

"We watch out for each other."

Phil frowned to show me he wasn't a sentimental fool. He kept his eyes fixed on the food in his hands: "How'd your session with the DA's people go today?"

"As far as they're concerned, the case is closed."

"I told you. DA's office took a call from Washington Monday afternoon. They wanted their players free and clear. Their idea is, their guys set up a bust, and when you interfered it went wrong. Game's over. No hits, no runs, no errors."

"Two hits," I said. "Mitch and maybe Ryan Kassiotis. And two very close fouls—me and Dawn Ashland. And as I told you, the cops let them erase the tape in my minirecorder."

"Not likely."

"Want to hear the blank tape?"

"Besides, like I told you, no proof. The hombre you call Carlos or Felix, he denies any knowledge of the Kassiotis kid, photographs, the works. It's your word against his. And somebody in Washington wants us to believe him."

"The two of them mauled Ryan in that parking lot in Revere, and when that didn't shake loose the photos, they took him out. Just as they would've dropped Dawn. And me. No witnesses."

"Ah. Here's your friend." Phil's eyes never left the sandwich.

Kevin Hollings stood in the doorway in his patrolman's uniform, self-consciously scouting the place for us. I waved. This time Phil Auburn rose to shake hands—impress the new guy. He slid Kevin the last Viking sandwich. They made small talk, feeling each other out.

Finally Kevin got bold: "I hear the gunslingers have gone back to Miami."

"Why blame Miami?" Phil Auburn clucked. I said:

"My guess is, Carlos is a Miami Cuban with some kind of ties to DEA. When Joe Mazey passed on Barshack's tip about the photos, the campaign tapped Carlos so respectable fingers could grab the goods without leaving fingerprints."

Phil Auburn studied the ragged bites he'd taken out of his sandwich. His eyebrows twitched: "You can be sure Carlos has anti-Castro contacts in Miami. Only his name, the name I hear, is Julio Reyes. And he's a Nicaraguan."

"A Contra?"

"Used to be. His old man was a military boss for Somoza—one of those guys embarrassed when, what was it, back in the seventies, when the CIA got caught teaching South American cops torture techniques in Virginia. Remember that?"

"Not me," Kevin Hollings said, wolfing his sandwich. "I was still in gradeschool."

"The son spent the Reagan years in the U.S. raising cash for the Contra war. Now he's on the payroll for the drug war."

"Smart," I said. "There's nothing for him back home in Nicaragua now but hard work. He probably figures he's a patriot sabotaging Merriam's presidential shot since in the Senate Merriam fought to kill funding for the Contras."

Phil examined the thumbnail of his right hand and swallowed: "Nobody's talking about his relation to DEA. But his buddy now, he's a former INS agent named Cables. Him you can actually trace to DEA."

"Then why the hell did he try to slide his badge past me that day at Concord Bridge?"

"Figure he wanted you to take him seriously, yet not be able to make him if a political storm broke."

I slid my sandwich onto Kevin's plate: "Whoever they are, they were playing both sides, freelancing stuff to Mitch. It's total free enterprise."

Phil swallowed. His eyes studied the fingers where his sandwich had been. "What do you expect. It's politics. Forget it."

"Who the hell is running the country?"

"Be realistic. DEA's got what, three thousand agents? And each one teased by big money every day. They got internal investigations going on all the time – thirty-something right now, I hear."

"You know as well as I do, the coke was to cover the photos and turn a little profit for Carlos too. That's why Joe Mazey was introducing Carlos to Mitch."

"Maybe. But Mitch is out of the game. It's no great win. But our side's happy."

"When I told the Boston cops that Carlos was in business for himself, they threatened me."

"Don't exaggerate."

"All of a sudden they start quizzing me – like I'm trying to score some of the coke myself."

"The cops, the DA's people, nobody wants Washington on their backs. With all the budget cutbacks in this state you'd have to blow up the Prudential Center to get their attention." Phil Auburn crushed his sandwich wrapper into a neat ball: "One more time I'll say it. This is America. Money talks. And evidence talks. The rest is fairy tales and horse manure."

"And one dead kid."

"That's what I wanted to remind you," Kevin said. "The autopsy report on Ryan Kassiotis is in. I just called again."

"Good thinking. I forgot."

"You want a look at it?"

"Put it on our list of chores."

"I think it's worth checking out."

215

"I'm sure it is."

"Seriously. We could check it out this afternoon. My shift doesn't start for a couple hours."

"I'm supposed to be getting an ultralight plane ready to fly. I have spot-welding to do, and control cables and—what the hell, it's my last chance for a summer vacation."

"Well, we don't *have* to—"

"Okay, okay. I feel guilty. I'll go. You satisfied?"

As we hunted for a parking space in Cambridge, the Volvo's radio caught a new tune by Steam Thieves. The refrain went something like:

> *Bite the hand that feeds you,*
> *Fight the hand that needs you,*
> *Fright the man that bleeds you—*
> *Don't let them drink your blood.*

Thanks to summer vacations, the DA's office gave the impression of slow motion frenzy—like sleepwalking at rush hour in the subway.

The autopsy report confirmed that with his mouth taped shut and his nasal passages swollen and hemorrhaging from blows to the face, Ryan Kassiotis had suffocated.

More revealing was the peculiar junk food in the list of stomach contents. It included a lemon jelly donut, corn chips, and raisins. And an oval medallion of the Virgin Mary, gold plate, one inch long. The Virgin hadn't made it as far as his duodenum, so there was high probability that she had been ingested no more than a half hour before death, in the course of the assault."

"There's your proof," I grumbled.

"Proof of what?"

"The Virgin. Just what you'd expect to find around the neck of a Nicaraguan Catholic with a taste for blood."

"I never thought of that."

"Where's the chain?"

With a magnifying glass we squinted at eight-by-ten blowups of the murder scene. In the first photos the tortoise shell lay on the rug like an army helmet. In later shots it gazed at us from a million years ago with an eye full of reptile rapture, and Kevin said:

"Did you know you can hypnotize certain reptiles?"

"I just tried it over the weekend and it almost got me killed."

"No, really. Cobras, say, and—"

In the final photo the tortoise had moved maybe four inches, just enough to reveal a loop of gold chain. It wasn't listed in the scrawled inventory of the room's contents, but the magnifying glass corroborated it. Kevin wiped off the magnifying glass on the sleeve of his uniform: "So what have we got?"

"A cannibalized Virgin and a tortoise with a taste for gold costume jewelry." I shuffled the photos. "The only thing I've been worrying about is why Ryan would've let Carlos in. After all, he never touched the collection of knives on the wall. And never called the cops. Whereas when Rachel and I called on him, he gave us the hairy eyeball."

"But like you said. A Latino Catholic. What could be more likely?"

We stared at one another in consternation.

"You were right," I admitted. "We needed to do this."

Kevin glanced at his watch: "Shoot. I have to be at work in ten minutes."

"I know I've seen that medallion. If I could only picture what Carlos was wearing that night."

"Maybe we could try hypnosis. Sometimes in investigations they have luck with that."

"Just because you can hypnotize a reptile doesn't mean you can hypnotize me."

The hall outside the DA's office has pay phones. Before heading back to New York, I could report the autopsy results to Rachel and score a few brownie points. She was still growling that at the critical moment in the investigation I'd dumped her. Put her down. Cut her out. Treated her like a kid. Which inspired me to flatter her now:

"Listen, the autopsy report on Ryan Kassiotis is in. I need some feedback. Got a minute?"

"Sure. More minutes than you have these days."

"Tell me what you think."

I summarized the data for her. And when I came to the payoff, the detail that locked Carlos into the murder once and for all, I said:

"You ready for this? In his stomach they found—he must've torn it off the neck of whoever killed him—they found a medallion of the Virgin. Just what you'd expect to—"

"Wait. A gold oval?"

I grunted.

"Like you'd hang on a chain around your neck? That kind of thing?"

"Right."

She hesitated. Then suddenly she placed the idea: "You mean, like Frank wears?"

50

$\triangledown$

IN THE HOT BREEZE a few sailboats skidded quietly on the Charles River. I nosed across the BU bridge and cut right, then crossed the rail yard past the old Braves Field, into Brighton. On the lazy summer sidewalks a few mothers were pushing strollers. When I stopped to ask directions near the Kennedy Children's Hospital, an echelon of nurses came off duty eating red and yellow popsicles.

The apartment squeezed up under the attic of a big Victorian house that had been divided into efficiency broom closets. Judging by the pair of ten-speed bikes in the downstairs hallway, some of the tenants were students.

Up under the roof the tenant was Sherry Fascelle, who answered the door in a blue chambray shirt and jeans folded to form a wide cuff. Her face looked freshly scrubbed as well as pretty, and her thick black hair glistened. In one hand, like a magic wand, was a fresh yellow pencil. It struck me that she was all dressed up to study. "Actually we met one night at a rehearsal of *La Ronde*," I reminded her.

"Frank's not here," she blurted.

"Just as well. I need to talk to you."

She stood her ground: "We're getting a divorce—maybe you knew. I don't want to say anything that might mess it up. Everything's real delicate just now."

"You want the divorce."

She blinked at me. For that long split second her eyes seemed to confess pain as they searched me out. Her mouth gave a twitch that said *yes* without making a sound.

"Can I come in for a minute?"

"Huh? Sure, I guess. I was just studying." A stack of books on the sill partly blocked the kitchen window. Textbooks and childcare guides, including *Be Glad It's Twins*. On the kitchen table a clear plastic cookbook holder propped open an *Introduction to Modern Logic*. Beside it was a glassful of fizzy seltzer. The bare tabletop dramatized fierce resolve.

The rest of the apartment choked on furniture evidently scooped from the dissolved marriage. Too many modern chairs and end tables and lamps and doodads.

On the kitchen counter a mini-TV was rerunning "The Dating

Game" with the volume down low. "It's just for company," Sherry said. "Helps me concentrate on my reading. I really need a degree now, with two kids to feed."

"Frank chipping in some child support?"

"Want some soda water? Caffeine scatters my thoughts too much."

"Where are the kids?"

"Napping." She found me a glass and took a swig of her own seltzer. "You take the chair, sit down. I'm getting new kitchen chairs tomorrow."

I ran cold water in the glass and leaned against the sink. You and Frank know a kid named Ryan Kassiotis?"

Neither of us sat down. Sherry combed the yellow pencil through her thick black hair. Her lips said: "I have my eye on these very pretty chairs like they had in ice cream parlors — "

"Didn't Ryan used to do publicity photos for Frank?"

Sherry looked at me with empty, star-gazing eyes, and I thought maybe she had heard the twins stirring with that ESP some parents have. All at once she said: "I suppose Ryan's the reason Frank and I got married in the first place."

"Oh?"

On TV smiles and grins on "The Dating Game" gave way to a toothpaste ad whose teeth filled the screen. Sherry snapped off the set and sat in the chair. "Dawn was living with Frank when she first started fooling around with the band. I was just a sophomore. Just trying out, not even a theater major. And when Dawn took off with Ryan, Frank really needed somebody, and I happened to be there."

"On the rebound."

"I hate that term." Even as she balked her tongue raced ahead: "Anyway, I got pregnant almost on the spot. I mean, what else? We were together all the time, like total immersion. We'd go out to eat, he'd eat off my fork. We'd feed each other. I never imagined anything could be — "

"This wasn't the first time Dawn had left Frank."

"No, they'd been real tight off and on for years. Since she was in high school. He almost lost his job over it."

"Frank ever lose his temper?"

"And when Dawn left, I was just finding myself. Really, I had no idea I could act, and Frank brought it out in me, this tremendous feeling of power, like, that could hold people's eyes on me, and go on forever. I'll never have another experience like that."

"But you're not going into the theater now."

She pressed the yellow pencil against her nose and mouth so it split her face in two: "It was all maya. Like the Hindus say. A beautiful dream. The kids weren't even real to me then, I was so caught up in acting."

"You loved it."

"What it was—what I see now is—it wasn't me and Frank who were coming alive. It was more Frank living on the excitement he'd gotten from Dawn. These crazy, intense feelings. They were always onstage together. Every second trying things out."

"Were you jealous even after Dawn left?"

"Oh no. Not really. Not really much. It took me a long time to see you couldn't live like that all the time. Up all night partying and doing freaky things."

"Such as?"

She blanked.

"Frank ever tie you up to make love?"

"She, they had these games—she encouraged him. He had a way of tying her up with the plastic loop thingy from a six-pack of beer, it was as good as handcuffs. You put your hands over your head, by the bedpost or something. That way you'd be very open down there."

"Which would turn him on."

"It was, well, it freed him somehow. He could say these wonderful things to you then. Sometimes."

"And the other times?"

"Huh?"

"He ever play rough?"

"Frank? Don't get the wrong idea. When they were together, him and her, they were like in a cartoon world where the flowers turn into waterfalls and dragons and pink bunny rabbits."

"And one of the pink bunny rabbits turned into Ryan Kassiotis and the lights came on in an empty theater. And there you were, so Frank married you."

"I don't regret it. Frank's got so much to give. So much talent—he was in the Sunday *Times*, in the 'Arts' section, did you see him? He's such a terrific . . . you know, force."

"The force ever hit you?"

"Did what?"

"Did Frank ever hit you. With his fists."

"What makes you ask that?"

"He flies off the handle sometimes."

"Well, he's under stress, he sets high standards. He gets frustrated with people who can't see what he's—"

"He ever hit the kids? Is that why you want out?"

"Oh now, wait. Frank's not pathological. I'm very aware of the battered woman syndrome, I have a friend who's worked in a shelter —. Look. Once in a while Frank gets carried away a bit, but it's only for a moment. And afterward he always feels horribly guilty."

"Frank still a Catholic?"

"He feels guilty and he doesn't go to Mass. If that's what you mean."

"Does he still wear his religious medallion?"

"The Virgin Mary? I guess so. Why?"

"She's turned up in connection with a Central American tortoise, in an unlikely place."

"What, a zoo?"

"More incriminating than that."

51

Dawn SPOKE FIRST.

"Duncan! What the hell are you doing here?" She swung her arms wide to match her smile. In one of Frank's white shirts and peach underpants, barefoot and long-legged, she could have been frolicking on a beach. One foot still wore a bandage — a grubby gray patch — and I thought I detected another bandage beneath her shirt. Her eye took in the sports coat on my arm and the revolver it covered. "Let me take your jacket."

"That's okay, I can't stay."

"Too bad you can't have some supper with us."

She meant it, but she couldn't hide her relief.

Since Sherry had taken much of the Fascelles' furniture, the oak floor in the living room was bare as a stage. By the door were several cardboard cartons labeled and sealed with duct tape, as if for the moving man. In the near corner the phone and a glitzy lamp rested on a folding TV tray.

The walls were hung with black-and-white eight-by-tens of productions Frank had directed. I glimpsed a young Donna Biondi as Juliet on a balcony, breaking light by yonder window. Backlighting cast a thin halo around her, yet the theatrical gloom seemed to devour her long black hair, so that her uptilted face invited ecstasy.

Throw off that virgin livery.

I wondered if it was one of the publicity shots Ryan had done for Frank Fascelle.

Frank was slouched in a leather sling chair munching fast-food fries and sipping vermouth from a plastic cup with a fast-food logo and a badly drawn pirate on it. Barefoot, in red tennis shorts, with his shirt off, he advertised athletic energy. He held the vermouth bottle tucked between his thighs, and in his lap a book, *Play, Death, and Heroism in Shakespeare.* The table beside him held a wedge of cheddar cheese, Wheat Thins, and a slicing knife. Under the sling chair sat a stack of travel books, a guide to London on top.

The tall open window behind him looked directly into the murky stained glass of a church: one of those hundred dark stone churches of yesteryear that mark Boston's neighborhoods like exclamation points. They were about to gut the building. Out on the street I'd passed

222

workmen carting out organ pipes, silvery sixteen-footers that could have been the cannon confiscated from a defeated army. From up here you could sight across the slate roof to the belfry and the ominous black bells. A row of pigeons sat mumbling on the roof. In some of these old churches the stained glass is gorgeous. You can't tell anything from the outside. Frank was Mr. Good Cheer.

"How's it going? Join us for some cruddy vermouth? Get him a glass, Dawn."

Her long legs skipped into the kitchen. Then she called: "The glasses are in the dishwasher. Let me rinse one."

"It's okay," I said. "Don't bother."

"No bother," Frank insisted. "Listen, your daughter, Rachel. She's great. The way she throws herself into roles—and with no training. I couldn't believe it. You should consider letting her study, audition in New York. Normally I wouldn't recommend that to my worst enemy. But Rachel's different. Hell, I didn't even realize she was your kid. I suppose she wanted to get the part on her own, mmm? You can't be too tough in this business."

"She can be pretty fragile from some angles."

"Aren't we all." To Dawn he called: "Hey, bring the man a chair. And some ice."

"I'll stand; I can't stay long."

"We're emptying this place out," Frank explained. "Taking a quick vacation while they deliver the new stuff."

Dawn carried a blue director's chair in one hand and in the other balanced a wet glass on a tray of ice cubes. The grubby gray bandage explained the hint of a limp. She'd let her hair down and it was magnificent.

"Frank tell you?" she chirped. "Next week, as soon as *La Ronde* opens, we're going to London. For three months, maybe more. They may ask Frank to revive his *Romeo and Juliet*. You can imagine what an honor it is to be asked, they're so snobby toward American theater people over there."

Frank poured vermouth and I congratulated him. Dawn said:

"And guess who might—just might—get to do Juliet."

Sun, moon, and stars filled her eyes. My heart slipped off a window ledge and plunged. She leaned affectionately into Frank and raised his cup for a sip. With a lovely ripple in her throat she swallowed. "Oh churl," she intoned. "Drunk all and left no friendly drop to help me after!"

When she plokked ice cubes in the plastic cup, a few water drops spattered on his chest and beaded up in the dark hair. She had enough presence of mind to ask again to take my coat, so I laid it on one of the cardboard boxes bound for London and changed the subject:

"You recovered from your accident?"

"Can't you tell?" She grinned. "The cut in my side took two hundred stitches, it feels like. They had to give me — what do they call it — units of blood. Sorry I couldn't wait for you the other morning. I had to get out of that hospital before it totally freaked me out. And Frank was willing to come for me. I've been trying to call you. How did things turn out?"

"You didn't see the papers?"

She shook her head: "We've sort of forgot to go outside since I got here from the hospital."

"Sounds like it's been a memorable reunion," I said.

Frank patted Dawn's rump and rolled his eyes in blissful exhaustion. "You clown," Dawn crooned to him. She was twisting ringlets in his thick, curly hair.

"It's been utterly intense," Frank said. "Once in a lifetime feeling comes perfectly together. You almost don't dare to move, let alone go out on the dirty street."

When he tried, he had a baritone fit for scripture or a thrilling soliloquy.

Across the alley the pigeons were ruffling on the roof's edge, cooing. In the golden light the afternoon was full of life: kids squawking, rush-hour hungry for supper. In spite of everything I felt a weight of guilt on me. The world was full of life, it was good to be alive. But we were running out of time.

Finally I heaved a deep breath:

"Where's your medallion of the Virgin, Frank?"

He felt around his collarbone as if he still felt its phantom presence. With perfect evenness in his voice he stunned me: "I gave it to someone. An old friend of ours."

"Oh?" Dawn kept teasing ringlets. "Who?"

"Ryan."

"Oh you guys are friends again. I'm gla—" She stopped so short I wondered if she'd suddenly remembered: Ryan was dead now.

"A long time ago," Frank said.

"Why give that to Ryan?" I asked.

"It's a long story." His voice spun word after effortless word. "It was Ryan's trinket originally. He gave it to Dawn and later she gave it to me. So it was really just a matter of returning it to its rightful owner."

Dawn gaped: "What?"

If he'd expected her to play along, he'd reached too far. Now his manner changed. He stifled a yawn, stirred, and pushed to his feet. Dawn was stricken. Her eyes darted meaninglessly here and there as she struggled to grasp a new logic. I said:

"Sorry to bug you about it. But if I don't, the cops will."

With the knife Frank sliced off a crumbly wafer of cheddar: "Why's that?"

"Because at the autopsy the medallion turned up in Ryan's stomach."

Silence.

"The gold chain for it turned up too. Broken. Indications are, he tore it from the killer's throat fighting for his life."

"Maybe it was the other way around. It was torn off him."

"Frank," Dawn blurted. "It's not true, is it?"

He snicked another bit of cheese with the knife. "Why would I bother Ryan, for christsake?"

"To punish him for beating you out with Dawn," I said. "And for keeping you from getting her back."

"Well that's not true," Dawn cut in with relief.

"But Frank thought it was true," I said. "And when I first told him Ryan had been beaten up, Frank decided he could teach Ryan a lesson that lasts forever. Then let the world blame it on the bastards that had jumped you and Ryan earlier."

"That's a bunch of—"

"It's first degree murder."

Like a sleepwalker Dawn backed toward me, away from Frank. I had to keep the pressure on:

"Didn't you once tell me you and Frank liked to play bondage games?"

"Oh bullshit!" Frank fumed. "What is this insane shit! Now I really am getting steamed."

"Take it easy," Dawn soothed. "Duncan's not talking about anything to be ashamed of. I never told him we did anything really weird."

Her voice died in her throat as the logic unfolded for her. "I wonder," I said, "will the cops find that the duct tape on these boxes matches the tape used on the kid's hands and feet? To make it easier to kill him."

"Impossible," Frank complained. "You're dreaming."

"Let's call the cops and see."

"Go ahead, idiot. The tape's all used up."

"There's enough here for a lab sample."

All three of us looked toward the boxes by the door and the phone just beyond them. But Dawn was the one who moved. She did it so quickly, so decisively, I was caught stupid, dazzled to see my jacket sail into the corner and the Smith & Wesson suddenly in her hand. The hand pointed at me:

"Leave us alone, Duncan."

"Look, kid. This guy's been slugging his wife. It's one reason she left him."

"Duncan, I've been here for days and it's been beautiful. The most honest time of my whole life."

She backed toward Frank keeping the pistol pointed at me. "Look at it this way," I said. "If Frank beat Ryan to death and he knows you know it, you'll never be able to turn your back on him."

"Come on," Frank said. "Let's lock this lunatic in the back room and head for the airport. Give me the gun."

"Wait," Dawn breathed.

"Give me the goddamned *gun*," Frank barked. "I'm losing my patience with this—"

"In a minute," Dawn said. "Why did you make up that bit about the medal belonging to Ryan? Why didn't you just tell the truth?"

"Come on, come on," Frank complained. "First we do the play, then write the stupid reviews."

"I don't know," she sighed.

"Well I do," I said. "If you go with him, you'll never sleep safe with him again."

"Jesus Christ," Frank pleaded. "Wake up, let's go."

Dawn hesitated. Her eyes were focused behind me, beyond the wall itself. "Ryan—"

I walked over to the phone.

"He's going for the goddamned phone!" Frank argued. "Give me the gun."

"I can't."

"Dawn!"

"*No!*" She pulled away from him. I reached for the receiver, tasting my own fear; telling myself she wouldn't pull the trigger.

"Ryan—" Again the word caught in her throat. Her eyes blazed with pain.

I began to dial 911. Suddenly Frank grabbed and Dawn shook the pistol loose, away from him. As it clunked to the floor she tried to kick it away. But by then Frank had her by the neck, the ridiculous cheese knife at her throat. He saw me gauging the distance.

"She'll get hurt," he warned. I shrugged:

"Come on, Frank. This isn't a hostage drama. Let's do the sensible thing." I let my hand drop to my side.

"Put the phone *down!* *Down!*"

I heard Dawn gag for air as the phone clicked into its cradle.

My eyes met his, and in that instant the playacting collapsed. He shoved Dawn aside and dropped for the pistol. I got only a step before the snubby gun barrel was on me.

"Let's go," he said to Dawn. She stared at him, rubbing her throat. "Get some things together. We can have the tickets changed at the airport."

"They extradite theater directors even from London," I said.

"Not if they don't know."

"You think killing me will keep the world out of your play?"

"It's not my fault."

"Then you can convince a jury."

"It was an accident. I just went there to talk to the idiot. To see if he was the one threatening Dawn. Find out where she was. Get her back from him. And he was so arrogant, you wouldn't believe the crap I had to take from him. What a little prick. All I did, the only thing I did, I slapped him in the face a few times. That's all."

"With his hands tied behind his back."

"I had to be sure he'd listen. How was I supposed to know he'd die?"

Rage and self-pity tangled in this throat. I lowered my voice: "That makes some sense. Give me the gun. We can talk."

"Like hell." He was gripping the pistol so furiously it trembled. What were the chances he hadn't flicked off the safety? He gave Dawn a nudge. "Come on, sweet. Get your things. I'll put this idiot in the back room."

"You're not going to hurt him?"

"Hell no."

He said it with slangy carelessness, a little too casual to work. And Dawn must have sensed that even as I did. Because when he nudged her into motion, a little roughly even, her hand dipped down to meet the handle of the cheese knife, and came up as the gun was rising to give him a firm stance to fire. His left hand started to sweep her aside. In that instant I launched myself at him, realizing that I was already too late to reach the pistol before he fired. I threw myself at the floor.

The gunshot roared in the bare room. I heard the pigeons flutter off the church roof in a panic. For a second I wasn't sure if I'd been shot. But as I rolled I could see Frank collapsing, and Dawn, the two of them

227

twisting into each other with groping, clumsy arms. My body surged toward them in protest.

He lay on his back, eyes fixed on the empty window, a sinister wet gurgle in his windpipe. The knife had entered from the side. As I pulled Dawn off him, the noise in his throat subsided. Faltered.

Fell silent.

Dawn opened her eyes and I could see her terror. The best my voice could do was a croak:

"You hurt?"

Her hand rose to her throat as if she could still feel his arm choking her. When I went to pull her up she shrank from me with a dry, frozen stare. "Don't," she begged. "Don't touch me."

"You all right?"

"He wouldn't have hurt me."

"Is that what you think?"

"But he grabbed for me. When he panicked, the first thing he did, he grabbed for my throat."

"You all right now?"

She nodded her head, in a trance: "Mmmm. I'll never be all right again."

52

COLUMBUS DAY MORNING THE tiny airstrip was sunny and sleepy. Some dozen planes were moored behind the tin operations shed, but the only takeoffs were crows skirmishing with a red-tailed hawk over the brilliant October oaks and maples on the edge of the runway.

After breakfast we'd brought the homemade plane a half mile down Connecticut back roads, the Volvo and its trailer creeping along with half a dozen local kids following on dirt bikes. In this corner of the open field the plane's nylon wings caught every feint at a breeze and from time to time gave a frisky flutter.

Phil and Kevin helped me check the plane's center of gravity one last time. You suspend the craft from a critical point at its wingtips, though in a contraption this simple there isn't much to adjust. You have to trust that you've laid out the wing and tail surfaces without any warps. You have to trust yourself to have measured exactly. By now we'd gone over the preflight checklist so many times that even I could see it was pure superstition. I had the manual more or less memorized.

Rachel needed a few minutes to reinforce a seam in the rudder fabric. Amy brought over the red plastic gas can—she'd arrived not with Rachel but with Kevin. The gasoline poured with a delicious-sounding trickle.

Sitting on the grass under her floppy straw sun hat, Vera was sunning the pages of a book and sipping iced tea. Rachel had talked Meg into joining us for the launch, but at the last minute her new boss—partner, she called him—had invited her to St. Kitt's in the Caribbean, and she'd taken wing like the bluebird of happiness. Oddly, I too was feeling it as a liberation. Something had shifted in her soul, a happiness that was hers and not ours, and I was glad.

Vera was doling out more tea from the jug when Dawn's red Alfa buzzed us. She parked at the edge of the runway as if waiting clearance for takeoff. In jeans, cowboy boots, and sunglasses, her long dark hair in a bouncy ponytail, Dawn paused in the grass to size us up. She threw me a shy little wave.

Her passenger trailed behind her, a watchful young woman with a crinkly perm and a quick smile. The woman already had her hand out to meet mine when Dawn said to me: "I thought I ought to give you a taste of the reality."

"Which one?"

"This is Lynne. Lynne Dresser."

"Ah," I said. "We're already fictional friends. Come meet Vera, say hello to everybody."

Lynne had what Granny Ames would have called a frank handshake. Dawn tilted her elegant cheek, Hollywood style, to be kissed. Her sister and Rachel she hauled into hugs. I introduced her to Vera.

For a few minutes we loafed in the grass slurping iced tea, Dawn full of restless energy: "Is it true Meryl Streep and a lot of other film people have houses out here? I wonder if they go into town to buy ice cream or something. God, this is actual iced tea, teabags in it and everything. I love it."

"That a Dan Merriam bumper sticker on the Alfa?" I asked.

"I hope he wins," Dawn vowed. "I want to see Caddy Merriam in the White House."

"They keep insinuating all this garbage about her," Rachel griped. "Trying to make her husband look henpecked. It stinks. Those guys have so much money for ads."

"People will have to see through it," Dawn said firmly.

I wondered what Rachel, who couldn't ignore the dark side of things, thought of Dawn's crazy upbeat determination. Good influence, I suspected, though Meg would be horrified to hear me say that. Some people you can imagine ten, twenty years into the future: more of the same, just a little fatter. Not Dawn.

Under the floppy sun hat Vera's eye met mine and we shared a wink. Dawn said:

"Lynne's staying at my mother's house. Makes an easier commute into BU."

"I'm trying to talk Dawn into going back to school," Lynne said. "She could take a screenwriting workshop."

"I'm too old," Dawn protested. "Too many requirements. Too bo-o-oring. Amy's the brain in the family."

"These days," Amy said, "you better be born rich. Do you know what college costs?"

Dawn turned to me: "I did take your suggestion. About my old man."

"Paid him a call? Did it work?"

"It wasn't easy. His new wife's too ashamed even to let me in their house, so I had to catch him in his office. But at least he didn't call me any names this time. What I did was, I flattered the hell out of him. And told him what a selfish slob he'd been. So he agreed at least to pay Amy's tuition. That's a start."

"What about you?"

"Cyndy's still got that cheap rent in L.A. And I have this little piggybank to help me write screenplays. You can live forever on eighteen grand if you're careful. And if it doesn't pan out, what the hell. Maybe I can hit up the old man for some kind of tuition deal like Amy's. I wonder if Meryl Streep does her own grocery shopping, where people might meet her."

"Maybe you'll meet her professionally," Rachel said.

"How's *La Ronde* going?" Simple question, but it surprised me. It was the first time Dawn had directly acknowledged Rachel, as if they were both grown women now, not rivals competing for scarce applause. Rachel sensed the opening:

"Tonight's the last night. I'm loving it."

"It's a great production," Dawn murmured.

Nobody mentioned Frank Fascelle. For an instant his shadow haunted the mild October air. Dawn broke the spell:

"I'll miss you guys."

Phil called over: "Ready when you are."

Vera passed around a box of biscuits, beginning with Dawn: "I hope you're sticking around for the big takeoff today?"

"You trust Duncan to get off the ground?"

"That's Daedalus," Vera said. "A ball of wax and a handful of turkey feathers, held together by a sticky insurance policy. Just don't you go up there with him."

"I thought you couldn't take passengers," Dawn said to me.

"I can't. No room. And no license. You don't need a pilot's license for an ultralight."

"Can you really fly that thing?"

"We'll see. I took a few flying lessons once, but I ran out of cash."

Rachel shook her head, munching a biscuit: "Well, I want to learn to fly too. That's the deal, remember? So bring it back in one piece, okay? And yourself too. I mean — "

As Vera stuck a couple of biscuits in my craw, she squeezed my wrist and finished Rachel's sentence.

And it was Vera's words that kept going in the back of my mind as the motorcycle engine pushed the flimsy crate down the runway and into the wind, wobbling ever so slightly till the airspeed stabilized us and the rubber wheels lifted off the blacktop. It was the third taxiing test. The third attack of the jitters — time to give the beast some throttle and pull back the joystick a bit.

Well, imagine that.

In the slow circling climb, the air cooled off and twittered in the ears of my borrowed helmet. Meadows and ponds and stone walls came into sight, even a serious white New England spire among the blazing October leaves; and the familiar faces on the runway below grew smaller and more indistinct — or maybe more vivid if you count the faces of the people you love in your mind's eye — including Vera, still wisecracking there in sort of a prayer:

Don't let gravity get you down.

If you have enjoyed this book and would like to receive details of other Walker mystery titles, please write to

Mystery Editor
Walker and Company
720 Fifth Avenue
New York, NY 10019